HER LAST BREATH

Debt Collector 9

JON MILLS

DIRECT RESPONSE PUBLISHING

ISBN-13: 978-1974284689
ISBN-10: 1974284689

Also By Jon Mills

Undisclosed
Retribution
Clandestine
The Debt Collector
Debt Collector: Vengeance
Debt Collector: Reborn
Debt Collector: Hard to Kill
Debt Collector: Angel of Death
Debt Collector: Prey
Debt Collector: Narc
Debt Collector: Hard Time
Debt Collector: Her Last Breath
Debt Collector: Trail of the Zodiac
Debt Collector: Fight Game
The Promise
True Connection
Lost Girls
I'm Still Here

JON MILLS

Dedication

For my family.

Prologue

Jack Winchester was strangling the man when the phone interrupted him. At first he ignored it, but when the buzzing started again for the third time, he released his death grip to answer. "Damn it," he snapped and pointed two fingers at the man. "Don't you go anywhere."

The muscle head rolled around on the floor, gasping and clawing at his neck, sucking in lungfuls of air. Outside light attempted to poke through the blinds. The noise of the city seeped through the thin walls. Jack stepped over the coffee table that was turned on its side, along with two chairs. The entire motel was in shambles.

He'd been hiding out there after his girlfriend filed a report against him. There were clothes strewn all over the floor, the TV was smashed and most of the cutlery was scattered. He was usually clean in his work but this guy had got under his skin. Though he had to give him some credit, he sure put up one hell of a fight.

He fished into his leather jacket and glanced at the caller ID. In the darkness of the room, the display was bright — almost too bright. It was the middle of the day but by the color of the guy's pasty skin, it didn't look as if he'd ever opened the blinds. Jack squinted at his phone. *The same number? That made eight calls in the past six days. What was the deal with this woman?* He raised a finger to the tattooed tweaker and told him to wait while he checked his messages. It was rare that he didn't reply to potential clients but he'd been trying to stay off the radar after his recent run-in with the law in Texas.

Jack leaned against the wall and kept a good eye on the asshole. He tapped the phone a few times and brought up his voice mail.

"Mr. Winchester, this is Jenna Whitmore. I'm not sure if my messages are getting through but I really need to speak to you. Look, I'll pay you whatever you want. I'm in over my head on this one. A friend of mine gave me your number; she said you'd be able to help. Please call me back." She reeled off her phone number and when she would be around.

Now under most conditions, he would have called her back immediately, especially since she said she'd pay him whatever he wanted. That was an offer too good to refuse. However, he wasn't done with this fool. He slipped the phone back into his pocket and ambled over to the meathead.

"Please. No more."

"So, sissy boy has finally found his tongue. Now you want to tell me where you put the dog?"

He groaned and muttered something.

Jack cupped a hand over his ear. "Speak up, I can't hear you."

"In the shed at the back of my house."

"And where is the leash?"

"Why? What are you going to do?"

Jack grabbed him by the neck and hauled him to his feet.

"Please."

"Not such a big man now, are we?"

"I didn't mean anything by it, I was just trying to get her attention."

"By strangling her dog on a live video?"

"I was pretending. I didn't kill it."

"Pretending? You better hope that dog is alive otherwise I'm going to finish what I started."

Jack tossed him on the bed and went over to the camera and peered through, adjusting it ever so slightly for the best angle. He played back the recording of strangling the guy. He was going to send it to the guy's ex-girlfriend who'd hired him to get her dog back. It was a crazy situation, she didn't want him dead but she wanted him to suffer. The guy was a complete meathead. He was loaded up on steroids, and by all accounts not the kind of person anyone in their right mind would have approached. But it was all a front. The very second Tina had told him what Bradley had done, he took the job. Nothing pissed him off more than someone taking out their frustration on a helpless animal.

He looked up from the camera and smiled.

"Strip."

"What?"

"Are you deaf? I said strip."

"Oh no, you're not—"

"Hell no. I wouldn't touch your ass with a barge pole."

The guy at first was reluctant as if he thought Jack was joking. He wasn't.

"Do I need to come over there again?"

"No," he said, his neck red and raw from being taken to the edge and brought back again. Strangling a person wasn't as easy as it looked. But after his time in the mob, he'd perfected the art. He knew how to take a full-grown man down to his knees and bring him to the point of where he blacked out, only to bring him back and do it again. Meathead was wearing tight jeans, and a black T-shirt. Once he stripped down to his undies he stood there, holding his hands over his privates and looking vulnerable.

Jack gave a nod. "And the underpants."

"No, come on, man."

Jack walked over to him and he flinched before quickly dropping them. Jack couldn't help but see the amusing side to what he had in store for him. Occasionally he liked to toy with them, change things up and make each job a little interesting.

"Where's the dog food?"

"In the cupboard over there."

Jack whistled to himself as he crossed the room and pulled out several cans of wet dog food. He searched around on the counter for a can opener and took the tops off before returning and handing it over.

"Right, smear that shit all over you and make sure you get it into every cavity in your body."

"Are you joking?"

"Do I look like I'm fucking joking?"

The guy stared down at the can. He grimaced but slid two fingers into the nasty smelling sludge and began smearing it over the front of his own chest. Jack went back to the kitchenette.

"You got any beers?"

"In the fridge."

He opened it and pulled out a cold one, cracked the top off and took a hard swig. He strolled back into the room, took a seat across from him and watched.

"Now don't hold back. I want to see you covered from head to toe."

"Do you get off on this?"

"Oh yeah, I just love to see grown men covered in dog food. Nothing else gets me hard like the smell of Pedigree Chum." He chuckled and took another swig before pulling out a pack of cigarettes and lighting one.

"You know, Bradley, this could have all been avoided if you had just gone on your way."

"I love her."

"Strange way to show your love."

"She wouldn't listen to me."

"Well, there is a surprise. You're a fucking idiot. What the hell she saw in you originally is anyone's guess. But here's the thing... Taking your frustration out on her dog." He made a clucking sound with his tongue. "Bad move. I have a good mind to go back to strangling you. But I think that would be too easy. So I'm going to do you a favor. Hell, I'm going to do dogs all over this town a favor."

Bradley's face screwed up. "I don't get it."

He leaned forward. "Of course you don't. But you will. And here's the thing. If I discover that you have gone anywhere near her or her dog after this, or any animal for that matter, I will hunt you down and make what's happened here today seem like child's play. Do you understand me?"

He didn't nod but just got this scowl on his face.

"You better wipe that scowl off your face and butter up those balls with that dog food before I make this far worse for you."

Once he was slathered in chunks of stewed meat, he looked as if he'd taken a bath in dog shit. Jack went over and picked up the leash off the counter and tossed it at him.

"Put it on."

"But—"

"Don't make me repeat myself. I hate repeating myself."

"I was just going to say I don't have the collar."

"That's okay, I can remedy that."

Jack hopped up, placed his beer on the counter, took a hold of the leash and tied it around his neck so tight it was almost cutting off his ability to breathe. "Now, get on the ground."

The hulking man's expression changed, and a chunk of meat fell from his face. Jack was tired of him dragging ass so he kicked out his feet from beneath him. "There we go. Now we're going for a little walk. How about that, huh? But before we do that, let's give you something to make you more compliant." He crossed the room and picked up a bag of heroin belonging to the man and took a few minutes to heat up a spoon of it before filling a needle with the dark liquid.

"Put your arm out," he bellowed.

Again he was slow, so he tugged it out in front of him. Jack stuck him with the needle and watched as his eyes rolled back. He then proceeded to drag him out the door of that shitty low-end motel and over to a clapped-out old car. He tossed him in the trunk and wiped his hands clean on a towel before dropping it and starting the engine. It sputtered to life, and he reversed out. As he was backing up, the owner of the motel gave him a strange look. Jack gave a nod and drove away.

Ten minutes later he pulled into a busy dog park in Chicago. It was an expansive green that was full of all kinds of dogs running off the leash. He let the car idle until he saw an area where he could pull in without being noticed. He pushed out of the car, popped the trunk and dragged the man out. He was disoriented and barely able to resist. That was exactly how he wanted him. From there he took him down to a small gate and tied him up to a chain-link fence. He breathed in deeply as he looked at his naked body lying there in the grass with dog food all over him. Jack turned and walked a few feet away, around a cluster of trees to an area where there were tons of dogs. Owners were busy chatting, drinking coffee or watching their dogs play. He brought two fingers up to his lips and whistled as hard as he could. Dogs perked their ears and turned his way. He did it again and then proceeded to run. He glanced back to find six or seven of them racing his way. Perfect, he thought.

As soon as he got around the corner, he hopped over the fence and watched as they burst around the bend and came rushing up to the gate. Jack chuckled as he watched them lick the guy all over. One of them bit him as it tried to get a chunk of meat out of his ass. Bradley let out a howl in agony as Jack walked off with a smirk on his face.

He could see the headline now: *Naked Man Found in Dog Park Smeared with Dog Food.* It was humiliation at its finest and a hard lesson but some people only understood the hard way.

* * *

When he arrived at Bradley's home, he let himself into the backyard and spotted the shed in the far corner. The asshole had placed two large tires against the doors to prevent the dog from escaping. Jack went over and peered in through the window. The dog was lying on his side panting hard. There were no bowls of water or food.

Bastard.

After pulling away the tires, he opened the door. The dog didn't move. He was breathing hard and looked like he was suffering from heat exhaustion. Jack went in and scooped him up and quickly made it back to his vehicle. There he took a bottle of water and managed to get him to drink some of the liquid from his hand. Not wasting any time, he placed the dog inside, and drove to the nearest veterinarians. On the way he made a phone call to the girl who'd hired him and instructed her to meet him there.

The look on her face when she saw her dog was full of both horror and joy. She cried into his fur as the vet went about treating the dog.

"Is he going to be okay?"

"He's dehydrated, and malnourished but he'll bounce back," the vet said before heading back into the room where the dog was laying on a table. The girl turned to Jack before he headed out.

"Are you sure I can't give you some money?"

"Use it on the dog. Get him some toys."

He extended his hand, but she leaned forward and hugged him.

"Thank you."

He offered a faint smile and then exited. Outside he pulled out his phone and made a call to Jenna Whitmore. He slowly paced back and forth in the parking lot waiting for her to pick up.

"Jenna, it's Jack."

"Oh God, thank you for calling back."

"How can I help?"

Chapter 1

The conversation was bizarre. Five women had gone missing over the past two years and had washed up in streams and creeks. She'd been investigating it because according to her, the cops were doing little to nothing because of the type of women they were. Jack probed her for specifics but she was too nervous to speak on the phone and wanted to meet in person. Initially, all he could manage to get out of her was that she was a small-town journalist living in the sleepy West Virginia town of Marlinton.

He generally didn't take on a job without getting the full scoop. It was sloppy and hard to gauge the true level of risk. Of course, missing people was his expertise. Years of working for Gafino in New York, and hunting down debtors had honed his skills. But they were usually alive. What did she expect of him?

"Look, Ms. Whitmore. I'm currently in Chicago. It's a

good ten-hour drive from you and without specifics, I really don't want to go to all the trouble of driving that far only to turn you down."

"If money is a problem, I can wire you some this morning."

He snorted. "Money isn't the issue, I don't take on every job that comes my way. There are a lot of factors to take into consideration. You mentioned you have compiled a lot of information on people of interest. Why not just take that to the police?"

Her voice became muffled. The hum of a highway could be heard in the background.

"Things work very different down here, Mr. Winchester."

"But surely with five dead women, the FBI is involved?"

"If you call showing up for a few days and interviewing the families, sure. But they are not here now." There was silence, then she sighed. "You don't get it, do you...? It's because of what these women did for a living that they aren't getting the attention they deserve. Police are a piece of shit down here. Several have been caught picking up women. As far as they see it, this isn't a murder investigation."

Jack stood back from his black Shelby GT with two silver lines over the top. He'd wanted to get another since his got destroyed in Maine. He'd finally bit the bullet. He ran a hand over his stubbled jaw.

"Look, I need a day or two to consider this. This is too rushed for my liking. I still have a few things to wrap up here before I give you my final decision."

"Okay, I'll wire a quarter of the money through Western Union."

"You don't need to do that."

"I want to show you that I'm serious," she said. "Just..." she paused for a second. "Don't take too long to think it over."

With that said she gave her address in Marlinton and hung up. Jack exhaled and leaned against his car. There was nothing left to tie up in Chicago, he'd lied to her simply to get her off the phone. That was thing about the clients he took on. He had to filter out the crazies, and those who were trying to screw him over from the legit. He wouldn't know what category she fell into until he went back to his hotel and looked into the disappearances himself.

It wasn't like her situation was any more extraordinary than the thousands that disappeared every day in America. But call it a gut feeling, Jack got a sense there was more to this than she was ready to disclose.

* * *

The Skylark was considered a seedy one-star motel on Archer Avenue. The ugly, two-story, flamingo-pink building stood out like an eyesore. He pulled into the Walgreens across the street to get a bottle of Tylenol. For the past ten hours, he'd been fighting one hell of a headache. It was another reason why he wasn't ready to agree to the woman's request. Right now, all he wanted to do was toss a few pills back, hide his head under a pillow and wake up in a couple of days. The past few months had been non-stop. Back-to-back to jobs, mostly small ones to keep him ticking over. As much as he wanted to slow down and rest, work kept his mind occupied. Downtime was never good.

After returning to the motel, Jack parked at the far end. His room was on the ground floor. Outside sitting on a bench was a black woman who'd been sitting there from the time he left that morning until now. Chicago was full of street people looking for handouts; most were winos struggling with drug problems. She glanced at him as he locked up his vehicle.

"Spare a few dollars?"

It was the same line he'd heard since arriving there three weeks ago. Jack wasn't hard up for cash, the last few jobs had netted him a tidy profit, and he knew what it was like to be down on luck. Whether she would use it for drugs and alcohol was immaterial. Jack fished into his pocket and yanked out a crumpled twenty-dollar bill, he stuck it in her palm and walked on to his room. He caught her glance at it, then she muttered something along the lines of God bless you.

Juggling keys and a bag full of drinks, Tylenol, and noodles, he felt the bag slip out of his hand just as a woman by the name of Serena came out of her room. She hurried over and started giving him a hand. She was a good-looking woman, probably about ten years younger than him, thirty-one, maybe thirty-two with dark wavy hair, and green eyes.

"Ah thanks," he muttered as she tossed the pills into the plastic bag.

"Do you have a neti pot?" she asked.

"A what?"

"You know, one of those teapot devices you jam up your nose to wash the sinuses out with saline. Works wonders for headaches."

"No."

"Oh, well you can get one across the road at…"

"Walgreens," they said in unison.

She took a step back and smiled. "You've already been there."

He nodded and there was an awkward pause.

"I'm just off to do my shift. You need anything?"

"A real air conditioner?" he said with a smile.

She smirked. It was a running joke of theirs. The damn things installed in the rooms were ancient. His unit had been leaking and for what it was worth, it was pointless having it in the wall. He got more air from opening his windows on a humid day than from anything that pumped out.

"I'll get that while I get you a gourmet dinner," she said in a sarcastic way as if she was working at some fancy hotel. From the little she'd told him, she had run away from home when she was seventeen and spent her time working odd jobs in Chicago until she landed herself a well-paid job at the motel. They even gave her a room at a discounted rate.

"That would be nice," he said pushing his key into the lock and turning it.

"Well, I should get going." She made it a few steps, then turned. "Oh, by the way, I got back in contact with my folks like you suggested."

"And?"

"They just want to see me."

He shook his finger. "I told you."

She winked and ambled away.

Inside the room a wall of humidity and the familiar smell of mold hit him. The place was in need of a serious overhaul. Jack tossed the bag down and went over to the drapes and pushed them back. The windows were cramped and barely any light poured in. Outside, he had a view of the Burger King, Angie's bar, a gas station and Julie's restaurant. In the day it looked dreary with the gray skies, and at night, the neon lights made it hard to sleep.

In the solitude of the room, Jack wandered into the washroom and took a quick shower. After exiting he slumped down on the bed and pulled out a tablet from his bag and powered it up. He set it on the side table to charge a little while he attempted to kick-start the air conditioning. It was unbearably hot inside. He flipped the switch on the unit and gave it a thump with the side of his hand. It let out a groan, then a high-pitched whirling noise.

He could have stayed in a nicer hotel. Heck, there was a lot to choose from but he hadn't intended on staying in Chicago longer than a few nights. That soon turned into weeks once he got to know Serena. It wasn't that he liked the motel. It was a shit stain, but she offered company and that he couldn't pass up. So, he took on a few jobs locally and settled into a simple way of life. Besides Serena, everyone else left him alone. That's the way he liked it.

After making himself comfortable, he poured himself a drink of bourbon and sat back on the bed with his tablet. Usually, his clients would give him a name, an address or a number for a person who was causing them trouble. The odd time he would have to go and knock on a few doors to find out where they were, but eventually, after a day or so of searching around, he'd find the problem and deal with it. This time was different. She hadn't stated what kind of help she wanted, only that she was investigating the murder of five women in the town of Marlinton, West Virginia.

Jack brought up Google and did a search for "Dead Women in Marlinton, West Virginia." It didn't come back for a hit on that town but there was an article about "5 Women Found Dead in the Small Town of Green Bank." He brought up Google Maps to get an idea of where it was located in relation to Marlinton.

Green Bank was located almost forty minutes north. He continued to read the article.

Is a Serial Killer At Large in West Virginia?

It has been almost two years since Rachel Dixon, the first of five women, disappeared from Marlinton, West Virginia. Only two months ago, a woman out walking her dogs found the body of Brenda Norris, the fifth woman, in Deer Creek. The deaths have shattered the families of the women and left a small town with more questions than answers.

Today a missing flyer, attached to a telephone pole, flaps in the wind, showing the faces of the five women from photos that have been circulated to media outlets. Despite the small amount of attention, the Pocahontas County Sheriff Department is still searching for clues and trying to determine exactly what happened in what has been called "The Quietest Town in America."

Each of the five women was found lying face down in local creeks and streams. Though reports have suggested the women knew each other through their involvement in drugs and prostitution that has still to be confirmed. All of them are said to have been missing shoes, pocketbooks, identification and cell phones.

Sergeant Tom Berringer has been quick to dismiss any talk of this being the work of a serial killer, and each death is being treated individually. The FBI has refused to comment at this time.

The families of the women are furious with the way the police have treated this investigation and are desperate for answers.

"These are our daughters we are talking about. Regardless of what they did for a living, we want to know what happened to them. Who would do this? They were dumped

like trash. The police say my daughter drowned but there is no way in hell that's the case. She was petrified of rivers, she wouldn't go near them. I know they are trying to blame this on her drug use but I know my kid. I just want them to catch who is responsible. Someone out there knows. We demand answers," said the father of Paula Roberts.

Rachel Dixon went missing two years ago while heading out to work, according to her husband, Peter Dixon.

"She left home around six that evening from Marlinton to meet a client at the Lodge at the Edge of Green Bank," Dixon told the Pocahontas Times. "She was meant to see her mother before she went there. I spoke to her on the phone and then that was it. I was expecting her back at just after eight. She didn't come home. Someone must have seen her."

It's still unknown if she ever made it to the lodge. Two weeks later her body was discovered in the North Fork River in the neighboring town of Green Bank. The medical examiner ruled the cause of death as drowning even though she was said to have had alcohol, morphine, cocaine, and amphetamine in her system at the time of death. It's also believed that she knew the other women that went missing later. According to those that knew them, they were all drug users who engaged in sex work to support their addiction. Two of them had spent time in jail on various charges.

Though the families don't deny they were troubled and their lifestyles put them at risk, they still want people to know that they were daughters, sisters, wives, and mothers.

Still, it appears that the residents of both Marlinton and Green Bank are divided.

"That's drug use for you," one woman who wished to remain anonymous said.

"I used to see them standing on the corner. What do they expect?" said another.

"It doesn't matter what they did, it's terrifying to think what these women went through," yet another said.

However, according to the families, it appears the investigation has now gone cold. Phone calls to the district attorney's office only resulted in being stonewalled, said the mother of Brenda Norris.

"We are not commenting on the Green Bank investigation

until we have additional information that serves the investigation or the public by its release," Gina Lopez told the Pocahontas Times.

Marian Holt's daughter, Susan Holt, 28, disappeared from Marlinton on June 12, 2016. She was the second woman found dead, only two weeks after the first. Her body was found just south in a nearby creek that flows through Green Bank. The exact location is close to where Rachel Dixon was discovered.

The autopsy report listed her cause of death as "undetermined." Yet her mother believes she was already dead prior to being placed in the water.

Jillian Carlton's daughter, 34-year-old Paula Roberts, disappeared a month later, followed by Dixie Stokes almost a year later on May 16. Both women were found with large amounts of narcotics in them but apparently no signs of sexual assault.

Chapter 2

The call from Jack Winchester came a little after ten to confirm his arrival for the next day. Jenna Whitmore had been out walking the streets of Marlinton, retracing the steps of the five dead women.

Though their bodies had been found in the nearby town of Green Bank, all of them were locals and Jenna had a hunch that whoever was responsible knew both areas. It had become a nightly routine, a means of exercise as well as another chance to spot something she may have overlooked. She had done it countless times since moving there eighteen months ago, a move that was intentional. Jenna had grown up in the area, and after six years of being a journalist in New York, she'd ventured back home to put down some roots. She wasn't getting much younger. She was thirty-eight and her mother had been harping on at her to find a man. Dates she could find. Good men, well that was the problem.

She looked both ways before crossing 8th Street, the main vein that ran through the town of just over a thousand residents. Marlinton was the largest town in Pocahontas County, West Virginia. Situated between the free-flowing Greenbrier River and the famous 78-mile-long trail, it offered more than enough for locals and visitors. At one time in the 1920s dozens of small railroading towns had dotted the landscape, now there were only nine in the rural county. Jenna was born a few miles outside Marlinton, in a town called Durbin, the second largest of the nine. Besides the recent string of deaths, the only time Marlinton had made headlines was back in 2013 when a fire destroyed an entire block of buildings on Main Street. Since then they had restored the area, and a restaurant called Tudor's Biscuit World had been built where the old McK Building once was.

She'd moved into what was considered a fairly modern apartment on 3rd Avenue, a few blocks away from the heart of town. It was a five-minute walk to City National Bank and there was a quaint café across the street called

DirtBean. Farther down was the Pocahontas County Opera House, a yellow building that looked more like a church than a location for theater buffs. On her way back she passed by the building that housed the *Pocahontas Times*, her place of employment until recently. She'd been let go for reasons that weren't exactly clear. They cited that she had become too involved in the Green Bank case, and it was conflicting with her ability to perform her duties, but that was just bullshit. Never once had she slacked off or fallen behind on her other work even when covering the story of the women's disappearances. They knew that but it didn't seem to matter. According to them, she was attracting unwanted attention. More bullshit. She was pretty certain that Tracey Reid, one of her co-workers, had played a role in her dismissal. She'd been vying for her position with the paper since she was hired.

Though she fought tooth and nail to get them to change their mind, she eventually backed off and took on a few freelance jobs, mostly writing articles. It wasn't as well paid as her last job but it paid the bills and kept things ticking over. Besides, it gave her more flexibility to work on investigating the Green Bank Five.

As she walked back to her apartment, she reflected on how different life in the small town was to the big city. New York was everything she had imagined, full of life, buzzing with activity and full of the promise of adventure. Marlinton, on the other hand, was a small town, with a slower pace. The nearest Wal-Mart was an hour and a half north in Elkins. With a little over a thousand people here, people generally knew too much about each other. Unlike the Big Apple, folks would wave, stop and speak to you in the daytime and would take the time to share every little detail about their mundane lives. At night though, the place took on a different feel. There was a dark underbelly; something that most locals wouldn't admit. It was easier to turn a blind eye, keep lips closed than to taint the small-town atmosphere and its heritage. Mind you, it wasn't always like that but a darker element had crept in and brought with it an increase in drug use, criminal behavior and sex work. It had begun to change the feel of what had become known as a safe place to raise a family. It felt different from nearby Durbin where she'd been born and raised along with her younger brother Corey.

If rumors were true, those in prominent positions in Marlinton, from the mayor all the way to the police, were involved in coverups but she didn't buy it. She'd met them and from what she could tell, they were as a straitlaced and vanilla as anyone could be.

Jenna arrived at the apartment block, an ugly gray building that looked as if it crouched at the edge of the road. There was a total of ten apartments inside. Though the owner of the property was pleasant, her son wasn't. He flat out refused to do any maintenance or even hire someone to fix issues. He said he didn't have the money. Fortunately, the bulk of the issues occurred on the ground floor. With the addition of the second-floor apartments, she'd landed herself a nice one-bedroom apartment. With her bag slung over her shoulder, she entered the stairwell.

The fluorescent lights blinked on and off. She cursed under her breath. How hard would it be to change a light bulb?

Farther down she noticed the exit door was ajar. Jenna frowned. That shouldn't have been open. She heard movement in the dark and a cold chill came over her. Jenna double-timed it up the concrete stairs aware that one of the other residents might have left the door open. It struck her as odd because it was only meant to be used in case of a fire. She cast a nervous glance over her shoulder. Her nerves were fried. Since investigating the case, she'd received a threatening letter warning her to back off, and several mysterious phone calls in the night. Each time it happened, the person didn't say anything. There was just the sound of heavy breathing. To say it had unnerved her would have been an understatement. It was pure intimidation; she knew it and so did whoever was doing it. She'd been to the police about it but their lack of interest in following up was evident from the first time she gave the report. She caught the officer at the front desk rolling her eyes. It was like they thought she had mental problems or that she was just seeking attention.

After a fair amount of pestering, an officer had been out to check on her apartment but that was it. He did nothing more than check the windows and doors and then make some off-the-cuff remark that she might do well by not dressing so provocatively. Jenna couldn't believe what she was hearing. Sure, she'd worn a low-cut top, but it was scorching that day and it was nothing compared to some of the attire she saw locals wearing, with their ass cheeks sticking out the back of daisy duke shorts or tops that were practically see-through. It was almost like the cop was suggesting that she was a street girl.

After letting herself into her apartment and driving home the chain on the other side, she placed her bag down and peered out the window into the darkness of night. She'd never been one to get frightened, especially after living in New York, a city where muggings occurred on a daily basis. But here now, after all that had happened, it felt dangerous.

Next, Jenna went through her daily routine. She checked the bathroom, her bedroom, and closets while holding a can of pepper spray. Once satisfied that no one was lurking in the shadows, she breathed a sigh of relief and crossed the room to the open kitchen and poured herself a glass of red wine.

As she poured, her eyes darted to the table. There in a tidy pile was her laptop, notebook and folders. On top of that was a digital voice recorder. She'd bought a top-of-the-line model to keep a record of tidbits, statements, observations and potential suspects. It could hold over four thousand hours and since the investigation had started, she had backed it up numerous times to a hard drive. Jenna slumped down on a sofa and took a large gulp from her glass before poring over her words. She hit rewind and then play and listened again to a conversation she'd had with a woman named Bailey Montgomery. A john who'd picked her up outside the Locust Hill Inn and

Restaurant had attacked her. At first it seemed like a typical encounter. She charged two hundred for an hour, and a hundred for half of that. Based on her description of the man, he was clean-cut and charismatic. It was only after they parked down a deserted trail on the outskirts of town that she saw the other side of him. He grabbed a hold of her throat while trying to slap on a pair of steel handcuffs. One minute she was engaged in conversation, the next fighting for her life. Fortunately, she'd managed to escape because she scraped his neck with her keys. In those brief seconds that he released her, she pushed out of the vehicle and scrambled into the surrounding woods to the safety of a nearby home.

Jenna listened intently to the conversation.

"And so you reported it to the police?"

"No."

"Why not?"

"I'm not even supposed to be out there. I have two kids. If they found out what I was doing, they would call child welfare. I can't risk that."

"But he tried to kill you."

"Some guys get rough. It's just the nature of what we do. I usually have a driver who takes me to the outcalls, but he wasn't available that night. If he'd been there, it would have been a different outcome."

"So he follows?"

"He stays close. Out of sight and I keep him on speakerphone. The first sign of trouble he's in."

"And how long ago was this?"

"A month, maybe two."

"And have you seen this man who attacked you since?"

She shook her head. "I've only just got back out there in the last couple of weeks. It shook me up but I need the money."

Jenna hit stop on the recorder. It had taken her the better part of six months to get some of the girls to trust her. At first, some were belligerent, others didn't mind, but they wanted money first. But that was part of the problem; once money was involved, it was hard to tell if they were being truthful or not, of if they were just telling her what she wanted to hear. Over the course of the past three months, it had felt like she was chasing her tail. It had been a month since the body of Brenda Norris had been found. He was out there, watching, waiting and would eventually strike again. That's what niggled her the most. She couldn't keep going without help — especially with the recent string of phone calls and the letter — she was starting to think that perhaps she had become the next target. That's what had driven her to call Jack Winchester.

She pressed play again, and for the next twenty minutes pored over snippets of statements from family, friends, and co-workers. It seemed as if everyone had something to say. Theories and allegations were rampant, some were merited, others outlandish. Jenna rubbed her eyes and headed into the washroom to splash some cold water over her face. It was rare that she got to bed before two in the morning. It wasn't that she wasn't tired, quite the opposite, her body was exhausted but her mind wouldn't shut off. She pulled back her long dark hair and put it through a hair tie. Her eyes were large, dark, and she had crow's feet at the corners from losing her temper too many times with ex-boyfriends. At least that's what she told others, as she hated to admit she was getting old. Still, her eyes were sharp and full of purpose. *You're getting close,* she told herself as she gripped the sides of the wash basin and stared at the water trickling down her almond-shaped face. Her mind was occupied with the story that would break the case wide open. This was the one that would get justice for those girls.

As she dried her skin, the sound of her phone caught her attention; she went back into the living room and scooped it up. The glow of the caller ID revealed who it was. Jenna pecked the screen.

"Corey."

"Hey, sis, heard you were down at the church today asking questions."

She sighed and wandered into the kitchen and pulled out some cheese from the fridge.

"Just following up on leads."

"You know all this digging around is liable to land you in hot water. I've already had to speak on your behalf."

"About?"

"People are concerned. About your well-being."

She let out a chuckle. "No, they just don't have anything better to do with their time than stick their nose into other people's business."

"Funny you should say that as that's exactly what they said about you."

"I'm a journalist, Corey, it's my job."

"But it's consuming you. I've never seen you like this. Surely, losing your job at the *Times* would have snapped you out of this…"

"This?" She paused. "What are you saying, Corey?"

He sighed. "I'm just concerned. I'm your brother; I have a right to be worried about you."

"I know." She nodded before cutting into some cheese and pulling out a box of crackers from the cupboard and tipping it. Several slipped out and she pushed the phone into the crux of her neck.

"Anyway, why the phone calls?"

"I got word that Tim had seen Brenda on the night she went missing."

There was a pause, then a snort on the other end. "Please tell me you are not thinking what I think you are."

"I'm not saying he's involved. But he runs the home for wayward women, and Brenda's mother received a call from him a couple of days after she went missing to say that she'd swung by that night after seeing a client. She was acting erratic and wanted to speak. I just wanted to know what that conversation was about."

"You know as well as I do that he runs a very transparent program."

"Then there shouldn't be any problem answering my questions. He doesn't even pick up."

"He's busy."

"You know that's not true."

He sighed again. "There are people that handle these kinds of things, Jenna. The police."

"Yeah and a fine job they are doing of nailing this sicko."

"Sicko? They haven't classed any of the recent discoveries as murders and according to the reports in the media, these women were known drug users. In fact, the jury is still out as to whether this wasn't just some drug deal gone wrong. You know yourself the town is ripe with all manner of sin."

"Corey, this conversation isn't going to turn into a sermon, is it? Because I really have a lot to do before tomorrow."

"If you showed up on Sundays, I wouldn't need to. Anyway, what's happening tomorrow?"

"A friend is visiting. Someone who'll give me a hand with the investigation."

He groaned. "For goodness' sakes, get some sleep, Jenna. And call mom tomorrow. She's been worried sick about you. Both of us have."

Chapter 3

It was almost midnight when Jenna sat in front of her computer. She was still waiting on a message from one of the girls who had got in contact a couple days ago after responding to a post she'd left on the backpage.com website in the escorts section.

Backpage was a free classified ads website similar to Kijiji or craigslist. According to those who knew the missing women, it was commonplace for women to post ads and connect with men looking for services. In one night they could earn what would take them two weeks slaving in some fast food joint. It was enticing to those with a drug habit and a vicious cycle for those needing cash. Once they'd gained a taste for how quick money could be made, walking away was tough even for those not on drugs. She kept refreshing her email, but no further messages came in. She wasn't sure if the girl had got cold feet or if the recent murder of Norris had made her think twice about coming forward.

The headline read: JOURNALIST SEEKS ESCORT FOR INFORMATION. Beneath that she had written: *I am looking to speak with escorts who were offering services in Marlinton over the past two years and think they might have come across someone linked to the disappearance of the Green Bank Five. I have discovered a possible link and believe I know who may be responsible. All I require is someone to confirm my suspicion.*

It was a ballsy move. She was hanging it out there, baiting him to see it, by posting in the same hunting ground that other women had said he used to find the five. Jenna knew the risk involved, and it was possible that the recent letter and phone calls in the middle of the night had been him responding, taunting, and deciding what he would do next but she was at the end of her rope and tired of going around in circles. One minute she would think she was close to nailing whoever had done this, and the next it was like being back at square one. She needed to speak with someone.

She stared at the screen. The last message she got from a girl named Meghan was dated two days ago. It was short and straight to the point.

"I have information that might help. I will be in contact soon."

Soon? What did that mean? An hour, a day, a week?

She wondered if she had scared her off. Maybe she thought she was a cop. Jenna nibbled at the corner of her thumb, a nervous habit she'd got from her mother. Her mind was awhirl with facts surrounding the case, and the statements released by the police. She didn't understand why this wasn't getting national attention and yet on the other hand, it made sense. Marlinton officials didn't want to appear ignorant of the presence of a killer among them. The members of the Pocahontas County Sheriff Department had already had their name tainted on several occasions by allegations of heavy-handed policing and mistakes made in criminal investigations. Having a spotlight shone upon their work, or lack of it, was the last thing they wanted.

Besides, these women were society's write-offs who operated with burner phones, cash transactions, and multiple identifications. They breezed in and out of towns and cities; some operating independently, others pimped out. They were the kind of women that wouldn't be missed. Drug users, single mothers, their lives had a track record as long as the black marks that littered their arms. The few that had confided in her had painted a dismal picture of their lives. They didn't do anything beyond work. They had no hobbies, goals or fun. What they did was a matter of survival, a vicious cycle of earning cash to feed a drug habit.

She blew out her cheeks and glanced at the time. She'd give it until just after midnight and then turn in. If she didn't get some sleep, she would be of no use to Jack when he arrived. A scrap of paper on the table had his number on it. A friend of hers from New York knew someone who had hired him to find his daughter. They spoke well of him. For the most part he was liked and respected but more than anything, he was good at finding people and protecting those in need. The fact was she needed not only muscle but also someone with new insights, someone who could look at the case from a different angle. Admittedly she was too close to the case and without the team from the *Times*, she felt singled out, like a fish in a sea of sharks that was circling her and waiting for the right time to strike.

Jenna thumbed through the flyers she had created and handed out in some of the sleaziest parts of town. She'd gone to bars, motels and even visited a local massage parlor that was rumored to be offering more than a massage. She'd posted them in windows, and on telephone poles. All of them were plastered with the faces and names of Rachel Dixon, Susan Holt, Paula Roberts, Dixie Stokes and Brenda Norris.

Handing out flyers hadn't come without a fair amount of heat from residents as well as local police who were getting complaints from those who felt it was bringing the town down. Soon, their faces started to disappear and all that was left was a few torn flyers on posts.

Several times she had come close to giving up the search for answers. Not even her own mother or brother understood what she was trying to accomplish. It would have been easy to forget or turn a blind eye, just as the residents or police had, but after seeing the families, talking to them and holding framed photos of the victims, it strengthened her resolve.

Another click on the keyboard to refresh her inbox. Nothing! *Damn it.* She got up and crossed into the kitchen to get another glass of wine. Pulling out her phone she flicked through the various photos of potential suspects. They each had a reason and yet in all honesty it could have been anyone. These women were seeing two or three guys a night, some even more. Outcalls, incalls, the escort section on backpage was like a buffet for a killer. As she poured another glass, she misjudged the amount of tilt and ended up splashing the counter. *Shit.* Frantically she looked around for some paper towel but was all out. The kitchen was a mess. The sink was full of microwave dinner trays. The trash bin was overflowing and badly in need of being emptied. She glanced around at the once-pristine apartment. She'd prided herself on being organized and keeping her home and workplace clean. She caught her reflection in the glass door. *What are you doing?* After wiping up the wine and tossing the dirty rag into the sink, she shuffled to her bedroom and collapsed on the futon. She was exhausted both mentally and physically. Was this really worth it? The doubts kept creeping in.

Corey was right. This was consuming her and for what? This was the reason why she didn't have a husband or boyfriend. Who would honestly put up with this? Even if she did manage to find out the truth, how would that change anything? Sure, the parents would get some closure, but the women would still be gone. Nothing would change that. She shook her head and allowed her eyelids to close.

In that instant, her computer dinged. She opened one eye.

No, leave it.

But it could be her.

Leave it, she told herself again.

But the investigation could put an end to this killer.

This went beyond the lives of five women. If someone didn't catch him now, others would die and then she'd have that on her conscience. She couldn't bear to think that she had got close and then bailed.

Jenna pushed off the bed and went back to the living room and took a seat in front of the laptop. She rubbed her tired eyes and tapped a key to bring the computer to life. The glare of the light made her squint. She narrowed her eyes and focused on the message that came in from the girl.

"Meet me tonight at twelve thirty and I'll tell you what I know. I'm at the corner of Smith and Delta Road."

That was it. No description of what she looked like. Jenna glanced at the clock on her computer. The time was just after ten past twelve. Anxiously she bit down on her lip. *This is what you've been waiting for. This could be the last chance you get. Go. Speak to her.* Jenna scooped up the car keys off the counter and was about to dash out when she stopped and went back to the voice recorder, the backup hard drive and cell. She had no idea what she was getting herself into or who might be following her, for all she knew this could be some attempt to lure her out. Perhaps that's how it was being done. Was a woman responsible? It would at least explain why none of the women had been sexually assaulted. Or was a woman being used as a means to lower their guards until they were out of earshot and then someone else stepped into the picture?

The content she'd accumulated was too valuable to leave out in the open. She raised a hand to her mouth and bit down on a fingernail. They were worn down, barely visible. Thinking fast, she took the small voice recorder, hard drive and cell and entered her bathroom. Her eyes scanned the ceiling tiles. She got up on the toilet seat and pushed up one of them but then got back down. *No, not there*, she thought. That's when she went back into the kitchen, placed them in a zip-lock bag, covered it with another one, then pushed it inside another plastic bag before heading back into her bathroom. She took the top off the back of the toilet and placed it inside the tank. It was above the water, tucked between the side and the valve. Once satisfied that it wouldn't slip in, she covered the tank back up and put a vase of flowers on top of that.

She felt she'd done her best to remain as anonymous as she could but there was no telling how sophisticated this killer was, or whether there was more than one. As she snatched up her keys and headed out, she chewed over the idea of there being a group involved in the abduction of the women. It certainly would have been easier to control them.

Outside it was extraordinarily quiet, save for the crickets, frogs and forest critters that could be heard and the odd vehicle returning home in her neighborhood. It was drizzling; a fine layer of rain covered the windshield on her 2008 Ford Escape. She ducked out of the apartment block with a hand over her head and slipped into the vehicle.

Jenna contemplated calling the cops, her brother, or a friend — anyone who she could at least tell where she was heading. Who knew what she was about to walk into? But they would only gripe, and the cops would think she was overreacting. She'd pretty much worn out her welcome to the point where she was sure they had blacklisted her number.

Five minutes later she was pulled onto Delta Road 1. It was just off Route 39. All around, smothering the landscape were thick fern and oak trees. Not a smidgen of light was in the sky that night. No moon. No stars. It was like death itself had drifted in and swallowed up the small town.

Jenna gripped the wheel so tight her knuckles turned white. The headlights splashed across the road capturing the silhouette of a pitiful-looking figure off to the right. The rain was now coming down harder, and she had her wipers on full speed. As she got closer, she could tell it was the woman. She was about five seven with protruding features. The rain plastered hair to her face and drenched her clothes. She eased off the gas and veered off to the hard shoulder. The door opened, and she got in shaking off droplets of water. She flashed a grin and under the glow of the inside light Jenna could see she was a meth user. Her teeth were badly in need of a dentist, though her face was pretty. It was a sad state.

"Meghan?" Jenna asked. She nodded.

"Drive on."

Jenna pulled out and kept an eye on the woman by shooting her a sideways glance every so often. *What are you doing inviting a stranger into your vehicle after midnight? This is insane*, she thought. Meghan's makeup was running. She pulled out a case from her purse and flipped the visor down. A small light either side of the mirror provided just enough illumination to allow her to clean her face.

"Do you have the money?"

"What?"

"Your ad. It stated you would pay for information. Money first."

"Oh. Right."

Jenna reached over and felt around for her handbag.

"I'll get it," Meghan said. She had visions of her jumping out or striking her with the bag just so she could take the money. Nope, instead, she rooted through it and pulled out the purse and handed it to her. Keeping her eyes on the road, she placed it between her legs and fumbled with the zipper before pulling out a couple hundred dollars and handing it over. Meghan tucked the notes into her bra and then pulled out a packet of cigarettes.

"Got a light?"

Jenna pushed in the button on the car lighter. Though she had a number of vices, smoking wasn't one of them. When it popped out, the girl put it to the end, and it glowed bright orange. Smoke filled the inside, and she brought the window down. She never asked if it was okay, then again it was to be expected, most of the women she'd met did whatever they wanted.

"So what can you tell me?" Jenna asked, eager to hear.

"You'll know soon enough. For now, I need you to drive me to one more client, then I will tell you."

"That wasn't the deal. I said I would pay you."

"Listen up, lady." Her tone changed and became sharp. Jenna immediately regretted letting her into the vehicle. "The two hundred is for my time, I still have a job to do and I'm not going to lose this client on account of you."

Jenna didn't agree but what other options were there? Kicking her out? Not after paying her.

She sighed and pressed on the gas. "Where do you need to go?"

"Green Bank."

Chapter 4

Deputy Sam Larson entered his darkened home on the outskirts of Marlinton at around twelve-thirty that evening. He carefully hung the keys to his Ford Crown Victoria cruiser on the hook, tugged off his boots and headed into the kitchen to get himself a glass of water before he turned in for the night. A light switched on and his wife, Kerry, was sitting in a rocking chair with their young daughter. At twenty-six, he'd been married to her since he was twenty-one. She had been his high school sweetheart. Both of them had grown up in small towns in West Virginia, though he'd never imagined he would remain there. He had his heart set on Charleston. Kerry had other plans.

"Still up?" he asked, surprised to see her awake.

"Baby wouldn't settle. I've only just managed to get her to fall asleep."

He turned on the faucet and filled a glass before

chugging it down and leaning back against the granite counter. They'd moved into the two-bedroom home as soon as she got pregnant. It was a step up from the dive of an apartment they'd been living in on the west side. He unbuckled his duty belt and took it into the living room.

"What's up?" she asked.

He shrugged but didn't reply. He slumped down in his chair and yawned hard. He was exhausted but found it difficult to go straight to bed when he got in. He needed to unwind as his mind was still preoccupied with the last few calls that had put him into overtime. Mostly domestics, dealing with drunks and those who thought it was fine to beat on women. Policing in a small town with just over a thousand people wasn't all it was cracked up to be, certainly not what he had in mind when he entered the recruitment process. He'd yearned for policing in a big city, something that would give him variety and keep him busy around the clock.

Here, in Marlinton, it was a joke. The twelve-hour shifts moved by painfully slow. The calls were all the same. But he had taken the position because of Kerry. She was worried about him not coming home, and with the newborn, her concerns had only increased. The fact was it didn't matter whether he was working in a city or a small town, every time he headed out that door there was a possibility he wouldn't return. Things could go south real quick. In his first year alone, back when he was on probation, he'd already stared down the barrel of a rifle on two occasions. Fortunately, he was able to talk his way out of it. Next time he knew he might not be as lucky. Of course, he hadn't told Kerry that. She would have had him hand in his badge the same day. No, there were some things he didn't share with her. It was better that way. She had enough stress on her plate.

"Was there another death?"

"No."

Kerry struggled to get out of the rocking chair. He was about to give her a hand but she got up and disappeared out of the kitchen. Sam leaned to one side and retrieved the *Pocahontas Times*. Local events, awards and achievements took up most of the front-page news. It lacked the punch he was hoping to find. Though the recent string of disappearances and deaths of five women had managed to garner some attention, once it got out the kind of lives the women were leading, it soon faded into the background. Sam had been biting at the bit to get involved but the chief said State Police and the FBI were now handling it. That was a crock of shit. He'd yet to see any of them in Marlinton for longer than a day after the discovery of each body. Sure they had shown up, asked questions and gone through the bare minimum required, but what then? Even the families were baffled by what was being done. It pissed him off. The chief wasn't the one that had to deal with the public on a day-to-day basis, he didn't have to make excuses or look into the eyes of heartbroken family members.

Kerry returned to the kitchen, cracked the fridge open and stood there for a minute in the glow before taking out the milk. She tucked a strand of her long dark hair behind one ear and gave him a smile. Even when she was tired, had dark circles around her eyes, and probably felt like crap, she still looked beautiful.

"You want a glass of warm milk?"

"No, I'm good."

She put a pot on the stove to heat it up.

"About time we get a microwave, isn't it?" he asked.

"And cause interference?" she said without even looking at him.

"You know that ban only applies to Green Bank. We're out of the restricted area."

"But still in the quiet zone."

He shook his head. While the National Radio Quiet Zone's thirteen thousand square miles covered the eastern half of West Virginia, only those inside a ten-mile radius of the National Radio Astronomy Observatory were prohibited from using devices that emitted a frequency. Marlinton wasn't included. It frustrated him to no end. They lived twenty-six miles away from Green Bank and the most restricted area, and yet a large majority of folks still lived as though it was the 1950s. As much as he respected his wife's concern for the Green Bank Observatory, he drew the line at cell phones and wireless Internet. He cast his eyes down at the paper to a small article with the headline:

NO LEADS IN THE DEATH OF MARLINTON RESIDENT

The Pocahontas County Sheriff Department and the WV State Police are still investigating the death of Marlinton local Brenda Norris. She was reported missing two months ago. She was in her late 20s to early 30s and was last seen at the Locust Hill Inn Pub on the night of May 11, 2017. She was wearing a green shirt with dark khaki pants and had shoulder-length hair. Her body was found in Deer Creek by a Green Bank resident while out walking her dog.

If you saw her in Green Bank or have any knowledge related to this case, please call the Pocahontas County 911 Center.

Kerry wandered in with a mug in both hands, she glanced down at it.

"You'd think by now they would have found

something."

He folded the paper, sighed and tossed it on the floor. "I should have gone through the recruitment process for a position with the State Police."

"Is that what's bothering you?" She took a seat across from him and curled up her legs.

"They want anyone who has information to call us, and yet we aren't even the ones handling the case. WVSP are. All we are doing is passing on leads."

"And the FBI?"

"Oh please, they showed up for a day and the last I heard that was only to save face. Their resources are maxed out. Since 9/11 most of them are working on cases related to terrorism. The Bureau is not what it used to be. They simply don't have the time."

He shook his head, juggling his inner frustrations.

"But we discussed this, Sam. You could have been posted anywhere. I wanted us—"

"To be close to family. I know." He sniffed and took a sip of his water. "It's just..." he trailed off. They'd had this conversation numerous times. There was no changing it now so he didn't even know why he bothered to mention it.

"Look, there is more to policing than spending every waking hour chasing down criminals. Your recruiter told you…"

"It's hours of boredom and seconds of sheer terror," Sam said before she could get it out. "I guess I was just hoping for a little more action."

"Can't you speak to the chief and see if you can be involved more with the investigation?"

He groaned. "It doesn't work like that, Kerry."

She shrugged. "I don't know how it works. I'm just fed up with you coming home looking frustrated. If I had known you were going to be like this, I would have…"

"What? Would have what?"

She shook her head. "I'm going back to bed. I have to be up early in the morning."

He nodded. She left leaving tension in the air. He hated going to bed angry, and yet he only had himself to blame. He should have kept his mouth shut or put his foot down and signed up with WVSP, at least then he would be in the thick of it. As he sat there contemplating heading off to bed, he got a text from Ethan Rigby, one of the officers on the night shift. He checked his phone only to find another one of his gags. The guy was full of them, except they were groan-worthy. He tossed it down and engaged the La-Z-Boy chair. The number of nights he'd fallen asleep in there were too many to number. His phone buzzed again, and he snatched it up out of habit. This time it was a phone call from the department.

"Sam, you asleep yet?"

"I will be in about five minutes."

"You think you can come in for a couple of hours?"

"I just got off a shift that ran into overtime."

"It's Ethan. He's taken a turn for the worst."

Sam's brow furrowed. "But he just texted me a few minutes ago."

"So can you?"

He groaned. That was the problem with being the new

guy. Shit rolled downhill and the hill in this department wasn't very steep. There were only six uniformed deputies, one shift commander, one patrol sergeant, one captain, one chief deputy and a sheriff.

"What about Matt?"

"He's in Durbin dealing with a dispute. Look, I wouldn't ask but you know how these things work."

"Of course, I'll be there in five."

"Good man."

He hung up and texted Ethan back. "Asshole."

This wasn't the first time he had done it. Ethan had been with the Pocahontas County Sheriff Department the longest, and as shift work operated on seniority, he tended to get away with a lot of shit, especially when it came to nights. He hated doing them. It wasn't like it was hard work. Most of the time the guys would park up, do some paperwork and turn the radio down and catch a few winks. Not Ethan. The problem was Sam wasn't in a position to argue. Sure he was out of his probationary period but in their books, he was still wet behind the ears and Ethan was milking it for all it was worth.

He rubbed his eyes and pushed out of the comfort of the chair and went about getting ready to head out. Kerry must have heard him puttering around as she made her way back down.

"I thought you were coming to bed?"

"They've called me back in."

"Another one?"

"No, just Ethan."

"You need to tell Brian about this. It's not right, Sam."

"Yeah, well, it is what it is." He snapped in place his duty belt, and finished making a coffee. "That's life in the fast lane, isn't it? Maybe I'll get a promotion to head coffee maker," he said in a sarcastic manner. She narrowed her gaze as he leaned in to give her a kiss. Kerry pulled her cheek away and put up a finger.

"Be careful."

"Always."

The baby started crying again and Kerry sighed. "Just when I thought I was going to get some sleep."

"You and me both."

Despite their disagreements, he loved her and would do anything to keep her happy. In many ways she was right. He had his kid to think about now. His idea of solving murders, chasing after criminals and being at the helm of some newsworthy investigation was just a dream. Some grandiose, unrealistic idea that ended the second he stepped inside the academy. Kerry headed upstairs to take care of Anna-Belle, and he finished up twisting the cap on a flask of coffee. It was going to be a long night.

* * *

She was breathing hard and not making any sense. It was a rambling incoherent mess. Words and tears jumbled together. It seemed like nothing more than the babbling of an insane person. The call had woken him out of a deep sleep. It took him a few seconds to get his bearings, let alone understand what she was shouting. Was it a prank? A wrong number? Hell, a few times he couldn't even tell if it was a female. There was a lot of crying, and desperation in the voice. In the background was the distant sound of a vehicle.

Jack held the phone to his ear and perched on the side of his bed. "Who is this?"

The person was barely able to string two words together. By any measure she sounded like she was high. He had encountered a lot of drug users in his time. When they were really out of it, they couldn't speak clearly, it was like they had a mouthful of marbles or were dribbling after dental surgery.

He put a finger in his other ear. "Speak up, I can't hear you."

It was like her mouth wasn't anywhere near the receiver.

Words blended together as if she was in a rush. She was completely incoherent. At first, he just thought it was a joke, and he hung up. But she called back again within a matter of a minute. This time he caught a few words. "Meghan Palmer."

"Your name is Meghan?"

Again, back to dribble from her lips. "For God's sake,

woman, it's the middle of the night, who are you?" The reply was mixed together with tears and intense crying. Whoever it was, they were putting on one hell of an act. But why him? Why now? He stared at the clock. The red luminous numbers flashed back two seventeen. It was too damn early for this. He was planning to leave for Marlinton at six. It would take him until early evening before he reached there and that was if he didn't stop.

"Look..."

She muttered again, this time words of pleading.

That's when he thought he caught the name Jenna but when he asked her to confirm, he got no response. She'd gone quiet. Then slowly he could hear her mumbling. It was almost as faint as a whisper. Getting annoyed, he was seconds away from hanging up when she started to flip out. A scream echoed so loud he had to pull the phone away from his ear.

"I'm sorry, I think you've dialed the wrong number."

"Jack," she croaked out.

"Who is this?"

"No. No!" the woman yelled, her words blending together. Next, it sounded as if she was fighting for her life. In the background, Jack could hear a male voice. It was firm and gruff.

"Give me that."

"Let me go."

Several knocks could be heard as if plastic was hitting plastic. Then he heard one more thing. "Jack, it's…"

Several large thuds were followed by a groan, and then a few more as if someone was being struck with the phone. What came next was the close-up sound of a male's voice breathing hard before he hung up.

Jenna? Jenna Whitmore?

His mind went into overdrive. He dialed *69 to get the last phone number. Once he had that, he rang the operator and asked if they could tell him where the number was from. The operator put him on hold for a few minutes and then returned.

"Green Bank, West Virginia."

Chapter 5

After the operator hung up, Jack tried Jenna's cell. There was no answer. Each time it just went to voice mail. Exhausted and disturbed by the call, he leaned back and closed his eyes, contemplating his next step.

Jenna had already paid him a quarter of his fees. Although his initial reaction to save time was to pack a bag, book a flight and hire a car when he got there, could he really be sure that it was her? It was incoherent at best. He cursed under his breath, rolled over and jotted down the one name he'd heard, Meghan Palmer. It was the only thing he could discern amid the jumbled mess of words. He swore he'd heard the name Jenna but he couldn't be certain. It certainly didn't sound like the woman he'd spoken to earlier that day.

As he chewed it over, he slowly succumbed to his tiredness.

* * *

The following morning, after gathering together his belongings, Jack handed in his keys to the front desk and headed towards his car.

"Hey there, are you leaving?" Serena called out to him.

"Afraid so."

"For how long?"

Jack held the door to his vehicle open. "Not sure yet."

"Well, if you are ever in the neighborhood, swing by."

He smiled and gave a nod. It was strange, but he felt more at home in that dingy motel than he had in a long time. The connections he made with strangers in that short time had more depth than those he'd known for years. Though he never mentioned what he did for a living, he never got the sense that he needed to hide his past or lie about his work. He had a feeling they were all running from one thing or another. Over the past year he'd traveled around the States, stopping for only a day or two in motels until a job was completed or he became restless. The idea of putting down roots was no longer in his mind. He enjoyed the open road and the eclectic variety of people that crossed his path. After spending so many years in New York, seeing some of the United States was like a breath of fresh air. When he was driving on the open road, talking with strangers or taking on jobs in some small town in the middle of nowhere, he felt at peace and no longer bothered by the demons of his past.

He slipped into the Shelby and the smell of new leather put him at ease as he turned over the key. The engine rumbled, and he eased the car out of the parking lot. He tapped the address into the GPS and headed southeast. He figured if he only stopped a couple of times, he'd be there by five at the latest. Three minutes later he was on the main road, and an hour after that he was well on his way to Marlinton.

He crossed the country by way of US-35 east and I-65. The farther away from the city, the more the landscape changed into wide-open spaces. Either side of the highway were farmhouses, and old barns set back from the road, along with the occasional run-down diner or gas station. The vast landscape shimmered in the morning sun, and for a short while, his mind was at peace. No longer in the past, or the future, just in the present. He passed through Merville, Lafayette, Indianapolis, Dayton, Charleston and a whack of small towns that seemed stuck in the dark ages. In the last leg of the journey, he passed through Monongahela before making his way into Pocahontas County. It was like stepping back in time. Over five hundred and seventy-eight square miles of scenic beauty. In the distance, he could see the Allegheny Mountains surrounded by an ocean of red spruce, balsam fir, and mountain ash trees. Every few miles he would see signs for Snowshoe Mountain Resort, Greenbrier River Trail, Droop Mountain Battlefield State Park and the Cranberry Glades. The place was an absolute gold mine for outdoor enthusiasts. Not that he would get to enjoy it the way others would. He liked to keep his mind on the job. In. Out. No messing around. However, he had a feeling that this wasn't going to be so easy.

Still, it would be home for the next few weeks.

* * *

Jack stepped out of his car and surveyed the Locust Hill Inn and Restaurant on the outskirts of Marlinton. He'd been driving almost non-stop for ten hours and it felt good to stretch his legs. The tension in his neck and shoulders remained, a reminder that he should have stopped more frequently. It was a hot day, even though the sun was beginning to wane behind the trees. The lodgings were set back from the road. A long winding road led up to the inn which overlooked the rich landscape and was framed by green mountains and mist. It was a short distance from the downtown and close to the Greenbrier River Trail.

As it was getting darker, the red-brick, two-story home was lit up like a Christmas tree. Jack wandered up the steps and entered the main door. Inside he was greeted by a young lady who offered refreshments. He declined and headed over to the main desk. A large, burly man in his late fifties was on the phone. He acknowledged Jack with a raised finger and quickly told whoever he was speaking to that he'd have to get back to them.

"Welcome. Welcome. And you would be?"

"Jack Winchester."

"Right." He flipped through a book in front of him, then tapped the keys on his computer and his face lit up. "There we go. Room for one, five nights."

"It may be longer."

"Sure, just let us know. If we can't keep you in the same room, we have a cabin as well as other rooms here in the house. I just need a credit card."

"I don't have one."

The man frowned. "That's a first. How did you book it?"

"The website said I could pay in cash upon arrival."

"Um. You wouldn't mind showing me which site that was, would you?"

"Is there a problem?"

"Well, it's just that guests usually book in advance with a credit card."

"Look, sure, I'll show you the site but I'm tired. I've driven for over ten hours. I would just like to go to my room."

The man pursed his lips and put his finger up again. He stepped away and disappeared out back. When he returned, he was with a heavyset lady who was wearing far too much makeup. Her earrings looked as if they were shower curtain hooks — thick, ugly, something from the 1980s era. Her outfit wasn't much better. A large flowery dress with one too many colors.

"Ed, I'll handle it. Just go and serve the customers."

He looked red in the face as he wandered off, flashing Jack one more embarrassed look.

"Sorry about that. My husband tends to do everything by the book." She looked him up and down. "I'm not sure where or how you managed to book a room but it would have meant using a credit card."

"I didn't use a card. Look, if this is going to be a problem. I'll just go find another place."

Jack turned to leave, and she was quick to stop him.

"No. No, it's okay. Years ago we used to let folks reserve a room without a credit card and it worked for a time but then guests wouldn't show up and it made filling rooms challenging. You probably came across one of the old sites. Anyway, it's been kind of slow this week, so you're in luck. We will, however, need all the money upfront if you are paying in cash. It's eighty-eight dollars for the night or a hundred and twenty-five for the cabin." Jack pulled out a wad of notes and thumbed off enough to cover a week. Her eyes lit up. If push came to shove, he could always find another place. A week would do for now. The woman was quick to snatch up the money and tuck it away inside her bra. *So it's that kind of place,* Jack thought.

"Follow me. I'm Beth Robertson by the way. My husband is Ed."

He noticed several couples were eating in a dining area off to the right. A pretty waitress flashed him a smile before threading around tables with a jug of iced tea. Beth led him up two flights of stairs.

"I hope you don't mind the attic. It's our newly renovated third floor. Queen-sized bed, bathroom and there is a balcony that overlooks the pond. If you get up early enough, it provides a breathtaking view of the mountains. Every one of our guests who have stayed here has said how much they love it."

"It will do fine."

All the floors were made of oak hardwood. When he reached the attic, it was quite spacious — nothing special but nice. A bed with a dark patterned spread was off to the left. There was a cream-colored sofa ahead of him and a bathroom with shower to the right. A large flowery rug covered most of the floor and a small flat-screen TV was positioned on a redwood dresser. Beth crossed the room to a dingy air-conditioning unit stuck into the wall and gave it a thump. It let out a groan revealing its age before the fan kicked in.

"It's on the brink of giving up the ghost, so give it a knock if you find yourself sweltering." She glanced around. "There are fresh towels in the bathroom, the Wi-Fi password is in the envelope on the dresser, there is a cozy robe behind the door and breakfast starts at seven and ends at nine. We serve a full cooked breakfast." She breathed in deeply while sticking her oversized hands into the front of the apron. "Any questions?"

Jack dropped his bag on the bed.

"Green Bank. How far is it from here?"

"About twenty-five miles north. You have friends there?"

"Nope."

"Not much to see up there. It's a very small town."

Jack fished around in his jacket and pulled out a scrap of paper with the address that Jenna Whitmore had given him. He handed it to her. "You know this location?"

"Of course. You have to go back the way you came. Stick to 8th Street and you will see 3rd Avenue on the left. Can't miss it. If you get lost, just look for signs for the Opera House. It's across the street from that." She paused before handing it back. "You here on business or strictly pleasure?"

He took it from her and placed it back into his jacket. "A bit of both."

She frowned as if confused by his answer. "Right, then I will leave you to it. Any questions, don't hesitate to phone the front desk or come down." She paused at the staircase. "Are you hungry? We have a nice restaurant that is open until nine. The weekends tend to get busy, so if you want to make sure you aren't disturbed I would suggest getting there at five." She turned and made it a few steps down before shouting over her shoulder, "Oh and we don't allow hookers here. So if you have any ideas about that, it's out of the question. There are no porn channels either. We run a clean house."

And just like that, she continued on down until he heard a door shut. Jack exhaled hard and perched on the edge of the bed for a few seconds before getting up and heading over to the window. Outside a 4 x 4 and a Chevy rolled in with fishing gear in the back. A couple of rough-looking fellas hopped out. One spat a wad of tobacco on the ground and headed inside.

Yeah, he certainly wasn't in Chicago anymore.

Jack removed his jacket and slung it over the end of

the bed. In the corner of the room was a small fridge. Curious, he went over and cracked it open. Sure enough, inside were several bottles of water as well as some snacks and small bottles of spirits. There was a note on top of the fridge that gave him a list of all the prices. He took out a small bottle of Jack Daniel's, twisted the cap off and took a hard pull on it before walking over to the window and looking out. A small amount of rain began to fall. He had a sense of foreboding. Small towns were nice to visit but he'd often found the people tended to operate outside the law.

A silver sedan crawled into the parking lot and parked near the front. A man and woman got out and covered their hair with their jackets as they made a rush for the house. While he surveyed the property, he gave Jenna's number one more try — again it went to voice mail. As much as he wanted to relax before going over to see her, he was beginning to think that perhaps that peculiar call in the middle of the night had more to it than his tired mind could comprehend. If it was her, this job had already become more complicated. As Mother Nature began to unleash her fury outside on West Virginia, Jack felt far from anything he was familiar with. He was alone in his thoughts as he finished off his drink and wandered into the bathroom. There, he stripped and got under the shower to wash off the grime of the day. Being in and out of the vehicle, smothered in heat one minute and in air conditioning the next, had taken its toll. The room soon became humid and filled with steam. After getting out, he wiped away the condensation on the mirror and gazed at his weathered face. Closing in on forty, he still had a thick head of hair, though the sides had a few silver strands. *How many more years can you do this?* He thought. He wasn't old but he wasn't getting much younger. The closest he'd got to a normal life was in Florida, or his time with Dana in Maine.

He unzipped his bag and laid out on the bed a fresh pair of jeans, a dark shirt, and his Glock. He took a few minutes to get dressed, then gazed at himself in the full-length mirror on the back of the bathroom door. Not too shabby. The last thing he wanted to do was draw attention to himself and yet in his line of work, it was hard not to. He had to poke his nose where it wasn't wanted, cross paths with the violent and dance with the law at every turn.

Jack pushed the Glock into the back of his pants before covering it with his shirt.

He snatched up some money, his phone, and keys and headed out the door a little after five forty-five. On the ground floor, Beth spotted him while she was giving instructions to the pretty waitress.

"A table perhaps?"

"Actually, I'm heading out."

"Oh. Tomorrow then, perhaps?"

He nodded and went out onto the porch. Rain hammered the vehicles in the lot and turned the muddy driveway into a slow-moving stream. There were several other couples waiting for the rain to die down before they dared step out. They looked him up and down while he stood there.

"Crazy weather, huh?" A gruff-looking man tried to engage with him. He looked over and gave a nod before making a dash for his car. He didn't want to get into it with anyone. Questions were always the same. Where are you from? Why are you here? What do you do? Too many questions could lead to trouble and right now he was enjoying the peace. Trouble would eventually rear its ugly head and when it did he would be ready, but now, he was content to observe.

Chapter 6

The drive from the inn to 3rd Avenue was a short ride. It took less than ten minutes. He might have got there sooner if it wasn't for a traffic accident. Some pickup truck had slammed into the side of a minivan just past 9th Street. Flares lit up the night as two cop cars and a tow truck cleared it up. One of the officers was redirecting traffic down 10th, along 9th and back up onto 8th. As he crawled behind a tractor, he took in the sight of the small, peaceful town. He passed by a Catholic church, colorful mailboxes that were positioned at the end of driveways, a shabby-looking gas station and an elementary school. Before entering the town, there was nothing but wide-open space, and now it was like the town itself had been nestled in the forest. He noticed a small building that was dedicated to providing tourists with information on the area, a post office that looked like it had seen better days and several small banks. He noted it was absent the big chain stores. Most small towns in America were like that. They pushed back against change and anything that might take away from the mom-and-pop stores that gave a place its character and charm.

For a town that was supposed to have problems with drug use and prostitutes, it didn't exactly appear to be noticeable. No women loitered on street corners. No one was hovering around cars trying to deal.

He reached the turn off for 3rd Avenue and continued until he saw a sign for apartments. Jack hung a left and brought the Shelby up just outside the building. He sat in the vehicle as rain wiggled down the pane of glass. Was this it? He turned on the dome light inside and glanced at the address, comparing it to the one outside. Yep, this was it. He glanced around at the parking lot and the path that led up to the apartments before hopping out and making a mad dash for the entrance. Once inside he shook himself like a dog. His clothes were wet, his hair and beard streamed with water. It smelled musty and like piss in the apartments as if some wino had staggered in and taken up residence. He glanced at the wall where there were some steel mailboxes. He spotted Jenna's name on one before entering the stairwell. Fluorescent lights flickered on and off, making the corridor on the second floor seem darker. He made it to her apartment at the far end. There were four other apartments farther down. He knocked a few times but got no response. Jack put his ear to the door; it was quiet. The only sound came from an apartment farther down. Someone had a TV on.

"Jenna," he said. Again nothing.

Jack bit down on the side of his lip. His brow knit together as he made his way to a large window at the far end. As he shimmed it up, some of the flaking paint fell away. The wood was rotten, and it badly needed to be replaced. Outside was a black steel fire escape. Jack slipped out and gave it a kick with his boot just to make sure it was sturdy. As he climbed out, he had visions of it coming away from the mortar. The rain continued to fall in sheets and his clothes would soon be drenched. The cold began to leach into his bones and he shivered. He leaned beyond the fire escape to a window ledge for her apartment. There was next to no lighting for him to see clearly. A large oak tree blotted out what light was coming from the moon. Jack eased himself over to a thick drainpipe, giving it a shake a few times before trusting it with his entire weight. *What the hell are you doing?* He shook the rain out of his eyes and stepped across to where the ledge of the window was. One slip and he was going to land in the industrial-sized dumpster far below. The lights were out in her apartment. He reached down and tried to pry the window open. It was locked. *Shit!* With one hand on the pipe, the other balancing precariously against the brick, he glanced around to make sure that no one was watching. He contemplated not doing it for a minute and then, against his better judgment, went ahead and shattered the pane of glass with a sharp kick of his boot. A sudden crash and it burst sending shards across the floor like stones on ice. Not wasting any time, he unlocked the latch, pulled it up and ducked inside.

He winced getting a few small slivers in the palm of his hand. Glass crunched beneath his soles as he made his way in. Once he made it to a light switch, he flicked it on and gazed around at the cramped quarters. Rain poured in through the window, soaking the laminate flooring. He searched for a sheet or towel, anything he could place over the window temporarily. Once done, he began a preliminary search. By all appearances the apartment was undisturbed. The bed hadn't been slept in, and there was nothing to indicate that anyone had broken in except for the damage he'd created. The first thing he did was to phone her cell to check if she'd left it there. It started to ring on his end but not in the apartment. So she left. *Where did you go?*

* * *

Deputy Larson was pissed. Not only had his shift started by being pulled into the chief's office to explain another complaint from Aaron Gance but they'd also screwed up the schedule and somehow he'd got lumbered with Ethan Rigby. He couldn't stand the guy, and now here he was trying to get some supper and the asshole was invading his bubble.

"I'm telling you, Larson, it's a good investment. You take an extra thousand bucks and put it in this stock and you are going to be made. I swear this company is on the up-and-up. It's easy money."

All he wanted was a little peace and quiet. Rigby sat across from him in Dories Lounge, picking at his teeth while gazing at all the women's asses as they walked by.

"Ah, I don't know. Things are tight right now. With the baby and all, Kerry wants us to save."

"Does Kerry carry your balls?" He snorted and reached across the table and slapped him on the arm. "I'm just kidding." It took a lot of restraint to not lunge at him and wipe that smirk off his slimy face. Rigby was in his mid-fifties, five foot six and his stomach threatened to burst the buttons on his uniform. His face sported a thick black mustache that made him look like a '60s porn star. "Seriously, don't tell her. I'm sure you spend money without her knowing."

Sam munched down on the BLT before taking a sip of his coffee. "Actually I don't."

"Shit, Larson. Do you wear the pants or does she?"

He was always making these kinds of remarks. Had it not been for the fact that he was still trying to make a good impression with the chief, he would have told him where to stick it. Instead, he pursed his lips and gave a faint smile as if he was somehow amused by it.

Rigby was about to drone on when his radio crackled and dispatch came over the speaker.

"Control to Car 1, 18-4-0."

"Go ahead."

"Respond to 819, 3rd Avenue for a possible B and E in progress, one male broke a window. There could be more than one intruder. Stand by. Trying to get further…"

"52-0. 3rd Avenue, right now, 819?" Ethan asked.

"819 3rd Avenue, um, suspect still in the house, unknown on the race."

"Is that the apartment number?" he probed.

"Apartment 9."

"C-13 to control, I'm over on 2nd Avenue, I will respond."

Sam shifted his chair back, tossed down a few bills on the table and both of them double-timed it out. In the cruiser a few minutes later, sirens blaring and lights flashing, Sam fishtailed it around a turn, almost losing control while slamming his foot against the accelerator. Marlinton suffered from all manner of criminal behavior, there wasn't much that didn't occur there, however, it was how frequently it occurred that separated it from larger cities. By all accounts, folks kept to themselves and most of his calls were related to domestics, usually fueled by alcohol. Boredom in a small town was rampant and with it came all manner of vices. Alcohol was the top one, drugs followed a close second. In recent years they had been trying to curb prostitution though it wasn't as easy as driving by street corners. They didn't operate like that. It was all done behind the scenes, over the Internet. By the time they got a lead, the john and hooker were long gone. Sam was pretty sure that the recent string of deaths had been somehow related to Aaron Gance, that's why he'd been keeping a close eye on him. His track record wasn't clean and despite him swearing that he was on the straight and narrow, Sam didn't trust him. He'd just got out of prison for beating a woman, drug use and pimping, and rumor had it he was back to his old tricks.

From Dories Lounge it usually took less than three minutes to reach the apartment block. With the siren blaring and no other vehicles on the road, he was there in two. A moment later Sam brought the car to a skidding halt, flicked off the siren and pushed his way out of the car. He surveyed the block as Rigby joined him.

"Go on up, I'll go around back," Rigby said before jogging off into the darkness. He wasn't one for placing himself at risk. Word had it, Ethan was eyeing the position of Shift Commander, a cozy little job to ride out until he retired, but that wasn't going to happen unless Harry retired and that old coot wasn't showing any signs of slowing. He unsnapped his holster and pulled his gun, keeping it low. As he entered the ground entrance, a female neighbor wearing a robe pointed to the stairs.

"He's still in there."

Sam took the stairs two at a time. Inside it was quiet, except for the rain pattering against the windows, the sound of a dog barking outside and the woman muttering downstairs. It was humid inside, a bead of sweat trailed his forehead, and one rolled down his back. His pulse raced and his breathing picked up. As he got closer to apartment 9, he noted the door was closed, but the window at the far end of the building was open. Staying as silent as he could, he headed towards the window and peered out. Rain battered his face. Rigby was at the bottom. He motioned with his hand for him to go back inside, he had it covered.

Heading back to the door, he moved to the side and used the wall as a shield just in case shots rang out. Standing in front of doors had killed countless cops. It wasn't just rookies. He rapped his hand on the wood and pulled back.

"Pocahontas County Sheriff Department. Open up!"

* * *

By the time Jack heard the sirens blaring, it was too late. The cops must have been close as within minutes of hearing them he'd exited the window and was scaling down the fire escape. Unfortunately, he never made it to the bottom as several neighbors began shouting, "There he is!" just as two cop cars screeched into view. Jack quickly retreated and went back inside and tried heading for the stairwell. He figured he could just pretend he was one of the residents, but another vigilant neighbor was quick to point him out.

Didn't these people have something better to do with their time?

Had it been one of the big cities, he would have taken his chances and run for it, hell, he probably could have walked. New York was a haven for breaking and entering. Muggings, rapes, and domestics were the norm. It wasn't unusual to hear someone screaming, glass shattering or a car alarm going off, but here... small towns were another thing entirely.

Minutes earlier, he'd slammed the door. "Sonofabitch!"

He paced back and forth for a minute or two, then it dawned on him. He didn't need to run. The way he saw it, he was just concerned about his client. He figured he could talk his way out of this. It wouldn't be the first time.

The cop bellowed his order again. He crossed the room and looked out the window and saw the other cop below talking to a resident. *Screw it.*

* * *

The door cracked open and Sam slipped the safety off and his finger hovered near the trigger. His heart was slamming hard against his chest. After a few seconds, the door widened, pushed by the hand of a guy of average height. He looked strong and drenched by the rain.

"On the floor now!" he bellowed.

Hands shot up. "Listen, I can explain."

"Now. Hands behind your back, face away from me."

He dropped to his knees and laid face down. Sam moved in fast and planted a knee on the back of his shoulder before getting on the radio and alerting Rigby.

"Suspect in custody."

"Copy that. Coming up."

Sam shook his head. *Yeah, you do that now that the threat has been neutralized.* After slapping a pair of cuffs on the man, he quickly assessed him for any weapons and found a Glock.

"This better be licensed."

"It is," the man croaked.

"You want to tell me what you are doing here?"

"She's my client."

"You a lawyer? Cause you don't look like one."

"No."

"Too bad, you're going to need one." He hauled him up and strong-armed him out. "So you break into most of your clients' apartments?"

Ethan appeared at the top of the stairwell out of breath. The guy seriously needed to lose some pounds. It was only one flight of steps. A man of his age, and with his job requirement, the department should have pulled him aside. It was embarrassing. He was leaning a hand against the wall.

"Good job."

"Take him down to the cruiser, I'll be there in a minute. I just want to check on the apartment."

"Why don't you take him down?"

The guy cast a glance over his shoulder at Sam and shook his head. Even he must have understood what a prick Ethan was. "Because I'm not out of breath."

Ethan scowled as he led the man away. Sam updated dispatch on the current situation before heading inside the apartment. His radio crackled and he turned it down a few notches. He surveyed the shattered window and noted that most of the items that were commonly stolen in a break-in were still there; the TV, DVD, an iPad on the table, a wad of cash beneath a pair of keys in the kitchen. By any measure, it didn't look as if anything had been taken. Then again, they had interrupted him. He crossed into the kitchen and looked at the corkboard on the wall. There was a list of numbers on the counter. Names he didn't recognize. He took out his phone and took a snapshot of it before running his gloved hands over a few personal effects.

Back outside in the corridor, he was met by the same woman he'd seen on the ground level.

"Is Jenna okay?" she said trying to peer around him.

"Jenna?"

"Jenna Whitmore, she rents the apartment."

"Ma'am, she's not there. Do you know her?"

"Of course, my son is the landlord."

"Is he here?"

"No, he's away on vacation."

"What can you tell me about her?"

"She's a good girl. Always pays on time. Is she hurt?"

"No, she's not there."

"Odd. Come to think of it, I haven't seen her for the past two days. I always see her. She's dropped off groceries on occasion for me because I can't get out as much as I used to and relying on my son is hit and miss. You know, my legs keep swelling up and whatnot. I keep trying to tell the doctor that the pills he's given me aren't working, but he doesn't listen."

"Right." He smiled. "I should probably get a statement from you. And you are?"

"Mrs. Welch."

He pulled out his notebook and took down as much information as he could. "You wouldn't happen to know if she has family nearby? The job she holds, etc.?"

"She used to work for the newspaper here in the town but they let her go. Terrible state of affairs, letting a young woman go, after all she did for them. I told her she should go to national media, you know; give them a taste of their own medicine. Shame on them. Anyway, her mother lives in Durbin but don't ask me where, oh, and she has a brother, Corey, he works for a church. Nice lad. Comes by often to check in on her."

Sam pulled out his phone and brought up the snapshot of the paper with all the numbers on. He scanned it and saw a number beside the name Corey Whitmore.

"Have you seen the man we took out of here before?"

She shook her head. "Never. By the way, who is going to pay for that window? I hope it hasn't damaged the floors. It costs a lot of money to run this place."

He nodded while she droned on about how money didn't grow on trees and that her son was thinking of hiking the rent because the cost of living was crippling them. Sam put up a finger to indicate he just needed a second. He dialed the number and waited.

"Deputy," Mrs. Welch tried to get his attention.

Sam raised a finger. "Ma'am, you'll have a chance to press charges. Just give me a second, please."

The phone rang and a young man answered.

Chapter 7

This cop was getting on his last nerve.

Aaron Gance stood outside his brother's garage under a carport, smoking a cigarette and staring at the message on his phone. It was the second message in two days. He'd reported him for harassment but that didn't seem to go anywhere. It never did. The pigs stuck together. His older brother Merle walked out of the garage, wiping his oily hands on a dirty rag before tucking it in his back pocket. The rain was still falling heavily, spilling over the gutter like a waterfall and splashing near his feet. Merle was three years older and since getting out of prison, he'd tried to go straight but there was no money in it. He barely had enough to keep the garage open, and support his family, let alone pay Aaron.

It was all a front, nothing more than smoke and mirrors to keep the cops at arm's length. Behind the scenes, Merle subsidized his income through an arrangement with a local biker gang to be a distributor for their narcotics. Of course, they didn't get their hands dirty, they left the actual selling to the guys on the street. It didn't pay much, but it was better than getting a real job.

A mosquito buzzed around his neck and he slapped it.

"Brother, you know how these cops are. They have nothing better to do than stick their nose in where it's not wanted. I'm sure something will come up in a month or two and they'll harass someone else."

"Two months? They are making trouble with my parole officer. Not to mention my little side gig."

Merle crouched over and pulled out a couple of cold brews from the cooler and handed him one. He ran the sweating can around the back of his neck to provide some relief before he cracked it open and took a hard swig. After, he took a long drag on his cigarette. The humidity was suffocating. There wasn't even a breeze in the air that night.

"I keep telling you. That gig is a one-way ticket back

to jail and next time they aren't going to be as lenient. Do you really want to blow it?"

He wasn't stupid but relying on minimum wage wasn't getting him anywhere. Now dealing drugs had been a beginning, a small step towards paying for the lifestyle he wanted — a lifestyle like those fat cats living in the suburbs. He wanted the nice SUV, the four-bedroom house, the cabin on weekends and a boat for those hot summer days. Why couldn't he have it? Why shouldn't he have it? Hell, he'd tried going down the road of doing shift work in factories, and waiting tables. But that was a chump's game. Never mind, humiliating. He hated seeing people he knew coming into the restaurant or bar. The smug look on their faces as he took their orders as if they were better than him. No thanks, 9 to 5 was for sheep, it was nothing more than eating the scraps from the table. He had plans, big plans and for a while, he'd been on track until that bitch squealed to the cop and he busted him.

"Anyway, what's in the past is in the past. Dwelling on

it does nothing. You need to knuckle down, keep your nose clean and maybe, just maybe we can build up this garage into a decent business."

"Decent business? Shit, Merle, you did one oil change today and replaced some spark plugs for a farmer. You call that business?"

He was getting a little tired of his older brother ordering him around and giving him the spiel about how Gance Motors was going to bring in the big money. It was nothing but bullshit. His brother had always been like that. A dreamer. Nothing more than someone who talked the big talk but when it came down to it, he didn't have the balls to make the tough decisions. He, on the other hand, was a go-getter. He always was and always would be. He wasn't one to rest on his laurels, or get ordered around by some asshole whose highest achievement was becoming manager at the local burger joint. No, fuck that.

"Mind your tongue, Aaron. All it takes is one call to your parole officer and…"

Aaron snorted. He couldn't even be bothered to reply to that. Lately, his brother was starting to step over the line. If he didn't watch it, he was liable to find himself face down in a ditch with a bullet in the back of his head like those who'd crossed him before.

"Anyway, you heard or seen Bonnie?"

Merle blew out a plume of smoke from his cigar and chuckled. "Aaron, just drop it. She's got a kid now. She's working down at Ali's Bar."

The thing was, he couldn't drop it. Sure, Deputy Larson had charged him but if it weren't for her, he wouldn't have done time. Kid or no kid, she was going to learn the error of her ways. No one fucked him over, and certainly not some cheap ass whore. Who the hell did she think she was kidding taking a job in a bar? He knew her better than that. With the small amount of cash they tossed at them there at the end of the week, he couldn't see that supporting her crack addiction. It was rampant back when she was one of his girls. It was how he was able to control them. He kept them stocked up on drugs while they serviced clients in the area. If they gave him lip about their cut at the end of the night, he slapped them back into line.

"Anyway, don't you have a few new ones working for you?"

"Yeah, Tina and Rita. Though I'm thinking of dropping Tina. She's a lippy bitch who keeps talking back. She's been hassling me about increasing her share. Says that she knows a few girls in town who are doing their own thing. She wants to cut out the middleman. Like I'm going to let her do that?"

"So what did you say?"

"I didn't. I just backhanded her and knocked some sense into her."

"Shit, dude, you are just asking for it, aren't you?"

"Who gives a fuck? I'm running this show, not them."

"They are the ones taking the risk."

"The risk?" He spun around on his brother unable to believe what he was saying. They weren't the ones who got put away last time. No, they were just given a slap on the wrist and sent on their way. But him, he had to endure days of looking over his shoulder in jail. They'd made an example of him.

"Calm down, man. You take things way too seriously."

"Yeah, well, you would too if you were in my shoes."

"I've been there. Done that. It doesn't pay, brother."

"Pays a helluva lot better than the shit you are paying me."

"I told you. Things are tight right now. Besides, I'm saving your ass. You could be working down at the diner or in some factory. Do you want that? At least here you don't have a boss over your shoulder."

"No, I have you. That's worse."

Both of them laughed. Aaron flicked his cigarette butt out into the darkness. The glowing embers fizzled, and he turned back inside thinking about what he was going to do about Deputy Dipshit. His brother was right to some degree, he had to be smart, however, that didn't mean he couldn't have some fun. They were going to have a little face-to-face, and he was going to regret taking a position in this town. But first things first: Bonnie had to be dealt with. He'd been waiting a long time to get even with her. There wasn't a night that had gone by that he hadn't thought about a fair punishment. Now that he'd heard about her having a kid, perhaps beating her up and leaving her in a ditch wouldn't hit her where it hurt. Perhaps he'd take it out on the kid. He ground his teeth as he went in and scooped up another beer. Because of Bonnie, he'd suffered greatly at the hands of inmates; because of her, he was now under the watchful eye of Larson and struggling to make ends meet. No one screwed him around and walked away. So now she was living a life outside of opening her legs, all content to earn minimum wage in some bar so she could raise her kid? Well, he was about to piss on her parade and no one was going to stop him. Not Larson. Not Bonnie and definitely not Merle. He was going to enjoy this.

"By the way, you know anything about who killed those women?"

"I heard they were overdoses."

"Come on, Aaron, you know better than that."

He scowled. "What are you asking?"

"Did you do it?"

"Why would you ask that?"

"Because I know you. All of them worked with you before you went inside. And it wouldn't be the first time you got rid of one. Maybe that's why Larson is on your ass."

Aaron spat a wad of phlegm. "I didn't do it."

He grinned. "Right."

Aaron grabbed a hold of his brother and slammed him up against a 1982 Chevy truck that was in the middle of getting a paint job. "You ever say anything to the cops about the past. And brother or not, I will put you in the ground. Do I make myself clear?"

His brother stared at him then slowly raised his hands. "Crystal."

He released him and handed him another beer as if nothing had happened. The inside of the two-car garage was a mess. Merle wasn't one for keeping a place tidy, no doubt that played a role in why he didn't get much business. Unlike the other garages in town that were professional, clean and fully licensed, Merle was breaking all manner of town codes and ordinances. Like disposing of old oil in the river behind his home, or burning tires out back in the fire pit. Or the new addition he'd placed on his home without informing the town.

"Aaron, you staying for supper?" Queenie, Merle's wife, a fiery redhead, stuck her head inside the garage.

"Not tonight, darling, I have a few things to do."

"Merle. Supper is on the table."

"Be there in five."

"It will be cold in five."

"Stop hassling me, woman," he snapped.

She flipped him the bird and disappeared.

"See what I have to put up with?"

Aaron walked past him without saying anything. The alcohol and his need for retribution dulled his mind. As long as he remained in this town his reputation would follow him. People would talk. The girls that worked for him knew his secrets. How many others had spoken? Told of what he'd done? He wasn't proud of it but neither did he regret his decisions. Those that crossed him made their choice.

Aaron grabbed up his truck keys off the counter and strolled towards the 4 x 4.

"You heading out?"

"Got some business to take care of," he said. "Going to pick up Billy and Dale."

"You want me to go with you?"

"And ruin your little dinner date with Queenie?"

"Ah screw that. It's probably burnt anyway, just let me get cleaned up first and I'll be right there."

His brother dashed inside and he could hear Queenie yelling a few minutes after. No doubt pissed at him for tossing his food in the garbage. He was right. She couldn't cook to save her life. While he waited for his brother to return, he hopped into the truck and leaned across to the glove compartment. Once it was open he removed the revolver from beneath a crapload of paperwork and then tucked it into his waistband, feeling

confident and excited about what he had in mind. It was

time to turn the tables and deal with this issue.

Chapter 8

Jack remained composed. It wasn't the first time he'd been busted and unlike dealing with big city cops who usually had something to prove; he knew it wouldn't be long before he walked out those doors. It was a broken window, nothing was stolen, and he had the voice messages left by Jenna Whitmore on his phone.

After being shoved into the back of a cruiser and detained by an older, pepper-haired cop with a stomach that bulged at the seams, he'd sat in the back waiting for the younger one.

"So what are you, a rapist? A druggie, looking to score your next fix by selling some stolen goods or just an idiot?" the officer said as he scribbled away on some report in the front of the cruiser. Jack stayed silent. He knew how it worked. Give them an inch, and they would spin it and draw it out for a mile. He didn't bother to ask what would happen next, he knew the drill. They'd go through the process of booking him, taking his prints and then grilling him.

"You do know that thirty minutes from now I am going to walk."

The cop glanced at him in the rearview mirror. "Confident. I like that. Stupid though. You aren't going anywhere tonight."

"We'll see about that."

"Yeah, we will."

The younger cop emerged and walked over to the cruiser. He leaned down and glanced at Jack before speaking with the other deputy. There was a brief exchange about who was going to do the paperwork, and how they were going to proceed and then he said he would meet him down at the station.

Upon arrival, he was photographed and then led away to give his ten digits. Of course, throughout the entire time, he told them that they were wasting their time. He hadn't done anything except break a window out of concern for his client. In reality, the evening could have turned out a hell of a lot worse. He could have easily overpowered the officer, or any one of the neighbors and walked away but that wasn't his game plan. He was here to complete a job, to find out what had happened to his client and get paid. This was just a small delay. Instead of making their job hard he let them finish up before he was given a seat inside an interview room. He sighed as the younger officer appeared with a cup of coffee.

"I'll handle it from here," he said to the other one who shrugged and exited the room. There wasn't much to the room itself; a table, two chairs, a clock that ticked louder than it should and a tiny camera. No one-way mirror. Perhaps they couldn't afford it? By all measures, the department looked as if it needed to be renovated. It could at least use a lick of paint.

The officer in front of him scribbled down on paper before leaning back in his seat and tapping the pencil in his hand on the desk.

"My name is Deputy Sam Larson." He took a breath. "Quite a predicament we have here. You say you know the owner. What's her name?"

"Jenna Whitmore."

He smiled. "Of course, you could have seen that on her mail. And where are you from?"

"All over."

"All over? You want to be more specific?"

"New York but I travel a lot."

"Yeah, I kind of caught the accent. That's a long way from home. So what brings you up here?"

"Like I said, I'm here because of my client. I showed up at her address, she wasn't responding so I broke in out of concern."

"Concern? I've heard a lot of excuses for breaking and entering but I have to say that is a first."

"It's true," Jack said looking unfocused. He still couldn't get over what a shabby setup they had. How many worked here?

The officer leaned forward. "You're in a lot of trouble, my friend, so it's best you come clean."

"Is this where you exit and your friend takes over? Let

me guess, you're the bad cop, he's the good?"

"A sense of humor. I like that." He paused, tapping his pencil in the palm of his hand. "Okay, let's go back to the beginning. So she's your client. For what? What do you do?"

He cleared his throat. "A bit of this, a bit of that."

"You know this isn't getting you anywhere. You want to get out of here?"

Jack returned to looking at him. "I help people."

Larson cocked his head. "You do? Go on."

"I received several phone calls from her over the past week seeking my help. She said she was looking into the disappearance and death of five local women."

The deputy's eyes widened, and he leaned back in his chair. "The Green Bank Five. Right. And?"

Jack inhaled deeply. "She was worried, I guess is the best word. She thought she was over her head and that possibly whoever was responsible was targeting her."

"Because?"

"She'd received phone calls in the night, and a

threatening letter telling her to back off."

He went back to scribbling down notes, mostly the short form of what he'd told him.

"And so what were you going to do?"

"Offer my assistance."

"Are you a private investigator?"

"Not exactly."

"An ex-police officer?"

"You're getting colder."

He narrowed his gaze. "How about you cut the crap and stop jerking me off?"

Quite frankly, Jack was enjoying the banter. It had been a while since he'd been pulled in and he liked to sit back and observe, study the different methods they tried to extract information. In many ways, he kind of felt sorry for cops. Civilians' rights and all manner of red tape tied their hands. The old days of turning off a video recorder and slamming a suspect into the wall were over. There was too much at stake. The reputations of departments all over the USA hung in the balance. They were on shaky ground from one too many problems.

"Listen, I have a unique skill set, you might say. It comes in handy when people go missing. I came up to meet her, hear her out and decide from there whether I would help."

"So when did you last speak to her?"

"About twenty-four hours ago. Though I did receive a strange call in the night that I believe was from her."

"Strange… in what way?"

"I was woken out of a deep sleep by a female's voice. Her speech was slurred as if she was drunk or high. It was mostly incoherent."

"So what makes you think it was her?"

Jack smiled. "Officer, call it a gut instinct but when a woman phones you to say she is scared and close to finding out who was responsible for the death of five women, and then she goes missing, it doesn't exactly take a rocket scientist to put two and two together."

"But it could have been anyone."

"She's missing."

"How can you be sure? She might have stepped out for the evening, gone to stay with a friend, or perhaps she's traveling."

"Maybe, or she's missing and the male voice I heard on the phone was the same person responsible for the other five."

"Male voice?" Larson asked. "You heard someone else?"

"Barely but yes."

"What did he say?"

"It was hard to tell, it was early in the morning and I was still trying to make sense of what she was saying."

"And did you?"

"What?"

"Make sense of anything she said?"

Jack thought about the name Meghan Palmer. He was close to blurting out her name but instead, he restrained himself. There was no telling who was involved. He'd come across enough crooked cops in his time, what was there to say that he wasn't sitting in front of one now?

"No." Jack exhaled and shifted the topic. "You think I could get a smoke?"

"That can be arranged." He got up and headed over to the door and hollered for someone to bring him a pack. Jack glanced down at his boots.

"Fresh out of the academy?" Jack asked.

Larson tossed a curious look over his shoulder.

"Your boots. Overly polished. Your uniform, far too crisp for a small-town cop."

Larson gazed down at his boots and returned to the table.

"It's been a year."

"How do you like it?" Jack asked.

There was hesitation before he replied. "While your story seems credible, Mr. Winchester, it's not exactly helping your case. Without—"

"Check my phone," Jack said cutting him off before he finished. "You'll find several messages from Jenna, I think that should at least clear up what doubts you have about me being hired."

"Hang tight, I'll be right back."

Larson left the room.

They had already taken his belongings. He didn't have much on him; a cell phone, the Glock, four hundred and sixty dollars in cash, and a pack of mints. Larson returned a few minutes later with the cell phone and a pack of smokes. He tapped out one; Jack took it and let the officer light it.

"See, that's what I love about these old towns. You don't abide by all those no smoking rules."

Larson didn't respond to that, instead, he slid the cell phone across to him. "Unlock it and bring up the voice mail."

Jack inhaled deeply then did as requested. He put it on speakerphone so he could hear it. After they'd listened to several calls, the officer made a few more notes.

"You know there are still going to be charges laid against you. The landlord will want to press charges."

"I'll pay for the window."

"Ah, it goes beyond that. You'll need to show up in

court. Damage to property is still a criminal offense."

Jack nodded. It wasn't like he could talk his way out of that one. Though he had hoped his connection to Jenna would at least take him out of the crosshairs.

This time it was Larson who shifted gears. "What did you do in New York?"

"I'm sure your database will bring up my file."

"Already looked. There's nothing. Not even a parking ticket. And yet I get a sense that there should be something on you. You care to shed some light?"

"Like I said, I travel a lot. My past is my past."

"You serve time?"

Jack mulled over the question for a few seconds.

"I could make a quick phone call and get that answer or you could save me the hassle."

"I did. But that's in my past. I've paid for my mistakes, officer."

Larson took a drink from his own cup of coffee.

"So you served some time. You now help people. You get a call from Jenna Whitmore asking for help. You show up and break into her apartment and now she's missing. You have to admit, this doesn't exactly sit well for you, does it?"

"Not sure what you expect from me, deputy. That's exactly what happened. I didn't take anything from her apartment, officer. And I don't know where she is but if given the opportunity, there's a possibility that I could find her, or at least whoever is responsible."

"And yet we still don't know if she's missing. Do we?"

Jack rubbed the bridge of his nose. This was going to be a long night. After another round of questions, all of which brought them back full circle, the other deputy poked his head inside.

"Larson, a minute of your time."

Larson stared at Jack as if searching for a hole in his story, something that didn't add up, something that would give him less paperwork, less of a headache and a reason to get a pat on the back from his boss. Without saying another word he got up and exited.

* * *

"Corey Whitmore is here. The brother."

"Good, maybe we can get some straight answers."

Rigby led him down the corridor to the waiting room.

"So what's his story?" Rigby asked.

Larson was still chewing over Jack's replies. As much as he wanted to get this wrapped up, there was something to his story that seemed legit even if his background was a little sketchy.

"Says he's innocent."

He laughed. "Aren't they are all?"

Corey Whitmore was roughly six foot one, buzzed hair, sharp features, and he was dressed in a windbreaker and large boots. The jacket was still covered in droplets of water from the rain. Sam extended his hand to greet him.

"Mr. Whitmore, I'm Deputy Larson, we spoke on the phone. Thanks for coming."

"I know who you are."

"You do?"

"Saw your photo a couple of months back in the paper — the announcement of the department taking on two new officers. About time they got some fresh meat in here." He looked Rigby up and down as if he was disgusted with him. "How do you like it so far?"

He smiled, studying him. "It has its moments. Come with me."

Larson led him through a doorway, and down the corridor to a separate room. He was keen to find out what he knew about Jack Winchester or the whereabouts of his sister Jenna.

"So what was this man's name?"

"Jack Winchester. Sound familiar?"

He shook his head. "No."

"Did your sister ever mention hiring anyone?"

"Not that I recall."

"When did you last speak with her?"

Corey's face screwed up, and he stopped walking. "Deputy, where is my sister?"

"That's the strange part. She's not answering her cell, it's going to voice mail, and she's not at her apartment. I thought you might know?"

"Well she could have visited our mother in Durbin but... have you tried there?"

"Already done that. She hasn't seen her. So when was the last time you spoke to her?"

He cleared his throat. "Um. On the phone the other night."

"Last night?"

"Yeah. It was just a short call to check in with her as she's been busy. I've been busy."

Larson frowned. "Um, what is it you do for a living?"

"I'm a carpenter by trade but I work part-time in a church up in Green Bank, alongside Pastor Tim Mathers. Perhaps you've heard of it. A New Hope."

"Doesn't he run a program for wayward women?"

His eyebrows arched. "So you are familiar?"

"Seen signs posted up in the town. Also, a few families of the missing mentioned that he had worked with them in the past."

Corey shifted his weight and nodded. "Yeah, he's a good man."

"And how long have you been there? Working, I mean?"

His eyes widened, and he looked up as if trying to recall. "It's got to be coming on three years now in August. It's a pretty small congregation. Not exactly a lot of money in it, so Tim can't afford to have me there full-time but I don't mind. I enjoy building things. I mainly assist with the church to help folks out. Actually, come to think of it, I do recall her mentioning the other night that she was going to have a friend come down and help her in the work she was doing with the missing women."

Larson nodded. "Well, then that confirms the messages your sister left with Mr. Winchester." He paused. "Just out of curiosity. Did you ever meet the five?"

"I did." He blew out his cheeks. "Yeah. Good women. Troubled but not outside the grace of God. It's a shame that it ended the way it did."

"And… uh… your sister. Did she ever inquire about Tim's involvement with the women?"

"Of course, that's actually what I was calling about the night we spoke. She had been trying to get hold of Tim, and I wanted to make sure that she wasn't going to cause any trouble."

"What do you mean?"

"Tim is a good man. A real man of God. He started that program for women out of a calling to help those who have been cast aside by society. The last thing he needs is to have someone pointing the finger at him."

"And by that you mean?"

"The women, deputy."

"You think your sister thought he was involved?"

"Not just my sister. Many people in the area. Let's face it, deputy; they all come to see him for one reason or another. As much as we try to help sinners, we also put ourselves in the crossfire of accusations. False accusations. Tim has a wife and three kids. He has a reputation to uphold and I would hate to see his name dragged through the mud."

"Just his? Were you not involved in the program?"

"No. Not me. My role is strictly Sundays and prayer meetings in the week. Beyond that, I'm a pretty much busy with my business. Which reminds me that I have a few errands to run. Look, is the man my sister hired here?"

"He is."

"Do you think I could have a word with him? You know. Perhaps he knows something."

"That might be arranged, though I wouldn't bank on getting anything out of him. Anyway, for now, we're trying to get in contact with the landlord to see if they want to move ahead with pressing charges."

"Press charges? For the window you mean?"

"That and breaking and entering."

"Oh, I'm sure I can speak with his mother, Mrs. Welch, and get it cleared up. We're good friends. I would hate to see this blown out of proportion and the court's time tied up with a misunderstanding. How much is his bail?"

Larson stared blankly at him. "Excuse me?"

"His bail to get him out? You're not going to keep him in over a broken window, are you, deputy?"

"But you haven't even met him."

"If my sister hired him, I trust her instincts."

He nodded slowly finding it a little odd but not completely out of the question. It hadn't been the first time that someone from a local church had stepped in to speak on behalf of someone arrested, or bail out those caught up in trouble. It would mean less paperwork and one less thing on their plate. "Look, I can't guarantee you anything, if you want to hang tight here for a few minutes, I will go and see what I can do. In the meantime, if you phone Mrs. Welch and she'll agree to not press charges, I'm sure we can get this cleared away tonight. Bail money might not even be required."

Chapter 9

When Larson informed Jack that he was being released, he assumed it was because of the voice mail recordings. While that had helped, he was surprised to learn that the brother of Jenna had spoken on his behalf.

"So I guess it's your lucky day," Larson said as he took the cuffs off him.

"He's here?"

"In the waiting area."

"And the window?"

"You'll still be paying for that but he's cleared it away with the landlord's mother. You're fortunate that Jenna had a good relationship with Mrs. Welch, and Corey knew her. She's dropped all charges."

"I suppose so." Jack rubbed his wrists and rose.

"Just a word before you go." He came back around and took a seat across from him. "I appreciate that you were looking to help but probably best you leave the investigative work to us. This is still an active case and you're liable to land yourself in hot water if you continue to pry."

"I wasn't aware the department was still involved. I thought it had been handed over to State Police and FBI."

Larson's eyebrow arched. "We're assisting them."

"To what extent?"

"To the extent that it's none of your business. Now, taking into consideration everything that's occurred tonight, you're fortunate that it's worked out the way it has. A little advice; go visit one of the many state parks in the area, take in one of the scenic train rides, and enjoy some of the county's food and wine, then move on. Leave the police work to us. Next time the department might not be as lenient."

Jack nodded slowly. He had no intentions of leaving. This wasn't his first dance with the law and it wouldn't be his last. If he shrank back every time he encountered resistance, he'd never make money in his line of work. So, he'd piss off a few locals and ride the razor's edge of the law, that was just par for the course. At the end of the day he'd been paid good money, and he never walked away without giving due diligence. And with her brother in the loop, at least now he might be able to make some headway in finding out where Jenna might be.

"Any questions?"

Jack didn't respond.

"Right, let's head out."

* * *

After retrieving his belongings from Larson, he was escorted down a corridor, through a set of doors out into a waiting area. There was a tall, broad-shouldered man standing with his back to them. He was admiring the different awards, and photos of baseball teams in a cabinet. Most of it was little leagues and different organizations that the police sponsored. Larson cleared his throat to get his attention.

"He's all yours, Mr. Whitmore." He extended his hand. "I appreciate you coming by." He turned back to

Jack. "Remember what I said, okay?"

Jack smiled but didn't give him a response even though he looked as if he was waiting for one. Larson headed back into the heart of the station and left the two of them alone.

"Mr. Winchester. Corey Whitmore."

Jack shook his hand. "Thank you for what you did tonight."

"Not at all. It was the least I could do under the circumstances. Would you be interested in getting a drink?"

"Um. I…"

Jack really just wanted to head back to the lodge and settle in for the night. He glanced up at the clock. It was just after half past nine. He couldn't exactly say no after the guy had gone to bat for him, and besides, it would give him a chance to find out a little more about the town, the disappearances and more specifically Jenna.

"Sure. I could use a drink."

Corey led the way, and he fell in step. They continued

talking as they stepped outside. The rain had subsided, and the air smelled clean. Corey shot him a sideways glance. "My sister mentioned you were coming to help. I'm curious, I gather you have experience with these kinds of situations?"

"By that you mean finding missing people?"

He nodded, his features creasing.

"I've assisted others in the past if that's what you're asking."

When they reached the edge of the curb, Jack looked around. "Where's my vehicle?"

"Around back. Though I can give you a lift to the bar. You hungry?"

"Probably best I take mine."

"That's fine. I was thinking of heading over to Ali's Bar. It's a local hangout just over on Highway 219. They do the best wings in town, and I don't know about you but I'm starving. Just head down 8th Street and hang a right. You'll see a BP gas station and Appalachian Sport. It's smack bang in between those. You can't miss it.

There's a sign outside of a woman—"

"I know. I saw it."

"Right. Well, I'll see you there."

He gave a short wave and headed off towards a black Ford truck. Jack pulled his jacket tighter as he started down the sidewalk at a fast pace. The sidewalk that evening was deserted. He circled around back to where there were several cruisers parked.

A minute later, the engine roared to life, and he peeled away. Though there were a number of cars parked along the streets, for the most part, there were no signs of life in the town. It was typical. Stores closed early and the only areas that got any attention were the 7-Eleven, restaurants and bars. Most of the folks living in the area were either farmers or blue-collar workers. It was deathly quiet and easy to see how people could go missing. No one paid attention because they had no reason to be on the streets.

Two blocks up 10th Avenue, Jack hung a left onto 8th Street and continued past the scene of the traffic accident. It was cleared up and they were no longer redirecting. It was a short five-minute drive to the mouth of the street. He crossed over 219 into the parking lot. About twenty feet back from the road, there was a one-story structure made from wood. It stood out with its brightly painted steel roof and a sickly neon sign that flickered like a mosquito trap. A handful of trucks and motorcycles were parked haphazardly in the lot. It certainly wasn't the kind of bar he typically would have chosen to visit. Even Corey looked too clean-cut to be seen there. He was sure Larson had mentioned the words church leader.

Though for a small town that had few options, it was clear to see how it would have appealed to locals, tourists and anyone that wasn't critical about where they ate.

A large sign with the name of the establishment hung above the buckled entranceway. It was stenciled in some ghastly looking neon red paint. It shimmered from the pot lights above it. At a glance, he figured whoever had been put in charge of the décor was either blind or perhaps the paint shop was out of regular colors. And yet on his way down from Chicago he'd seen similar dives, so perhaps it was common.

Jack killed the engine, pushed out and crossed the parking lot and went inside. The interior wasn't much better. It was dingy and the faint smell of mildewed wood and alcohol permeated the air. There was a large dance floor, three pool tables and a bar that stretched the full length of one side of the room. Behind the bar was a sign that read: *Don't mess with Marlinton.* The owner had taken an outdoors theme with the place. Thick natural tree trunks acted as pillars throughout the interior. A large canoe was positioned precariously across the rafters, two chandeliers made from deer antlers dangled from the ceiling and the walls were covered in paddles, skiing equipment, netting, fishing tools and the typical metal signage of brands of beer.

An old-fashioned jukebox flanked the rear exit, and a dozen tables were spread throughout. The floor was hardwood, covered in peanut shells and a thin layer of dust. Many of the chairs looked handmade.

It wasn't packed inside. At a rough headcount, there

looked to be about twenty-two. Patrons thronged at the bar and tables while a group of guys crowded around a pool table. A couple of women danced provocatively on the dance floor trying to get the attention of the guys who were making comments to each other and laughing occasionally.

He scanned the room looking for a place to sit. A hand shot up and Jack's eyes darted across the room and spotted him. Corey was sitting in a booth holding a sweating Budweiser. He smiled as Jack took a seat across from him.

"What can I get you?" he asked making a quick gesture to a pretty young waitress. She was wearing a small amount of makeup, and skinny jeans that showed off her tight body.

"I'll get it. I think you've done enough for me tonight."

"No, don't be silly."

He shrugged. "Okay, a Bud then."

While he placed his order, Jack noticed how upbeat he

was. For someone whose sister was missing, it struck him as a little odd. Unless of course, he didn't think she was missing. He turned his gaze back to Jack.

"So tell me about yourself, Jack. Where you from? What do you do?"

"You sound like Larson."

He chuckled. "Sorry, just curious to know how my sister came across you."

"She was referred to me."

"Is that how people contact you?"

"Not always. But it's becoming quite common."

"So you're good at what you do?"

"I get paid well if that answers your question."

He narrowed his eyes and Jack decided to shift the attention back to him. "Larson said you work for a church. I have a friend out in L.A. that does the same. Though he would argue that he's not religious."

He raised his eyebrows. "Is that so?"

The waitress returned and shifted over a crinkled beer mat and set the glass down. Some of the head rolled over the lip and formed a half-circle, soaking the mat.

"Anything else I can get for you guys?" Jack noted the name tag on her shirt. Meghan. He gazed up at her, curious. He was about to ask her what her second name was when Corey interrupted.

"Wings, Jack?" Corey asked.

"Um. No, I'm good for now."

"Just me then, I guess. I'll have ten barbecued wings. That's it." He folded up the menu and handed it back.

Jack noticed Corey eye her ass as she ambled away. Religious or not, they were all the same. Given a chance he would have had her in bed at the first sign of interest.

Corey clasped his hands in front of him and answered Jack's question. "Yeah, I took a position as a leader several years back. It's with New Hope in Green Bank. Always wanted to work in the ministry. Tim Mathers, the pastor, had a position open up, so I took it. I was already going there as a parishioner. It seemed like a good fit."

"Did Jenna attend?"

He chuckled and took a swig from the bottle. "She did

until all these women started going missing. Then she became obsessed with it. It took up a lot of her time."

"Obsessed?"

"She lost her job working at the *Pocahontas Times*. They covered the disappearances but she took her interest in the case to a whole new level. I guess her boss thought she was spending a little too much time on it. An unhealthy amount of time, I believe, Jenna said."

"That's too bad. And you haven't seen her in…?" he probed.

"In several weeks but I did speak to her the other night. That's when I learned about you. She said you were going to help. Though I'm still not quite sure why."

"Why what?"

"She said she was closing in on whoever was responsible." Jack gave a confused expression, and then clarified. "My sister believed that they were murdered."

"Strikes me as a reasonable assumption."

"The toxicology report stated they died from drowning, likely related to a large amount of narcotics in their bodies. Mr. Winchester, I don't know how much Jenna told you about these women or our town but they weren't exactly clean women. They were known drug users and women of the street."

Jack pursed his lips. "I didn't see many women on the street."

"I'm sure you know what I mean. Look around you. What do you see?"

Jack surveyed the bar then returned to looking at him, allowing him to clarify further.

"The two on the floor are prostitutes, the two behind the bar are as well."

"And you would know this because?"

He smiled. "My sister, Mr. Winchester. She was quite vocal about what was going on, and her ideas about how they were doing it."

"They?" Jack asked.

"They. One person. A figure of speech."

"So she believed they were targeted?"

"Of course. Except anyone from around here knows

that they aren't picked up on the street. It's all handled over the Internet via craigslist and backpage. Perhaps you're familiar with the term escorts?"

He paused as if trying to assess Jack's moral compass.

In an instant, Jack heard glass shatter. He jerked his head towards the bar, where a guy with long hair and tattoos appeared to be in a heated exchange with one of the bartenders. Jack eyed her with a concerned expression. Corey on the other hand glanced but then returned to the conversation.

"As I was saying. My sister spoke with a number of these women. She visited the families of the dead. Heck, she showed more concern for their well-being than her own."

"So where do you think she's gone?"

He shrugged with a concerned expression. "That's what I would like to know."

Jack chugged back on the beer until it was all gone. The first one always went down smooth. He could feel the alcohol kicking in and taking over. Jack shuffled out of his seat. "You want another?"

Corey gazed at his bottle, examining how much was left. "Sure."

Jack headed over to the bar, threading his way through the crowd of people. Wedging himself between two guys, he raised a hand to the bartender who appeared to be taking flak from some rough-looking individual at the far end. She shot him a glance and was about to head over when the guy grabbed her wrist and raised his voice.

"Bitch, don't walk away from me while I'm talking to you."

"Get off, Aaron, you're hurting me."

Jack noticed that no one was paying attention. There weren't many sitting on bar stools, and those that were were watching some baseball game on the flat-screen above the bar. It was like they were oblivious to what was taking place or used to it. Was this a daily occurrence around here? He looked away for a second, watching the interaction in the reflection of the mirror across from him. *Just stay put. Don't do anything. You've stirred up enough trouble*, he told himself.

The woman struggled for a second or two, then grabbed the nearest glass full of beer and tossed it in his face. "I told you, I don't work for you anymore."

The guy grabbed her by the back of the shirt and as she tried to pull away, he reared back his hand to slap her when Jack grabbed his wrist.

Chapter 10

"You don't want to do that," Jack said while tightening his grip. For a brief moment the guy stared back. Something in his expression, in the way he stared, seemed more than menacing — he was comfortable. There wasn't any fear. He had the kind of look that was formed from time inside. Instead of resisting, he released his grip on the bartender and gave a wry smile. Jack waited a few more seconds before he let him go. The guy sneered, shot the girl a look of death and snatched up his bottle of beer before crossing the room towards the pool area. Three other men greeted him with questions and he just barged his way through them before taking a seat.

A female voice behind Jack made him turn towards the bar.

"Thank you for doing that, but really, you shouldn't have."

"And let him slap you?"

"Well, no, but…"

"It's fine."

She extended her hand. "I'm Bonnie Ratlin."

"Jack," he replied before shaking it. It was soft, void of calluses, giving him a sense that she hadn't done many hard jobs in her time. There was a beat, a pause as they both looked over to where the guy was.

"Aaron Gance. Thinks he owns me. I wish he was still in jail."

"You, uh—"

"Bonnie, you okay?" The dark-haired pretty little waitress came rushing over and cut him off.

She gave a faint smile. "It's okay, Meghan. Really. Nothing I couldn't have handled."

"You want me to call the cops?"

"No. It's not worth it. It'll only rile him up more."

"Meghan Palmer?" Jack asked. She glanced at him while holding Bonnie by the shoulders.

Her brow knit together. "Do I know you?" she asked.

"No. But you knew Jenna Whitmore, right?"

Her expression changed and the color in her face vanished. "Are you a friend of hers?"

"I'm with her brother over there." Jack turned and noticed that the same man he'd had the confrontation with was talking with Corey. The exchange looked to be quite heated but from where he was standing he couldn't quite hear what was being said. He was about to go over when the guy walked away. "Um. Yeah, she's gone missing," he said turning back to her. "You wouldn't know where she is, would you?"

"She's... what? Missing? But I was with her only the other night."

"What night?"

Meghan turned to Bonnie. "Listen, if you want to go serve the customer at the end of the bar, I'll clean up the glass."

"You sure?"

"Yeah, go."

Bonnie went to walk away. "Thank you. Again." Jack nodded. She smiled and wandered off. Meghan turned her attention to the shattered glass on the floor. She turned her back momentarily and reached for a broom and dustpan. As she swept up, she looked back at him, conscious that he was staring.

"Look, she wanted to speak to me about…"

"The Green Bank Five?"

She nodded, casting a nervous glance around the room. "Look, I really shouldn't be talking about this here. I'm working."

"What was your involvement?"

She stopped cleaning up and cast a gaze down at the floor. Hesitation. Embarrassment perhaps? "I'm involved in the industry."

"So what happened the other night?"

Before she could say another word, there was a slight commotion behind him. Jack turned at the sound.

"Is this the guy?" a ratty-looking fellow said.

"Yeah, that's him."

He tensed automatically readying himself for what was coming. It was always the same. Egotistical pricks just couldn't walk away. Once pumped up on liquid courage they had to take it to the next level. The same guy who had grabbed the girl was standing behind him, holding a pool cue, his eyes glassy from having drunk too much beer. Beside him were three other guys. The way they shifted around, he could tell they were trying to decide whether to throw a punch or not. The crowd at the bar, sensing trouble, began to fan out.

Meghan immediately was up and jabbing her finger at them. "Listen, Aaron, you want to start something, you do it outside otherwise I'm calling the cops."

"Shut the hell up, woman," he said without taking his eyes off Jack. Seeing that things were about to kick off, Meghan hurried towards the phone but one of the men hopped over the bar and blocked her way leaving the other two flanking Aaron. Jack stared hard at them while they returned narrowed gazes without moving. The two arced out as if preparing to jump him. Jack was holding a bottle at the time; he brought it to his lips and took a hard pull on it before placing it down.

"Listen, this can go one of two ways. You can head over to the pool tables and continue on like nothing has happened, or you can leave here in an ambulance. Your choice."

Aaron snorted, and the others shook their heads. He turned to his buddy beside him and in an instant threw a punch. Jack blocked it with his left forearm and flipped up the bottle, grabbed it by the other end and smashed it across the top of his head. Chaos erupted as the other two lunged with pool cues. Moving fast, Jack grabbed Aaron, throwing him into his buddy, sending both of them down, while grabbing the pool cue that rained down on him. He stabbed his boot into the man's knee causing him to buckle and reel in agony; he followed through with a knee to the face, bursting his nose like a fire hydrant. By the time he was down, the one who had hopped over the bar tackled him to the ground. Jack took a jab to the face but parried the next with a hard crack to the ribs before pulling the guy's upper body down and slamming his elbows into the top of the man's head. Out the corner of his eye he saw Aaron stagger to his feet. He had to move fast. Jack plowed an open palm into the man's face and shoved him off before rolling out from underneath. He'd just managed to get to his feet when a chair hurtled through the air sending him flying back, crashing into a table. Beer glasses went everywhere. The next thing he knew someone grabbed him from behind and drove a fist into his kidney. Jack reached over his shoulder, latched on to his attacker and then jerked forward in one smooth motion sending him straight over the top. Still bent over, he saw another coming in hard from behind, he reared back his leg and drove a boot into his shin, sending him off balance and collapsing.

Once he turned to see who remained, he found all of them laying on the ground groaning in agony. As he was brushing himself off, he heard his named called.

"Jack!"

He whirled around just in time to see Meghan break a glass bottle over the top of Aaron's head. He'd gone for a gun in his waistband. Had she not acted in that moment, chances were he would have been dead.

"Thanks," Jack said.

Out of breath, she hurried over pushing him towards the exit. "You should go. I called the police, they'll be here soon."

"What about you?"

"I'll be fine. Go."

Jack nodded and motioned to Corey who had been watching the whole thing unfold from the safety of the booth. Before leaving, Jack told Meghan that he was staying at the Locust Hill Inn. "I'd really like to continue our conversation."

She pursed her lips, nodded and then looked around at the mess. Shattered glass was everywhere, tables had been overturned and one chair was broken. It was liable to cost them a small fortune to get it fixed up. Jack fished into his back pocket and pulled out a few hundred-dollar bills, he stuffed them into her hand. "Towards the damage."

"You don't need to…"

Before she could finish he'd turned and headed

towards the exit. As he and Corey stepped outside, sirens could be heard in the distance. As they made their way back to the vehicles, Corey seemed eager to educate him on the gravity of the situation.

"Do you know who that was?" Corey blurted. "That was Aaron Gance you put on the floor back there. Not a smart move."

"And letting him beat a woman is?"

"No, but most of those women in there are known for egging guys on."

Jack scowled at him. "What is it with the people in this town?"

"I'm just saying they're not worth going to jail over."

"I'll keep that in mind," Jack said, stepping out into the night's cool air. "Anyway, what did he say to you?"

"I told him to drop it. I've known him for a while. He's a hard man to reach but the Lord doesn't give up on any of us." His words went in one ear and out the other. Jack gave a nod and upon reaching his car hopped inside. Corey tapped on his driver's side window. He brought it down, and he handed him a scrap of paper with a number on it. "In case you get into any further trouble. Call me."

"You a lawyer now?"

Corey smiled and slapped the top of the vehicle before walking away. The Shelby tore out of the lot. Gravel spit as he headed north on 219. It would take him the long route around but he needed some time to blow off steam. His adrenaline was still pumping hard and his heart was pounding. He smiled ever so slightly as he gripped the wheel. It felt good to exchange knuckles. The look on those guy's faces after he was done with them was priceless. At least he would think twice before raising a hand to a woman again.

Jack drove for the better part of forty minutes, weaving his way through the back roads of West Virginia, lost in thoughts of the past and mulling over the challenge ahead of him. It wasn't until he was within five minutes of the inn that he noticed the vehicle following him. It was hard to tell how long it had been tailing him as the roads he'd been on didn't have many streetlights and he'd seen a number of vehicles on the road. It was a dark Chevy sedan with tinted windows. He was unable to see who the occupants were but after making several turns, he was confident that they were tailing him. As he pulled into the driveway that led up to the inn, he let the car idle and watched as the sedan rolled by. The window was partly cracked. A cigarette sailed out, landing a few feet from the back of his vehicle. Figuring they had been spotted, they drove home the accelerator and tore off into the night. He waited there for a few more minutes contemplating turning the tables on them and following but after what had happened at the bar, getting into a car chase through a sleepy town was the last thing he needed. He'd already drawn enough attention. He drove on deciding to turn in for the night. Though he wished he could have extracted more information from Meghan and Corey, at least he'd made some progress. There was no telling what tomorrow would bring but one thing was for sure, he wasn't going to let small-town intimidation shake his nerves.

Chapter 11

It was like taking candy from a baby; he thought as he prowled though the ads. He could have killed more if he wanted to but he had to be careful. The recent involvement of the FBI, and questions by State Police had set all the girls on edge. Before, they were careless, greedy, and it made it that much easier to control them. The sound of the woman's muffled cries seeped up through the cracks in the floorboards. He usually didn't let them live beyond the first few days as it was too dangerous but this one, this was different. For the first time since he'd started, this was one he wasn't sure about. She knew too much but... the man trailed off in his thinking, returning to looking at the laptop before him. The screen light illuminated his face in the darkness of the cabin. Long gone were the days of stalking women on the streets, the Internet made it so much easier. His eyes scanned over the many ads littering backpage. Searching for the one, the right one required time. With Susan Holt, it had taken six hours; Rachel Dixon, three days, and Brenda Norris, well that had taken him up to a year. He wasn't sure about her. He went back and forth just like he was doing now.

"Too fat, too thin, odd-shaped face, no ass, too much makeup, claw toenails, not enough meat. Ugh. Sluts."

He continued going through his list of the things he didn't like. It wasn't perfection he was after but a certain look. He didn't care if they were dark, blond, red-haired or using some of that fake coloring in their hair. They just had to have that look in their eyes.

He groaned again.

All of them were whores, worth nothing to him. How many of their family members knew what they did? He was doing the world a favor — ridding them of the filth one by one. Of course after they were dead, people acted as if they cared but did they? He chuckled to himself. No one cared about these women. They were the lost ones. The outcasts of society. Under any other circumstances, the public would have turned up their noses and shunned them. But murder one, and there was an outcry. He wasn't fooled by that fakery. He knew the truth. It infringed on their little bubble of reality. The suburbanites sickened him with their high-end cars, their white picket fence homes, their perfect lawns and their stories of what they were doing with their lives. Who gave a shit? He didn't, that was for sure. It was nothing but noise to him, noise that he wanted to smother.

He took a break for a second to load another computer beside him. He sipped at his glass of bourbon, relishing its taste as the woman whimpered in the background. He hadn't decided how he would kill her. Up to now it had been simple, he'd used narcotics and let the women overdose. From there he transported them to their final destination where they would later be found. He wanted them found. He wanted the town, state, and the world to take notice. This was art, and the rivers and streams of the world were the wall on which he carefully placed them. On a few occasions with Dixie Stokes and Paula Roberts, he'd returned to their watery grave to look upon their waterlogged skin, and bask in the beauty of their final resting place. But it was getting harder to do that. A neighborhood watch had been started, the public was mindful that a predator was among them. He smiled at the thought — predator. That's what he was. This was a form of big-game hunting — the greatest form.

He gazed at the local news article. *A possible link in the Green Bank Five.*

They'd given his work a name, and yet they didn't know the half of it. He'd been working for much longer than this. They thought five was a lot. Five? He chuckled to himself. Five was the number of women he'd allowed them to find. He'd killed much more than that. These were just the next level in his game. The ones before were buried out of sight and would never be found. Hell, they had barely got a mention in the press. Families had disowned them, forgotten they existed. Pimps moved on to the next girl, assuming they had run away. No one was searching for them. That's what made them the perfect target. All he had to do was choose them.

He returned to the second computer and scanned the ads:

NEW in Marlinton, baby. SWEET JUICY BLOND BARBIE 28

HOT, wet and juicy, I'm jaw-dropping sexy and sweet 23

Sexy THAI Busty Beauty to kiss and shower. Fantasy 20

Your #1 CHOICE Singaporean Josie 29

He clicked on one and it brought him to another ad. Six photos of the woman not showing her face were off to the right and to the left was an ad listing her stats. He clicked away. He avoided the ones that didn't show their face. That was an important part. He could tell a lot about a woman by her eyes, that and of course the fact that many had shown up at his door and turned out to be nothing like what their photos had shown. For their deception, he treated those with extra care. Their exit from the world was drawn out and painful.

He clicked on another ad, then another, over the years he'd gained a good sense for the ones that would be easy to manipulate. The ones that were addicted. There were signs. Even the best photos and makeup in the world couldn't hide the withdrawn, junkie look. They wore it like a medal of honor. He could almost hear them crying out. "Kill me."

He reached for his drink, his pulse pounding faster.

Another muffled cry from below and he slammed his foot against the ground in anger.

"Shut up!" he cried out.

She was throwing off his concentration. Didn't she know she was ruining it? He delighted in finding the next one as much as he enjoyed killing them. Of course, he didn't see it as murder. It was more of a cleansing, a purging of the scum from the world around him. This wasn't sexual in nature. He wasn't driven by the demons that other serial killers were tormented by. Oh no, he didn't touch them in that way. To do so would have been to lower himself to their standard. No, he made them think that he was going to touch them. He led them in with the high hopes of a wild time beneath the sheets only to ply them in his hands like putty. Before they knew what was happening, it was over. In many ways, he was merciful to them. He could have used any number of painful methods to snuff out their light but he gave them what they wanted. The deepest sleep. Rest from their miserable lives, a home on the other side where no one could touch them again. No one could label them.

His eyes fell upon his next victim. She was breathtaking. Perfect in every way. His mouth watered at the thought of watching the light disappear from her eyes. He leaned back in his seat and allowed his eyes to roll back in his head as he envisioned the moment, the smell of her skin and the sound of her last breath exiting her lips.

That last breath. It was exquisite.

Another muffled cry.

He slammed his hand against the table and kicked his chair back before crossing the room and pulling back a large rug to reveal a trap door. He took off the key from around his neck and inserted it into the steel lock. A twist of the hand and it came away, and he pulled back the heavy door. He stomped down the wooden stairs like an annoyed child, pausing only to tug a cord. A dim light illuminated the stony prison.

"You just don't listen, do you? I told you to be quiet. I told you that if you were good, I might let you live a little longer. But you just couldn't do it, could you? You're just like them. Full of lies. Filthy. The world would be better without you." The sound of his boots echoed in the cavernous hole beneath the cabin. There in the center of the room, handcuffed to a steel foundation pole, was the woman. He approached her, crouched down and placed both hands on the sides of her head. Her eyes were full of terror. Her mouth gagged. She was still fully clothed. He didn't need to see her body. He leaned in and smelled her sweet hair before slamming her head against the steel pole. That was all it took. One good knock and she was out. Her body went limp, and he stood there gazing at her form while a smile danced on his lips. He went back and forth on whether to kill her. He could dispose of her in the North Fork River. It was close. That had always been a location he'd enjoyed visiting. The fish he'd caught there were gorgeous. The idea of setting her body down into the water excited him. The visual image of her lying lifeless. Another photo to add to his collection. He crossed the unfinished concrete basement to a shelf on the wall that was lined with photo albums. He ran his finger across the spines, mumbling under his breath and trying to recall some of the women inside them.

"This one," he said out loud as he squeezed one out and laid it down on the workbench. There he turned on a small light and took a seat on a barstool. Like an artist reminiscing about his work from the past, he flicked through the album gazing at the multiple photos of women who had so freely given up their lives. For what? Two hundred bucks? He'd heard all their stories and he could remember them all.

He tapped the album. "Gina, a mother of two,

addicted to meth, majored in law but never entered her desired career because she got pregnant. Became an escort after the father abandoned her and the children." He paused. "Oh Gina, I see your kids in town. You would be proud. They no longer suffer the embarrassment of having a whore for a mother." He smiled and continued thumbing his way through the next.

"Abbey, a college dropout, addicted to oxycodone, a runaway. No one loved you but I did. I took care of you and showed you more love in your final few hours than anyone had in your entire life."

As he went one by one, he relived each interaction and recalled how he lured them in and got them to lower their guard. So many were guarded when they showed up. They thought they were in charge. Telling him what he could or couldn't do. Of course, he played into it. He wanted them to think that he wasn't a danger and just when they had let their guard down enough, he would flip the table. The look on their faces when he did it. It was priceless. It wasn't fear. It was shock.

No longer interested in the rest of the faces, he closed the album and placed it back on the shelf, taking a few seconds longer to make sure they were lined up perfectly. It never worried him that anyone would break in and find them as the cabin was in an isolated area of Green Bank. No one came to this town except those interested in the observatory tower or folks who had electro-sensitivity and were looking for peace. That's what Green Bank was to him — a place of peace and quiet.

Satisfied that the woman wasn't going to wake up anytime soon, he went back upstairs and closed the trap door, locked it and covered it with the rug. He was going to return home, but he had more work to do. Now that this man was here, he needed to know more about him. What did he know? He was dangerous, liable to bring an end to his work. He couldn't allow that. The man returned to his seat and typed in the name: Jack Winchester.

* * *

Larson wasn't buying her story. The call had come

through while he was in the middle of writing up a report for a domestic that had occurred in the south end. It had been the fourth one in the past five days. Now as he stood inside Ali's Bar gazing around at the mess, he wasn't convinced.

"Where did you say they went?"

"Aaron left here with his pals a few minutes before you arrived."

"And how many others were there?"

"Six of them."

He continued scribbling it down, taking just a few seconds to write down the description she was reeling off. According to Meghan Palmer, a group of bikers had rolled in around eight, had a few drinks when Gance and his buddies showed up. One of them had tried to pick up one of their women and had caused a fight. Was it true? If it was, it was the first time he'd heard of bikers passing through this town. It was in the middle of nowhere. There were only a few folks who stumbled across their town — Tourists, and those who had broken down. He didn't kid himself, it was a shithole that had nothing to offer anyone except those looking to hike, bike or find peace. There were better towns, ones with better bars in the surrounding area.

Of course like any good cop, he wasn't one for just taking one statement. He took several that evening, and that's when it came to his attention that perhaps she was telling a lie. Outside, a young couple was smoking nearby. Larson approached them and they got that familiar look of fear on their faces that all people did when they saw a badge and gun. He recalled what his Academy instructor had told him. *Remember, they don't see you. They only see the uniform.*

"How long have you been here tonight?"

"A couple of hours."

"Big fight, eh?"

They nodded but didn't expand. Folks around town were cautious around police, not because they thought they had done anything wrong but usually it was because they knew someone who had and there was always this lingering thought that they would get in trouble for who they knew. There was a real divide between the police and the public. It had been a gap that they'd been trying to bridge but had been unsuccessful.

"So did you see who started it?"

"Nope," the tall guy with long hair and a Metallica T-shirt on said before his eyes flitted over to his girlfriend who had a nose ring and looked like a pig. *Whatever happened to fashion?*

Did they know Aaron Gance? Everyone knew Aaron in one way or another. That kid had his fingers in every facet of the families in town. Teens knew him from drug dealing. Women knew him from his offers to help them earn money. He was a weasel that worked his way into lives and destroyed them. Since his release, Larson had been looking for any reason to put him away again. Just one thing. That's all it would take, and he was going back inside.

"Too bad, I heard those guys did quite a number on Aaron Gance."

"Guys? It was one guy," the girl blurted out.

Her boyfriend was quick to dismiss what she said. "What she means is one guy did the most damage."

"Cut the shit," Larson said. "Give me a name."

The kid blew out some smoke and navel gazed.

"A name?" Larson barked, snapping the guy out of his dream world.

He shrugged. "I don't know his name. Tall guy, bulky, short dark hair. You should have seen it. That guy took out four of them like he was brushing flies out of his face."

Larson frowned. *Surely it couldn't be. He wouldn't be that reckless, would he?*

"Was this guy wearing a leather jacket?"

"Yeah."

Larson thanked them and headed back into the bar. He made a gesture with two fingers for Meghan to come over to him. He could put up with a lot of shit, and lying was common in this town but lying for a stranger, someone who wasn't a local? He had to hear this.

Chapter 12

Jack had a sleepless night. In the early hours of the morning after hours of rolling around trying to get comfortable, he slipped out of bed and got dressed. The alarm clock was flashing a little after four. His mind was still preoccupied by his previous visit to Jenna Whitmore's apartment. Journalists were notorious for keeping notes and recording as much information as they could, and yet an extensive search of her apartment had yielded nothing. No laptop. No recorder. No notebook. For someone supposed to have been fired from her work because she was obsessed with the Green Bank Five case, it struck him as odd that she wouldn't have kept some record of her investigation. *You were scared and believed you were getting closer to finding out who was behind it. So where is this information?*

Outside his window, a heavy mist covered the landscape giving everything an ominous feeling. His reflection in the window was illuminated by the glow of the cigarette. Snatching up his keys he headed out. It was still early enough that he could slip back in without being noticed. Jack drove the short distance back to 3rd Avenue and parked a block down the road from the apartments. This time he didn't enter the front entrance, instead, he scaled up the fire escape, making sure to stay as silent as possible. Sure enough, the window hadn't been repaired. In its place was a thick layer of cardboard with a few pieces of duct tape holding it in place. He peeled it back before entering. The shattered glass on the floor was gone. As soon as he was in, he removed his boots and switched on his flashlight. *Where would you have put it?*

In his time working for the mob, when he wasn't hunting down people, he often found himself searching for money that had been stolen, or hidden away by those who owed Gafino a debt. Years of doing it had made him familiar with spots that were used by those looking to avoid detection. He shone the light up at the ceiling. Guns, cash, drugs or fake IDs were stored in all manner of tight storage areas; lockers at bus stations, secret compartments in vehicles, spaces below floorboards, cavities in walls, behind ceiling tiles, in cans of food and much more. But he wasn't dealing with someone versed in extreme measures. Jack stepped up onto the sofa and raised a few of the ceiling tiles and swept the light inside. He turned over the sofa cushions and stuck a knife into the bottom to check there. Next, he felt around on the floor for any loose floorboards. Nothing. He moved on to the bedroom and ran his hand around the top of the closet, under the bed. He lifted the mattress and tore it open with the blade. Nothing. In the past, he'd seen people install fake walls and hide all manner of shit behind furniture. Scared individuals went to great lengths to hide their secrets. Over the course of the next fifteen minutes, he checked each of the room's ceiling tiles, cupboards, bags, furniture and décor items that might have been able to hold recorded information. The bathroom was the last place he searched. He was starting to come to the conclusion that she'd kept it on her and was about to leave the bathroom when he saw several petals from the flowers above the toilet on the floor. He frowned and looked at the vase; he removed it and lifted the top of the toilet's water tank. His eyes widened. Bingo! Jack removed the bag, laid it on the floor and proceeded to place the cover back.

* * *

It was a little after five when he made it back to the inn. He was eager to find out what she'd discovered and how it related to her disappearance. He placed the bag on the small table in his room, then went about making some coffee. He stared at the bag from across the room. With the police not convinced that she was missing yet, it would have taken them a while to find that. He took his phone and dialed her cell number and waited for the one on the table to ring. It didn't. *That's why it never rang in the apartment. You used a second cell phone.* She must have known that whoever was keeping tabs on her was getting close to her otherwise she wouldn't have gone to all the trouble of hiding it.

The dripping of hot water and aroma of roasted coffee brought alive his senses. He rubbed a thumb and finger across the top of his eyes and yawned. He was going to feel it later.

Jack poured steaming hot coffee into a mug then took a seat in front of the bag. He slid it open and pulled out the voice recorder, a hard drive, and cell. He tapped on the cell and expected it to show a code that he had to enter but there was none. The first thing he checked was the last number she had phoned. It came up with the name: Meghan Palmer. There were several calls to her over a period of days leading up to her disappearance. Jack leaned back in his seat and scrolled through her contacts. He took a pad of paper and wrote down those she had called or had called her the most in the last forty-eight hours. He got up and went over to the window and cracked it open before lighting a cigarette. There was a rule that no smoking was allowed but following rules had never been a strong point of his.

Next, he browsed through photos. Besides those of her

family, there were many that had been taken of different men. There were four shots of a dingy-looking motel called the Lodge on the Edge of Green Bank. A large majority of the shots were taken from a distance as scantily dressed women were seen going to and from the lodge with different men. He didn't recognize any of them, except for the man he'd fought in the bar — Aaron Gance. Seeing his face wasn't a surprise. The guy had trouble written all over him.

Jack flicked the butt out the window and returned to the table. He laid the cell down and picked up the voice recorder. It was dark with silver buttons. Most prominent were a stop and a record button. Beneath that were the play, rewind, forward, volume, erase, folder and menu buttons. At the top was a mic and earphone socket, and on the bottom was a USB port. Before he turned it on, he hooked up the external hard drive to his laptop and powered it up. There was one main folder full of hundreds of photos, snippets of audio and video. *Holy cow.* It would take him weeks to get through all of this.

He didn't have weeks, so he used the sort by date option in the folder to get everything organized. He figured the closer it got to the date that she disappeared, the more audio, video and photos she would have on specific people of interest. Hopefully, he could skip her preliminary work and pinpoint those who were potential suspects using the most current information.

Over the course of the next two hours, he pored through interviews with locals, and girls involved in the industry, most of whom were very dismissive and guarded in their answers. He transferred photos of the men onto his phone and made detailed notes. It would be a process of elimination. He'd have to sift through those who were most likely to have been involved, find out who they were, where they lived, what they did for a living and what their connection was to the Green Bank Five.

He pressed play and heard Jenna's voice.

The Pocahontas County Sheriff Department released a statement today that announced the FBI and State Police will be now handling the case. So far their investigation suggests that no foul play was involved but they aren't ruling it out. I don't believe that they don't see the connection. They are holding back. I tried to corner Sheriff Riley but he was very dismissive. The only one that seems to keep an open mind to it all is Deputy Sam Larson. Not sure why he listens to me but I appreciate what he has shared about the case to date. If it wasn't for him, I wouldn't have known about them pulling in Karl Fraser. Note to self: Speak with him tomorrow.

Jack pressed stop. *Karl Fraser?* He flicked back through multiple photos until he stopped on one of a bald, unshaven man wearing light blue overalls with the name Karl on the breast pocket. Six of the shots were taken with him in front of the Lodge on the Edge of Green Bank. He noticed he wasn't listed in the contacts but the number for the lodge was. There were also numerous notes about him having a history of exposing himself to a maid and attacking an escort. Jack dialed the number and leaned back. He blew out his cheeks and heard his stomach grumble. It was nearly a quarter to eight in the morning.

He still needed some breakfast.

A female answered the phone.

"Lodge on the Edge of Green Bank. How can I help you?"

"Yeah, good morning. I was hoping to speak with Karl Fraser."

There was silence on the other end.

"Hello? Are you still there?" Jack asked.

"Is this a joke?"

"No, I—"

"Mr. Fraser no longer works here."

Jack was quick to ask, "You wouldn't have his phone number by any chance? An address, maybe?"

"Who is this?"

"Just a friend."

"Listen, do you want a room or not?"

"No, I..."

Before he could finish she hung up. Damn it. This wasn't going to be so easy. He thought about the path Jenna must have taken. *How many doors did you have slammed in your face?*

Chapter 13

After Jack returned from a short morning run, several of the inn's guests were sipping coffee in the dining area, some talking while others were reading free copies of the *Pocahontas Times*. The smell of toast, bacon and eggs wafted in from the kitchen as he climbed up the stairs to his room. With so many questions swirling in his mind, running gave him a way to clear his head and focus on the task at hand. It would be easy to get distracted, sidelined by some small personal issue or caught up in small-town drama that had nothing to do with this case. No, he needed to stay on point, so his plan that morning was to visit the lodge. After taking a quick shower and throwing on a fresh pair of jeans and a long-sleeved shirt, he headed down for breakfast.

Once he reached his table, most of the guests had left, so Jack ate alone. The quick run that morning had worked up quite an appetite, but the owner — Beth

Robertson — had done a superb job of filling up his plate, even though there was only fifteen minutes left before they would close up the kitchen.

"Do you mind if I join you?"

He scooped up some of the scrambled eggs. "By all means."

She sat down with her cup of coffee. "I don't usually infringe on our guests, or ask them questions about why they are here but I couldn't help overhearing from one of our local delivery guys that you were recently in trouble with the law — something related to Jenna Whitmore."

He paused eating, his fork hovering close to his lip.

"News travels fast. You know her?"

"Her mother is a good friend of mine, and Jenna used to work here years ago before she took that job at the *Times*. You aren't here to cause her trouble, are you?"

He snorted. "I'm here to help her," he muttered before filling his mouth. "Problem is she has gone missing."

"This is related to her work, isn't it?" She shook her head and sighed. "I told her she would land herself in deep waters if she wasn't careful. She wouldn't listen to me. That's Jenna for you, always so gung-ho."

"Did she ever mention who she thought might be behind it?"

"The Green Bank Five murders?"

"Is that what they are calling it now?"

"Locals are, the police are afraid to call it that."

"Why?"

"Cottage country, Mr. Winchester. There are only two reasons people come here. To vacation or to live and believe me, there aren't many that live here that aren't from here. You have to be a unique individual to want to live in this neck of the woods. So many folks are too attached to their technology."

"But you use cells."

"We do but depending on where you are the reception is spotty at best. It's not uncommon to have it drop completely the further north or east you go."

While he ate, she continued to give him a history lesson on the county and the observatory tower. How it affected businesses, especially places like the Snowshoe Mountain Resort. He learned they had purchased the inn here many years ago not because it seemed like a lucrative venture but because they were in love with the area and people.

"The town wasn't always bad, Mr. Winchester. There are a lot of good people who live here. Honest, hard-working folks that would give you the shirt off their backs to help you."

"So what's changed?"

"The lack of jobs in the area probably contributes, but drugs. I saw Jenna a few weeks ago and she was telling me that she was astonished at the kind of drugs that were making their way into this area. She said most folks didn't know the half of it. A big part of the problem is that motorcycle gangs are buying up properties and turning them into crack houses. It's big business," Beth said. She sipped at her coffee. "And the problem is that most aren't aware. These aren't places of ill repute where junkies hang out. No, they are your typical suburb households, with a couple and several kids living there. On the surface everything looks fine, but behind the scenes they are storing drugs and distributing them out to the sellers."

He smiled. "For someone that runs an inn, you know a lot."

"To stay afloat in this day and age, it behooves a person to keep their ear to the ground. Jenna has always been a good source of information. Even if others don't agree."

"Is that why they fired her?"

"They fired her because she wanted to print the truth."

"About?"

"The corruption in the sheriff's department, the mayor's office and what some key individuals are up to in this town."

He paused, then poked at his bacon. "This key information wouldn't involve escorts, would it?"

She got this big grin on her face. "Now you're getting warmer."

A voice bellowed from beyond the room. "Beth, where

are you?"

Her eyebrows shot up and she looked off into the hallway. "I must get going. Ed doesn't like me wasting time in the mornings. Not that we have much to do except make the beds and do some grocery shopping for the evening."

As she was getting up Jack asked her, "Did Jenna ever mention anything about a Karl Fraser?"

"No. But I know him. Everyone does. Dirty pervert spying on guests up at that lodge. He tried to get a job here after he had done time for that incident. I told him where to go. I run a clean house here and there is no way in hell I would allow a filthy swine like that to taint our legacy."

For a woman in her early sixties, she had one heck of a mouth on her. He liked her. She was feisty and didn't worry about speaking her mind.

"So he would have left a résumé here?"

"He brought one in but I refused to take it."

"Do you know if he lives locally?"

She leaned back on her haunches. "You think he's responsible for those five women?"

"I think Jenna took an interest in him. I need to rule him out."

"So you are here to look into the murders then? What are you, an investigator?"

"Not exactly."

He sighed.

She ran a hand over her face. Ed was still calling for her. She glanced that way. "Hold on a minute here. We might still have a copy of his résumé. Ed said he had swung by a few days after I saw him, but he told him that he had to speak with me. Can you believe the nerve of that man to think he could circumvent me?"

"You do the hiring?"

She nodded. "And the firing."

With that said she shuffled away, and he finished off his breakfast. While he was waiting for her to return, his phone started buzzing. He tapped to answer and there was a woman on the other end.

"Jack, it's Meghan Palmer."

"Oh hey, thanks for getting back to me. I was hoping you would call. How did it go last night?"

"Not exactly as expected. Deputy Larson knows about the fight."

"You told him?"

"Someone else did. I had no choice but to explain."

Jack sighed. The last thing he needed was some cop riding his ass.

"Listen, would you be around this morning?"

"Um, I have a few errands to run, but after that.... Why?"

"I was hoping we could meet to discuss the last time you were with Jenna. I have to travel up to Green Bank later, maybe you can come along?"

"Uh, I don't know about that. I don't mind speaking on the phone or meeting locally but... no offense but I don't know you and..."

"With the disappearances, and all..."

"Exactly."

"Sure." He glanced at his watch, it was just after nine. "Name a place?"

"Dories Lounge, at ten o'clock."

"I'll see you then. And Meghan. Thank you."

A few minutes passed and Beth returned with a single piece of paper in hand. It had been folded. "Here it is. He lives in Green Bank."

"Beth!" her husband yelled again. She smirked. "Hope you find what you're looking for, Mr. Winchester." She hurried out of the room leaving him alone. He glanced down at the résumé. It was littered with odd jobs, mostly handyman positions. The longest employment he'd had was with the lodge which had ended last year. If he wasn't mistaken that was in the middle of when the five women began showing up dead. Jack took a sip of his coffee. A crisp morning breeze blew in through the window. It was cooler than the day before. The rain had taken most of the humidity out of the air. As he scanned the résumé, he heard gravel spitting. Jack glanced up and through the dining room window, he saw a police cruiser coming up the driveway.

"Oh great," he muttered, more trouble with the law. He certainly didn't want them slowing him down today. There was too much to be done.

Now whether it went against sound judgment or not, Jack double-timed it up to his room, snatched up the voice recorder, the phone, his keys and some extra money and exited via the window. He slid down the drainpipe and ran at a crouch towards his vehicle. Once inside, he started the engine and rolled out of there. His heart was pumping as he peeled away. As he drove, he kept his eyes on the rearview mirror to make sure that Larson wasn't following him. He had an hour to kill before he would meet up with Meghan; he figured he could stay out of trouble until then.

Chapter 14

The day wasn't going as planned. Deputy Larson had shown up at the inn expecting to find Winchester and bring him in for questioning about the previous night's incident. Larson made a call in person last night but he wasn't around. He was going to return later that evening, but he got snowed under with paperwork and figured that Winchester wasn't going anywhere, anytime soon.

Even though Meghan and Bonnie had come to his defense, he couldn't believe the nerve of the guy. First, he broke into an apartment, then he got involved in a brawl within hours of getting released from custody. Was he looking for a one-way ticket to jail?

He cast his gaze around the room after he got no answer and Beth Robertson had let him inside. A small duffel bag sat on a table, a hard drive off to the right of that and a packet of cigarettes beside his bed. The window was wide open, and the drapes were blowing in.

She quickly crossed the room and closed it.

"Looks like we might be in for some more rough weather before this week is out," she said as he gazed around.

"He was here?"

"Like I said, he was here only minutes ago. Maybe he's gone for another run."

"A run?"

"He was out this morning running."

"Oh, I bet he's gone for a run," he said under his breath. He wasn't stupid.

Beth peered out the window. "Yep, doesn't look like his car is here."

Larson joined her and glanced out. Sure enough the Shelby he'd seen on the way in was gone. He smiled and exited the room with Beth on his heels.

"Deputy, Mr. Winchester brought to my attention that Jenna Whitmore has gone missing."

"That's not confirmed."

"But shouldn't you at least be looking into that?"

"We are."

"Like the way you are looking into the Green Bank Five?"

He continued down the stairs with his mind occupied by the next person he was going to see that morning — Aaron Gance. On a good day he didn't like swinging by that garage, but if anything would rile him up, it would be this.

"Thank you, Mrs. Robertson."

"Deputy, Mr. Winchester strikes me as someone who is trying to help. Shouldn't you be out there hunting down whoever is responsible for the death of those women, instead of bothering him?"

"Thank you," he repeated and let himself out. If he had stopped to engage with her, he wouldn't have got out of there. She was notorious for flapping her gums and holding people hostage with her endless conversations, which were mostly rumors that she'd heard. Outside he got back into his cruiser. His radio was crackling, and he heard Ethan come over the line.

"Larson, any luck with Winchester?"

"Negative. He's not here."

"You spoke with Gance this morning?"

"I'm on my way over there."

"You want some backup?"

He was about to say yes but then figured that he could deal with it himself. If he was going to make headway in the department, he needed to demonstrate he could handle situations as they arose. He hadn't had any problems bringing in Aaron for the last assault when he had thrown Bonnie through a window. Aaron spent time in prison for that — though it definitely wasn't as long as he should have got. Since then he had been putting on an act, trying to make out he was going clean by working at his brother's garage. That was just a farce. He knew he was still dealing drugs and pimping women out, he just needed evidence, and that was something he was short on.

No, it wasn't Aaron who posed a danger, it was his older brother Merle. Merle had one hell of a temper on him and had already done time before setting up his garage. Unlike Aaron, he shied away from drawing attention to himself, at least nowadays. He was smart, cold and calculating. He knew when to play or fold his cards. According to those in the department, long before Aaron got a taste for criminal behavior, Merle was constantly in trouble with the law. Mostly small-time offenses but it soon increased to car theft and drug dealing for a notorious biker gang. Rumor had it that he was still the main contact for the flow of drugs coming into the county and getting into the hands of youngsters, but the department had yet to prove that. Since he'd been busted over eight years ago, he had done his time, come out and had been leading a fairly peaceful life as a mechanic, though Larson knew that looks were deceiving. His name had come up numerous times but no matter how many times they raided his home or the garage, they had always come up empty-handed.

It was frustrating, but one of these days he was going to catch him red-handed and hopefully Aaron would be there at the same time. Nothing would give him more pleasure than putting away the Gance brothers. They were a stain on society's ass.

As he drove the winding streets towards the Gance garage, his thoughts drifted to the days after Aaron was released from prison. Ethan and several of the others in the department had told him to watch his back. They had warned him that busting him for beating up a woman was going to do him more harm than good.

Since Aaron had got out, all manner of weird shit had started to happen. He found his cruiser's tires deflated. His driveway had been spray-painted with obscenities and a vehicle had nearly knocked down Kerry. He was pretty sure Aaron was behind it and that's why he'd been riding him hard since he'd come out, making sure that he was meeting with his parole officer and spending his time working. Most days he would roll past the garage just to see if he was there. Many times he'd locked eyes with him standing outside smoking a cigarette. Aaron would toss him the bird. It was when a mysterious fire started in his cruiser after he'd parked it outside his home that he began to think that Aaron wasn't going to let up until someone got hurt. The problem was that without witnesses, there was absolutely nothing Larson could do about it. It was all hearsay. They would have thrown it out of court if it even made it into court. His lawyers would have had a field day.

"Look, Larson, I'm heading over there. Wait until I get there. I don't want you getting all up in his face. Hell, we got enough to deal with, don't go stirring up the hornet's nest," Ethan said.

"We have a job to do. I'm going to do it."

"Alright but don't make this about the past."

"You know as well as I do that he's behind the recent string of events. Now I have multiple witnesses that say he started the fight last night. I might not be able to get him for lighting fire to that cruiser but I sure as hell can take him in for last night. All I need is one thing to put him away."

"Larson, there is a brawl every night down at that bar. It's part and parcel of this town. People like to get liquored up and exchange a few words. The court will throw it out. You know they will. Look, wait until you have more on him before you go wasting our time by dragging him in. Besides, we are still dealing with that domestic from the other night and the hit-and-run. Don't go looking for trouble."

Larson ignored him. He focused on the road ahead. Nothing was going to deter him from at least having words with him.

"Are you hearing me? The guy has already filed a harassment complaint against you. The department doesn't need this right now. You want to make a good impression with the chief, this isn't the way to do it."

"So you're just going to let him think that he can do whatever he likes in this town?"

"It was a brawl. Who knows if that Winchester guy wasn't behind it? Perhaps it would be best to track him down. At least we had him in on a B&E."

"He came to Bonnie's aid. There is a restraining order still in effect on Gance."

"You don't get it, do you, Larson? You might have had that couple tell you about the fight, but no one is going to speak out against Gance. You know as well as I do their family's reach goes beyond Aaron. They have ties with that motorcycle gang. And before you say it… for all we know, they could be responsible for the Green Bank Five."

"No. I don't buy it."

"Because your judgment is clouded by a chip on the shoulder."

"Yeah, I'd like to see how you would react if you woke up to find your cruiser ablaze. I have a baby to think about. The sooner he is off the streets, the better."

Larson gripped the steering wheel tightly.

"That's right. You have a baby to think about. So I'm telling you… ease off the gas in your pursuit of Gance. We will get him when the time comes, but it's not now."

"So you just expect me to look the other way?"

"No. That's not what we do. But let's just feel this one out. I'm heading over there. Don't engage with him until

I get there otherwise we are going to have a riot on our hands. And listen, Larson, I'm telling you this for your own good. I know you think I don't give a shit about being a cop because I'm going to retire soon but it couldn't be further from the truth. Like a good gambler, you just need to know when to play your cards and when to fold them."

Larson sighed as he flicked his indicator on to turn left down the street that led to their garage. "Okay. I'll wait for you to get here," he answered. Even as he said it, he couldn't guarantee that his temper wouldn't flare when he saw Aaron.

* * *

An hour after leaving the inn, Jack pulled into a parking space outside Dories Lounge. It was a cozy-looking establishment on the corner of 2nd Avenue and 9th Street. Like any diner, it had the typical booths on either side with about ten tables and chairs taking up space in the middle. A bell above the door let out a shrill as he entered. Inside it was stuffy. Ceiling fans were on full blast. A few locals looked his way. Jack noticed Meghan wasn't there yet, so he slipped into one of the booths and waited for the older waitress to come over. The place had a bit of a funky smell to it. Not bad, just unusual. At the far end was the kitchen. He could see a lone chef working away behind a plume of steam while a young woman manned the cash register. Outside the window, across the street, was a used car dealership. Some oil-slick salesman was guiding a couple around. A few pedestrians walked by and gazed in.

A waitress appeared off to his right and handed him a menu.

"What can I get you to drink?" the older lady said holding a pad of paper and pen. She looked as if she had been working there for decades.

"Coffee is fine."

She shoved the pad into the front of her apron and walked off. Five minutes passed, then ten and he figured she wasn't going to show. He'd already drunk two cups of coffee when the door opened and Meghan came in. She hurried over and slid in across from him.

"I'm so sorry, I got held up at a friend's house."

"Can I get you a drink, maybe a little food?" Jack asked, hoping to at least give her a reason to stick around. Since he'd arrived he already got a sense that people didn't want to talk about what went on in the town.

"Coffee. Thank you."

"So… What can you tell me?"

She gazed around the room as if making sure that no one else was listening. "Look, Jenna was in contact with me for a few months but I really didn't want to talk about what I did. It's embarrassing. I have a kid. I'm a single mother. That job at the bar barely pays enough to pay my rent and groceries for the week. With the kind of prospects that this town offers, I certainly am not going to get anywhere."

"But selling your body?"

She frowned. "Are you here to judge me?"

Jack flung his hands up. "Meghan, I'm the last person to judge anyone for their decisions. Trust me. But I'm just wondering if that's the only option you felt you had?"

She stared back at him before biting down on the corner of her lip and fiddling with a packet of sugar in front of her.

"Do you know how much I make at that bar a week? Bearing in mind I don't work every day because they don't have enough people coming in to warrant it." She paused. "About three to four hundred bucks."

"And tips?"

"Tips?" She let out a laugh as the waitress came over and placed a coffee before her. "Nancy, he wants to know how much we make in tips in this town. You want to tell him?"

She just rolled her eyes and walked away.

"Does that answer it?"

He shrugged, then looked at her arm. She caught him staring, and she pulled up her sleeve. "No, I'm not a junkie. Not all of us are. Though I've considered it. Just trying to make ends meet and keep my head above water is enough to make anyone want to numb out. But no, I have a kid to think about."

"So did some of the women that went missing."

"If you did what we do, you would want to take drugs. You think I like doing it? There are some dirty old men out there, and many that are married."

"So how long are you going to keep this up? I mean, surely you must be worried about the recent string of deaths."

"Yeah, I am. But I have mouths to feed. I figure if it happens, it happens. Nothing I can do about it."

"So you work for someone, or just yourself?"

She smiled and shook her head. "Myself."

Jack took a hard pull on his coffee. He'd met all manner of girls on the street when he was living in New York. Among the many enterprises his old boss used to run, prostitution was one of them. He met the women. Most of them were clean, girls who just wanted to escape the streets. At least working with a pimp came with protection from the johns. Pimps would park outside and the women had ways of letting them know if they were in trouble, or concerned about the john.

"And what about Bonnie? What was all that about in the bar the other night?"

Meghan stirred her cup.

"Aaron used to be her pimp. He'd set up deals with johns and pocket the lion's share of the profits. When she got pregnant by her boyfriend and refused to get an abortion, he went ballistic on her. She spent several days in the hospital for that. Nearly lost her baby. The police hauled him in and tossed his loser ass in jail. In the meantime, she managed to get her life together. Contrary to what some people think, she doesn't do it anymore. She's worked out a pretty good deal with the owner of the bar and is the only full-time staff member. So it covers her bills. She could use some extra money but couldn't we all. I admire her grit for walking away from it."

"So he doesn't want her to walk away?"

"No, he doesn't give two shits about her. He wants her to suffer for turning him in. He has shown up several nights a week since he's been out. Usually, after he's had a couple, he tries to get into it with her."

"And the cops?"

Meghan sipped at her coffee and then chuckled. "The cops in this town are a joke. Well, I say that but Larson seems to be trying to change things. He's the only decent one in the department." She got this glint in her eyes. "Did you know that one of them even sleeps with some of the..." She made quotation marks with her fingers in the air, "'escorts' in the area? Did you know that?"

"It doesn't surprise me."

She smiled. "Now you are starting to sound like a local."

Four guys came into the diner, and Jack noticed that one of them was from the group that he'd roughed up at the bar the previous night. He had short hair, tattoos and was wearing dirty jeans and a white T-shirt. His lip was swollen, and he had one hell of a bruise around his eye socket. The man never took his eyes off Jack for even a moment.

"What can I get you boys?" Nancy said, leading them

into a booth on the far side of the room.

"The usual, Nancy."

One of them was telling some story to the others, and they all cracked up laughing, except for the one guy who kept leering at Jack. Meghan looked over and then back at Jack.

"Just ignore him."

Ignoring people in New York would get you killed. He always had to have his wits about him. He noticed the guy pull out a cell phone and slip out from the rest of the group to find a quiet space to speak. He stepped outside and every few seconds he would glance back in the window. Now it wasn't a hard guess to figure who he was contacting. When he came back in he threw a smirk Jack's way and sat back down.

"So you met up with Jenna then?" Jack continued.

"Yeah, sometime after midnight. I had one more client that I was meant to see in Green Bank but he bailed at the last minute, so she brought me back home."

"What do you mean he bailed?"

"We pulled up in front of a cabin in Green Bank. Jenna was going to wait outside while I went in. But my phone rang before I made it to the door. It was him, telling me he had changed his mind, and he wanted to cancel. I told him there would be a cancellation fee, but he just told me to fuck off." She shook her head and took a sip of her drink. "Now if I had a pimp, they would have gone in and got the money. But nothing I could do about it."

"Okay, so she brought you back home. Did she mention where she was going to go next?"

"Well that's the thing, she was acting all strange when I got back into the car. She asked me if I had seen that client before. I hadn't. I'd never been out there. Anyway, she dropped me off, thanked me for my time and said she might be in touch again and that was it."

"Which way did she drive off?"

"Back the same way we came. Out of town. Up Highway 28."

"And you never heard from her after that?"

"Nope."

Jack breathed in deeply and leaned back. He eyed the guy across the room. He kept casting an anxious glance over his shoulder towards the door. He was expecting someone — Aaron Gance, probably.

"Look, I have to head up to Green Bank this morning. I'm not too familiar with the area. Would you come along with me?"

"Um. I…"

"I'll pay you."

Her eyebrows shot up.

"Strictly just to have you as a guide. You're obviously familiar with the town and whatnot."

"How much?"

"How much is a couple of hours of your time worth?"

"Four hundred."

"I'll give you six."

"Six? Done!" A smile formed on her lips as Jack got up and tossed down some money to pay for the food and drinks. The guy across the room looked panicked. He looked away from Jack for a second or two and then back outside. As Jack passed by him he made a comment.

"Maybe next time." He made a gun symbol with his thumb and finger, winked and they exited the diner. He wouldn't have minded going another round with those idiots but he had a feeling the next time he encountered them they would be bearing more than fists.

Chapter 15

On the long stretch of road, Larson hit speeds up to eighty miles an hour, and by the time he turned off to the garage where the Gance brothers operated, his pulse was pounding. He was gripping the wheel so tight that his fingers had become rigid. Frustration surged through him. The department's concern for Aaron wasn't anything more than a need to keep themselves out of the media. He knew they would have tossed him inside at the first chance they got but their hands were tied by red tape. He'd always imagined that cops were protected against civil lawsuits. However, that wasn't the case. All over the country, officers had been called into court to account for the treatment of the public. Sometimes they got off though more often than not someone had filmed an interaction and shared it online. In the past most cases against an officer would be tossed out because there was no proof besides the word of the accuser. Now, with cameras on cell phones, it was a complete shit show.

He eased off the gas and began to slow down. He was nearly there. Larson had been waiting for this since the day Aaron got out — another opportunity to pull him in for creating a disturbance.

A few minutes later, Larson brought the cruiser to a stop in a graveled lot in front of the garage at the end of a dead-end road. It had always struck him as an odd place to run a business. It was off the beaten path, far from Main Street and less liable to get traffic from those who drove by, and yet with the history that the Gance brothers had, it seemed appropriate. They wanted to stay clear of prying eyes and the property backed onto dense woodland full of trails. If the flow of drugs circulating in the town was coming from them, he guessed they were using the surrounding forest as a place to stash them.

He pushed out of the car. Standing close to the open door, he surveyed the area and watched for movement. Usually, the garage would have been open for business but there was a sign on the door that read: CLOSED.

Larson ran a hand over his head. There was tension in his neck, and he needed to stay calm. Every time he tried to speak with him, he had come close to losing control.

He squinted at the windows scanning for movement. As a precautionary measure, he unsnapped his holster. Aaron had never owned a firearm, but that didn't mean he wasn't carrying.

Aaron Gance was a wild card.

A cold, unpredictable man capable of anything.

It was eerily quiet as he waited for Ethan to show. Besides the trees rustling in the wind, there were no other sounds. No birds. No critters. Only the thump of his heart. The sky was a dark gray, a far cry from the early morning, which was warm and sunny. Perhaps Beth Robertson was right. A storm was brewing. Larson cast a glance at his watch. *C'mon, Ethan.* He looked back up the road but there was no sign of him. He had a good mind to get back on the radio but he didn't want to become distracted. The last time he'd taken in Aaron, it hadn't come without a fight. He wasn't the kind of man that would return to jail twice. His eye caught movement, a drape in the window of the RV. The door cracked open, just a little, then fully and Merle was standing there wearing a dirty white muscle shirt, and garage overalls tied off around his waist. He had a few smears of oil on his forehead and a pair of specs resting low on his nose.

"Can I help you, officer?" The words came out slurred and gruff as if damaged by one too many cigarettes.

Larson noticed his nose was busted up. He had a strip of tape across it and some bruising under both eyes. He watched as he picked up a quarter filled bottle of Jack Daniel's off the counter and took a swig. *Great, he was drunk.*

"Need to speak to you and your brother about last night. The fight that broke out over at Ali's Bar."

"Don't know about any fight. We were here last night."

Larson scanned the tree line. If someone had a rifle on him, it would have been virtually impossible to know it. It was dense and seemed even darker from the brooding clouds that hovered overhead. The distant sound of thunder bellowed and Merle looked skyward.

"You and I both know you were there. There are multiple witnesses that place you at the scene and responsible for starting the fight."

"Sorry, deputy, they must have their wires crossed as we were here last night, playing cards and drinking with family. Listen, come back later, Aaron is not around. He'll be able to clear this up."

Merle hung one hand on top of the door and the other was hidden behind his back. Larson kept his hand on his gun, slowly easing it out of the holster but keeping it below the door. If shots broke out, he at least would be ready. He gave a nervous glance around him. Though he was wearing a bulletproof vest, he didn't like being out in the open. There were too many ways someone could creep up on him.

"Merle, don't make this any harder than it needs to be."

"You going to charge me for a fist fight?"

"You know how these things play out."

"I know that you keep harassing us. My brother has already filed a complaint against you. You want another?"

He made a gesture with two fingers for him to step out. "Step out and while you're at it, tell Aaron to get his ass out here."

"I told you…"

"I know he's in there."

He noticed Merle's head turn ever so slightly as if he was trying to communicate with someone. He staggered a little and then steadied himself against the side of the doorway.

"I want to know what we are being charged with?"

"Disturbing the peace, destruction of property, a breach of a restraining order and a threat made to Bonnie Ratlin."

He chuckled. "Shit! You have got to be joking. You know that isn't going to hold up in court. We'll be out on bail before the end of the day, and you are going to have another harassment complaint on your plate. You want that, deputy? Could tarnish that shiny new career of yours."

He was pissing him off. "Step out."

Merle scoffed and slammed the door shut. Right at that point, Larson knew he was fucked. It had taken a squad of six officers to bring in Merle many years ago. His reputation preceded him. Instead of moving in on him, which would have been a foolish move being as he didn't know if both of them were inside and armed, he got on the radio.

"Ethan, you there?"

"I'm two minutes away."

"You better move it. This is about to go south."

"Shit, Larson, I told you not to engage."

"I didn't. Merle did."

His eyes shot back to the RV at the sound of the door opening again. Strangely enough, he had a jacket on. Merle grabbed up some keys and stepped out as if he was ready to go quietly. He stumbled down three steps.

Larson's brow furrowed. "Where's Aaron?"

"I told you, he's not here. He got a phone call from a friend of his and shot off to meet him."

"Why's the garage not open?"

"Things have been slow."

"That's not what I've heard," Larson replied. "I hear you are still up to your old tricks."

"Yeah, well, people have big mouths in this town. Proof. That's what people need around here. Nothing but rumors floating around," he said as he made his way over.

"Keep your hands where I can see them."

He raised them up and got this big grin on his face. "Really, you that nervous?"

As they were speaking, Ethan's cruiser came rolling up. Larson slipped his gun back into his holster. Ethan hopped out expecting there to be some standoff. His eyes darted between the two of them.

"I ain't done nothin'!"

"Then you don't have anything to worry about, do you?"

"Ethan, you going to let him do this?" Merle said.

"I've always treated you and your family good."

"It's just procedure, Merle."

"Procedure my ass. I'd like to see the warrant."

"Don't need one."

"I have rights, you know. You can't just breeze in here and tell a man you're going to arrest him without proof. Where are these witnesses? Huh? Where's the victim of this crime? I'll tell you where the victim of the crime is. It's us. This is bullshit."

Larson gave him a command to stand by the vehicle so he could search him. Merle staggered from side to side, failing to walk in a straight line.

Larson scoffed. "Bullshit? Like the time you said you didn't steal that car?"

"You know as well as I do that people bring all manner of vehicles this way to be repaired. That wasn't my vehicle. I was just fixing it up."

"Oh, it wasn't your vehicle, all right. Giving it a spray job and changing the number plates. Yeah, right. You were just fixing it up. Now listen to what he's telling you and get over there," Ethan said.

"Anyway, that was in the past. I've done my time."

Larson latched onto him and kicked at his heels to get him to spread his legs before doing a routine check to make sure he wasn't carrying. He winced, smelling the booze on his breath as he exhaled hard.

"You got anything in your pockets that's going to stick me?"

"I'm clean."

"Who did Aaron go see?"

He shrugged. "I don't know. Maybe your wife," he said before laughing.

Rage overtook him and Larson slammed his head hard against the front of his car and pulled his gun, pressing it against the side of his temple.

"Larson. Enough. Put it away," Ethan said coming up behind him.

"You think that's funny. I know he's behind the destruction of my cruiser. I know he's the one that nearly ran over my wife. When I find him—"

"Larson!" Ethan yelled harder. In that moment he snapped out of it. His heart was pounding in his chest. It took everything not to pull that trigger. Unlike many of the larger cities in the area, their town hadn't incorporated video cameras onto the dashboards of all their cruisers. If they had, he would have had a lot of explaining to do. Larson slipped the gun back into his holster and began to read Merle his Miranda rights.

"You're arresting me? What have I done?"

"You know damn well what you've done."

Larson strong-armed him into the back of the cruiser and slammed the door shut before walking away to blow off some steam. He could hear Merle protesting in the back. His yells were muffled. A few times he kicked at the window with his feet but Ethan got him to calm down.

Larson knew Ethan was going to come down on him over it but he didn't care. The Gance brothers just kept pushing.

"What the hell was that?" Ethan asked crossing over to where he was standing by the edge of the woods.

"You know he did it."

"It doesn't matter, Larson. Do you want to lose your badge? This is about the fight not the cruiser, and definitely not your wife."

"Let's just take him in." Larson was done listening to him harp on. He didn't understand. How could he? He would soon be retiring. All he wanted to do was stay out of harm's way for the remainder of his career. He wasn't the one that was going to have to put up with them in the coming years, sifting through paperwork, red tape, and legal bullshit.

He hopped back into the cruiser, ignoring Merle's obscenities and spitting at the hard vehicle partition between the front and rear seats. Larson cast a glance at Ethan before pulling the cruiser around and heading toward the department.

* * *

The two cruisers tore away from the mouth of the road that led down to the garage. Aaron Gance sat in the front of the battered black Chevy truck. He'd been on his way back from Dories Diner when he spotted them in the distance. Riding shotgun was Billy and Dale.

"What do you think that's about?"

"The fight, you dimwit."

Aaron pulled into the road and floored it. The truck bounced around down the unfinished road and came to a grinding halt outside the RV. He pushed out of the truck and began shouting.

"Merle. Merle!"

He hurried over to the RV and let himself inside. There was a note on a pad of paper on the table, he picked it up and read it. It was short and straight to the point. *Larson showed up. Get out of town.*

"Fuck!" he yelled, scrunching it up and tossing it across the cramped quarters. Aaron went nuts and started smashing his fist into the cupboards. His fist punctured a hole in one. He kicked a chair and flipped the small table over. Billy and Dale entered to see what all the commotion was about.

"What's up?"

"Larson that's what. That sonofabitch has taken Merle in."

They stood still with their mouths agape. His thoughts were a mess. If he'd only been here, things would have been different. He wouldn't have gone in easy, or let him take Merle. Not again. Aaron shoved past both of them and headed out. He lit a cigarette and paced back and forth, one hand running over his head as he inhaled deeply. He had a good mind to head down to Larson's home and set the entire house on fire with his wife inside. He'd been egging Larson on since getting out but he'd shown restraint. Merle had made it clear that they'd eventually get him for putting him away. He'd always envisioned rolling up beside his cruiser while he was doing paperwork and putting a bullet in his head. Every day that he was inside, he'd thought about that man. But it wasn't just him. It was her — Bonnie. None of this would have happened if it weren't for her.

"You think she told them?"

"Of course," he spat back.

With the cigarette in the corner of his mouth, smoke curled up into his eye causing him to squint. He reached around and pulled out a Rossi snub-nose .357 revolver. He checked how many bullets were inside before he spun the cylinder and slapped it back into place. Aaron tucked it back into the small of his back and continued towards the truck. A clap of thunder threatened rain. He looked up momentarily before casting a glance over his shoulder.

"Well come on. Let's go."

"Where are we heading?" Dale asked.

"To deal with that bitch once and for all."

He stormed over to the truck and swung the door open.

"But what about the guy?" Billy asked picking up the pace.

"That's going to have to wait."

"But."

"Would you two idiots just get inside," he said. He was fuming. Rage pushed out what control he had left. The only one that had kept him from blowing her brains out and going after Larson was Merle. Now they had him, he was done pussyfooting around. And he sure as hell wasn't going to leave town. Tires squealed, and the truck kicked up grit as it sped away, leaving behind a plume of dust.

Chapter 16

Twenty minutes ago, the radio cut out as they crossed over into Green Bank. Jack adjusted it but Meghan told him not to bother. "You're in the Quiet Zone, 13,000 square miles free of electromagnetic pollution. And Green Bank is where it all happens." She brought the window down and breathed in the air. One road snaked its way through the Allegheny Mountains while on either side of them was an ocean of green rolling hills and dense emerald forest. On the way up they passed through several small towns, each one smaller than the last. Slowly but surely the forest parted and he could see the beginnings of the town in the distance. It was spread out in a valley full of cattle farms and old wooden barns. They passed a tiny post office, a library, a bank and Henry's Quick Stop; which Meghan was quick to point out was the gas station, convenience store, décor shop and only sit-down restaurant. Beyond that, across the street was a

Dollar General that had only been in business since 2011. Before that residents had to travel the forty-minute journey south to Marlinton or north to Elkins.

"Where what happens?" Jack asked.

She leaned back in her seat getting comfortable. "It's where they listen to distant galaxies at the edge of the universe." She said as if it was common knowledge. He'd never heard of it. She pointed to her left towards a megalithic dish that loomed over the tiny town with a population of 143. "It's the Robert C. Byrd Green Bank Telescope. Did you know that sucker is as tall as the Washington Monument, weighs 17 million pounds and you can fit two acres of land inside the dish?"

"I did not know that," he said, his lip curling up at the corner as they made their way toward Karl Fraser's home.

"Yeah, out here there is a ban on cell phones, radios, Wi-Fi routers, microwaves, you name it, and it's banned. At least within a ten-mile radius of the Astronomy Observatory."

"Why?"

"It would wreak havoc on the sensitive equipment. That's why they have someone who patrols the area in a white van. They're called the RFI Police."

"What do they do?" he said glancing out the window at the monstrosity of a telescope. It was one hell of an eyesore.

"They monitor frequency interference from cell phones, wireless devices and so forth. Every single one of these residents in the ten-mile radius has had to sign a waiver stating they will not use wireless devices. In fact, get this... many years ago they picked up some abnormal signals in the town. Turns out, when they managed to pinpoint where it was coming from, it was a dog's heating pad. Seems the pad had worn down and cracks in the wiring were causing super tiny electrical arcs. It wasn't enough to shock the dog but enough to cause issues. Anyway, they had to toss it and get a new one."

"So no one has Wi-Fi out here?"

She smiled. "If you ask people they will say no, but you can be sure there are some that are using it. I've heard from a couple of johns in the area that the RFI crew has shown up at certain neighbor's doors and had to get them to shut it down to prevent interference. It wasn't too bad back in 1956 when they created the site. Back then they only had issues with radio noise, spark plugs, and power lines. The problem is technology is so prevalent today; it's kind of hard to monitor everyone. Now having said that, for the most part residents abide by the rules in the Quiet Zone which of course includes Marlinton and the surrounding towns. Unlike Green Bank, we can have Wi-Fi in Marlinton, cell phones and so on but it gets real spotty when you start traveling in the county. There are even some folks who won't use a phone."

"For someone who doesn't work at the observatory, you sure know a lot about this."

"You have to, otherwise people are quick to remind you." She gazed out the window. Several cars shot by. "There you go..." She pointed off to the left. On the side of the road, there was an old-style telephone booth. A rusted-out box that looked out of place. "That's the pay

JON MILLS

phone that folks would have to use if they broke down out here. Or they can use a landline. Folks who live around here are pretty good people. I guess that's why the girls who went missing never worried about coming out here. This used to be a safe place."

She shook her head and frowned. Jack eased off the gas a little as they rolled by it.

"So no one has Internet out here?"

"No, they have dial-up Internet, landline phones, and ham radio. It's just wireless that is restricted. But the Internet out here is painfully slow."

Jack pulled out his cell phone and switched it on. Sure enough, no bars.

Meghan laughed. "It's strange, right? It's like living in the 1950s. I'm not sure how folks do it."

Jack mulled over the information and then it dawned on him. "So if you were seeing a client out here and you ran into trouble, you wouldn't be able to use your cell phone, right?"

"Exactly."

It was beginning to make sense why someone would kill women from Marlinton in Green Bank. All the homes were spread far apart. The chances of anyone being able to run to a neighbor's home were slim. Phoning emergency services would only be possible if the home they were in had a landline, or they were near a phone booth.

Jack slammed his brakes on and the tires squealed. Meghan jerked forward in her seat and put her hands out to brace herself. "What the hell?"

He shifted into reverse and spun the Shelby around and drove the short distance back to the phone booth. "How many pay phones are in Green Bank?"

"Um. I'm not sure. This is the only one I've seen."

He veered off to the hard shoulder and pushed out. Jack took out a scrap of paper that he'd jotted down a phone number on.

"What are you doing?" Meghan said getting out and walking behind him.

"Checking the number. On the night Jenna went

missing, I got a phone call. It was incoherent for the most part but that's how I got your name."

He headed over to the rusted old box. With the rise of cellphones, they weren't required as much as they had been. Of course in the city, pay phones could still be found in Greyhound stations.

A cold wind blew against them as he stepped inside.

"But she could have phoned from anywhere."

"I heard a vehicle in the background when she was on the line. And the operator said it came from Green Bank, West Virginia."

He checked the phone number against the booth, but it was scratched out. He couldn't tell if that was it. Had she phoned from there? He stepped out and scanned the landscape. There was a store across the road and two homes farther up. Had she come from one of those? Was she followed and forced off the road? Jack gazed at the gravel nearby and looked for any signs of tire tracks or anything to indicate that a vehicle had been there. But there was nothing.

"Do you recognize any of those homes?" Jack asked.

"You mean have I been there for clients?"

"Yeah."

"No."

Frustration was setting in even though he felt like he was making some progress. If she had made it to the phone that night in the state that she was in, it meant she couldn't have gone far. As they both hopped back in, Jack showed Meghan the address for Karl Fraser. "You recognize that?"

"I think so."

"Is it nearby?"

"Yeah, not far from here."

The Shelby pulled away, and he glanced back at the lonely phone booth in the middle of nowhere. In the day it seemed desolate but at night, for a young woman being pursued by a killer, it must have been terrifying.

Chapter 17

Aaron watched her drop off the kid with the babysitter. He thought back to when he first came across Bonnie. She was nothing until he picked up her sorry ass and gave her a reason to live. Had it not been for him, she would be lying in some gutter with a needle in her arm. Now, here she was acting like she was a good mother, holding down a regular job, turning her back on being a whore. Did she really think she was going to rat him out, get to play the doting mother and spend the remainder of her days flaunting her new lifestyle in front of him with no consequences? Since getting out of jail, he'd thought long and hard about how he was going to punish her. But all his talk had been shot down by Merle. Merle wanted to play it safe and look where it had got him. No, this was her fault.

Merle didn't understand. At one time he wouldn't have questioned him. Anyone that crossed them was tossed into the back of a car, taken out into the forest and either was beaten or ended up with a bullet in their skull. But that was before, back when Merle had balls. Now he was all about flying under the radar, playing by the rules. Meanwhile, he had to suffer the humiliation of watching the two people who had put him inside move on in their lives as though nothing mattered.

Billy and Dale sat quietly not saying a word as they waited for her to come out of the house. They knew better. These were two men he'd known since he was a kid. They were as loyal as they came. Some might have said they would have walked over hot coals and taken a bullet for him. Aaron puffed away on a cigarette with one arm leaning out the window. His fingers tapped the side of the truck, growing more impatient.

"Aaron, what are we going to do?"

"Teach her a few lessons."

"You aren't going to kill her, are you?"

He turned his head. "It wouldn't be the first." He smirked thinking of those that he'd disposed of. Some

were buried so they could never be found, others; well...
he didn't discuss those. But they all had it coming to
them. Every fucking one of them.

And now Bonnie was going to get crossed off his list
too.

As they waited for her to emerge, he wondered how he
could take his business to the next level. Marlinton had
been profitable but with the recent discoveries of the
Green Bank Five it meant more attention. In his line of
work, he didn't want that, especially not from Larson. He
vehemently hated his cocky demeanor. He thought he
was so big in that uniform, with that badge and gun, but
behind it all, he was nothing, a nobody, and he was going
to make an example out of him.

Hours. He'd spent hours mulling over the best way to
hurt Larson. At first, it was just simple stuff — walking
up to his cruiser and shooting him. But that was too easy.
He deserved so much more than that. Next, he thought
about pinning him in his cruiser and using lighter fluid
and gasoline to burn him alive. At least that way he would

suffer. But was that really punishment? He'd be turned into a martyr. Newspapers and media around the nation would be full of articles about how this man had given his life in service to others. No. He wanted him to suffer the way he had, something that was long and drawn out. He needed to strip him of the very thing that he hid behind — his reputation and family. He wanted him to lose everything and know what it felt like to be imprisoned. He thought about the Green Bank Five and smiled. *Oh, Larson, I've had plenty of time to think about how to get you back. You are going to wish you had killed me by the time I'm done with you.*

"Aaron," Billy said tapping him on the leg. Lost in thought, he snapped back into the present in time to see Bonnie exiting the home and getting into her rusted-out Ford. The engine spluttered to life, and she pulled out. Good. She hadn't noticed his truck as he'd made sure to hide it as best as he could down at the corner of 13th Avenue and Parrish Street. He figured he would tail her and wait until the window of opportunity opened. The last thing he needed now was to have anyone witness what was about to go down. Besides, he was still chewing over what he was going to do with her. All he knew was it was going to be a real bad day for her — the worst yet. That window he'd thrown her through was nothing compared to what was coming.

He gave the truck some gas and made sure that they remained a good distance behind her. He allowed a few vehicles to get ahead of them. Aaron could feel his revolver pressing into his back. His pulse began to race at the thought of pressing it against her skull and hearing her beg for her life. That's it. That's what he was going to do. Take her deep into the state park. Somewhere where no one would hear her scream. He'd toy with her. Make her think that he was going to let her go. Tease her into thinking that they were even, and then he'd take the shot, dump the body in a shallow grave and leave her for the animals. But what about her vehicle? He'd leave it. They didn't need it. Then again, it might raise some eyebrows if it was found abandoned in a parking lot. Screw it. He'd take it with them, scratch off the VIN and set it ablaze until it was nothing more than charred steel bones. He'd done it before. The cops didn't have the manpower or will to find a whore. That's why he was confident that he'd get away with it. Sure a few people might have seen him argue with her but that wasn't uncommon. All manner of guys got in trouble for slapping waitresses' asses. Anyone could have done it. And for all they knew, she might have walked away leaving her kid behind. Others had done it. He'd seen the news of some mother who had fled to Florida to start a new life, leaving behind her three children. Years later she showed up with some sob story. She was too young. Under too much stress. Addicted to drugs. He smiled. God, it was easy to make them disappear. The police could suspect him all they wanted, but they needed proof and that was one thing they had a hard job finding. Sure, he might come under scrutiny but by then, with Ethan about to retire, and Larson buried in some shallow grave, it would soon pass. The department would hand it to State Police and that would be the last they would hear about it. After that, he'd go back to doing what he was good at, Merle would probably be out on bail and life would go on as usual.

Aaron eyed Bonnie's vehicle pull into a parking lot on the northeast side of town. This was it. Time to make his move.

Chapter 18

The final stretch of the drive ended at a small clapboard home, on a dirt road just off Wesley Chapel Road. It was a weathered structure that had chipped paint and shingles that looked as if they were in desperate need of repair.

"Have you been here before?" Jack asked.

"Nope."

The driveway that wound its way up to the house was full of potholes. Out front were two rusted-out vehicles from the '80s and a child's swing set. The yard was overgrown and full of wildflowers. It was packed with weeds and the grass looked as if it hadn't been cut for several months as it was almost knee high. A hard sun emerged from the belly of dark clouds, then vanished almost immediately. After parking near the house, they climbed out and continued to take in the sight of the cabin-style abode. A cool wind brushed against his face.

The smell of fresh-cut summer grass lingered in the air and a nearby stream could be heard babbling.

"Hello," Jack called out but got no response.

Crouched down behind the front porch was a man painting one of the columns. He was slightly out of sight but Jack could tell he hadn't heard them as he was wearing headphones.

As they made their approach, a dog darted out from beneath a shady portion of the porch. It was a husky, vicious looking, and for a second he thought they were going to be attacked until the dog let out a yelp as a thick chain yanked it back. His heart slammed against his chest and Meghan looked equally startled.

"Can I help you?"

The commotion had caused the man to take notice. He now stood holding one of the earphones off his ear and gripping a paintbrush with his other hand. He had sharp features, a patchy beard and wore sunglasses. He couldn't have been a day over forty.

"Karl Fraser?" Jack asked.

"Who's asking?"

"Jack Winchester and this is a friend of mine. I was hoping to have a moment of your time."

"You from the newspaper?"

Jack wanted to approach the porch, but the dog was blocking his way. It was snarling, baring its teeth and wasn't showing any signs of backing off.

"Nope."

"Then what do you want?"

"To talk to you about Jenna Whitmore."

He figured he would just drop her name and see what his reaction was. While he knew Jenna had taken photos of him from a distance, there was no statement from him, just snippets of articles from the newspaper about his questionable past.

"Don't know her."

"You ever meet her?"

"Look, I don't know what you are doing here but I told the press everything they wanted to know, and they just twisted my words. I'm done talking. Now go before I set my dog on you."

He turned and went back to painting.

"I heard you were innocent," Meghan blurted out. There were a tense few seconds as he glanced their way, peering between the slats of the porch. "We were hoping to set the record straight, get your side of the story. The truth."

Jack smiled ever so slightly as he glanced at her out the corner of his eye.

"I already told them the truth," Karl bellowed back.

"Look, she was a good friend of mine and she's recently gone missing. We just want a few minutes of your time and we'll be on our way."

Karl didn't respond. He set his paintbrush down, lifted his sunglasses and squinted at them before stepping off the porch and heading over to where his dog was chained up. Jack muttered to Meghan to get back in the truck, thinking he was going to set his dog on them. Jack slipped his hand around his back getting ready to grab the Glock. There were a few seconds of tension and then he yanked his dog back, unlatched him and hauled the furry friend into his house. He slammed the door behind him and the dog started barking.

"Oh shut up, before I put you down."

He turned and beckoned them to come up out of the noonday heat.

Jack breathed out a sigh of relief.

Meghan smiled and looked all pleased with herself before leading the way.

Karl motioned for them to take a seat on the porch rocker. It creaked as they took a seat. The paint was peeling on it, much like the home.

"Trying to get on top of the work around this house before the winter. I was hoping to get it done today." He pointed out towards the dark clouds. "But looks like we are in for a storm." He sniffed hard. "Can I get you a drink? Iced tea perhaps? A beer?"

"No, we're good," Jack said.

"So who's this Jenna Whitmore and why are you asking me?"

"She is a local journalist from Marlinton investigating the case of the Green Bank Five. I know your name came up as a person of interest back when the first two bodies were found."

Karl leaned to his side and snatched up a can of Skoal chewing tobacco. He took a pinch and jammed it into the side of his mouth, closed the lid and fished around for a small, dirty spit bucket.

"Yeah, well they got the wrong person. I told them that from the start."

"So what happened?"

"My old lady told them that I did it."

"And did you?" Jack asked. He knew he would say no but a lot could be learned about a person when posed with an uncomfortable question. Jack had learned from years of dealing with liars the signs of someone trying to cover their ass. Even those who were good at remaining expressionless could still be caught out. There were common telltale signs, a person's initial response when accused, changing their story, not answering with a yes or no but giving long answers. It was a means of stalling. Others would offer too many details, lying about smaller stuff, or referring to a missing person in the past tense. Of course, then there was nonverbal communication. Though many debated how reliable that was, Jack had found it extremely useful.

"No, I didn't do it. And I'm not sure I want to speak about this."

"Please," Meghan said leaning forward with her hands clasped together. "Continue."

He sighed and spat into the tin. It made a popping sound and then he wiped his lips with the back of his sleeve. It was a gross habit. It certainly made his teeth look damn nasty. They were brown and one of the bottom ones was missing.

"Look, you want to know the truth. I worked at the Lodge at the Edge of Green Bank for over thirteen years as a handyman. I even had a place there. When these women started turning up, I lost everything. Not just a job. I lost my family, my freedom but most of all my reputation. It's shot. No one will hire me now."

"So how do you make a living?"

"I have a few friends. Those who knew me well enough to know that I wouldn't have done what they said I did. I do work for them from time to time. Farming and odd jobs. It doesn't pay much."

"And this place?" Jack asked looking around. "How did you afford this?"

He squinted, spitting again into the tin. "It was mothers. She's dead."

The words lingered in the air and Jack wondered if this guy was capable of killing his own mother. If surface details revealed what lay beneath, no wonder the police had him as a suspect.

"So they took an interest in you because your ex told them? Or because you had installed cameras in the motel you were working at?"

He scoffed as if finding Jack's question amusing. "Like I told the police, prostitutes used to use the motel all the time. My boss wanted them gone. Now I couldn't just go kicking out every single woman who looked like a whore, now could I? But I had a job to do, and so I installed cameras in rooms."

"That's an invasion of privacy."

He chewed hard. "My boss told me to do it. Of course, the bastard denied it later when someone found one." He shook his head and reached over and grabbed up a glass of iced tea and sipped at it. Once he set it back down, he continued. "The whole story changed. Now I was a pervert."

"So you didn't watch the videos?"

"Of course I did. Didn't you hear what I said? He wanted me to find out who they were and kick them out. I couldn't do that without seeing what was taking place. Some of the women didn't return and there were new faces all the time."

"And what about the images on your computer?"

"When this all blew up, they confiscated my computers and then word got out I had porn on them. Like, who doesn't?"

"Did you?"

"This is America, Mr. Winchester. The sex trade is the biggest business in the world. What I do with my time in the privacy of my home is no one else's business, certainly not those who would point the finger but do the same goddamn thing." He leaned back and took another sip of his drink before spitting again in the bucket.

"So who do you think is responsible?" Jack asked.

He sniffed hard. "You know what they call motels like the Lodge on the Edge of Green Bank?"

He shrugged.

"No-tell motels. And believe me, there is a lot that goes on in those places. If people knew the kind of men that frequented that motel to have sex with prostitutes, a lot of people in high places would be out of a job."

"So how did you learn about the Green Bank Five?"

"It was all over the local news and papers. You couldn't switch to a new channel without seeing something come up. I'd seen these girls. They came here on numerous occasions before my boss wanted them out."

"So it's possible you might have seen who was responsible for their disappearances?" Jack asked.

"Mr. Winchester. I can throw a few names out there, and I did but the police never looked into them. The media sure overlooked them. Why? Because no one would believe they were capable of doing it, except me. And that's another story. Look, I was doing my job. Doing what I was told, and now what do I have to show for it?"

"Names like who?"

He sucked at his lips before spitting another black wad into the tin. He studied Jack's face as if trying to determine whether he should entrust him with such information. In all the news clippings that he'd read so far, he'd seen the name Tim several times but there was no mention of anyone else except Karl Fraser. Though being fair, he'd barely scratched the surface of Jenna's files.

"Tim Mathers, the pastor of New Hope, Deputy

Rigby, and Peter Dixon."

"Rachel Dixon's husband?" Meghan asked.

He nodded.

"A pastor and a deputy?"

Karl got this grin on his face. "Like I said, Mr. Winchester, all types showed up at that motel at all hours. That's why they buried me. It was easier to just have me accused than for it to get out that two of West Virginia's finest are getting blowjobs in some seedy motel on the edge of town."

Jack blew out his cheeks and ran a hand across his face. He was beginning to see why Jenna was so afraid. This went beyond the search for a serial killer; it reached deep into the heart of a community. A community entrenched in secrets, lies and a cover-up.

"You wanted the truth. That's it."

Jack gazed off across the open fields towards a large barn. He contemplated the distance it would have taken to get from Karl's home to the pay phone. It was possible that she could have run. Jack turned his attention back to the house where the dog was barking non-stop. It seemed a little convenient that he would put the dog inside and not just leash it up elsewhere outside. Was he hiding something?

"You know there are some who would say that you could have been behind the murders."

"Yeah? Who?"

"What can you tell me about Bailey Montgomery?" Jack asked, remembering the audio he'd listened to between Jenna and Bailey. His name had also come up in one of the most recent statements Jenna had on the voice recorder from another escort who had been assaulted. Had two managed to get away?

He snorted, spat the remainder of his tobacco out and got this really uncomfortable look on his face. His cheeks went flushed, and he reached up and touched a small scar on his neck. He then took out a packet of Marlboro Lights and tapped one out. "I met her online."

"She said you met up with her close to the Locust Hill Inn, you took her to a secluded spot, had sex with her and tried to kill her."

"I didn't kill her. That dumb bitch tried to steal my wallet."

"So you tried to stop her."

"I tried to get my wallet back, she cut my face with a set of keys and raced off into the forest. I lost over three hundred and fifty dollars that night because of that whore."

Jack noticed Meghan's demeanor change. Her jaw clenched and her hands balled. The way he talked about them as if they were nothing but meat didn't exactly help his credibility.

"So they gave you nine months for illegal videotaping. That's it?" Jack asked.

"Yep."

Meghan's eyebrow arched. "Interesting how in those nine months no other women went missing."

Karl lit his cigarette and eyed her while squinting as smoke rose above him. He tapped his finger towards her. "I know you." He tapped the side of his temple a few times. "Yeah, I remember now. You're one of the whores that used to show up at the motel."

She shifted in her seat and Jack placed a hand on her knee and gave it a squeeze. She glanced at him and he shook his head. It was obvious she was insulted by the way he spoke about her, who wouldn't be? But they had to tread carefully.

"You think I can use your bathroom?" Jack asked.

Karl's eyes bounced from her to him. "Sorry, it's not working right now."

Jack sniffed hard. "Well, I guess we'll be going."

He didn't have to tell Meghan, she was already up and marching to the Shelby. He rose from his seat, thanked Karl for his time and headed back to the vehicle. When he slipped in and started the engine, it roared to life.

"Fucking nerve of the guy," Meghan said. She was seething.

As they pulled away, Jack looked in his rearview mirror and noticed Karl had come down off his porch to watch them leave. For someone who was apparently innocent, he didn't exactly help himself. His weird behavior and clear disgust of prostitutes would keep him at the top of Jack's list. At least now he had a few more potential suspects that he could cross-check with Jenna's case files.

Chapter 19

Bonnie had her head in the rear of her vehicle when Aaron crossed the lot. He knew that rushing in might attract too much attention, so he moved in cautiously. They had parked a few vehicles down and Dale was ready in the driver's seat if things went south. Aaron pulled the revolver from the back of his waistband and kept low, and out of view.

This was going to be easy.

She wasn't going to know what hit her.

Bonnie was bent over sorting through a load of washing when he shoved her inside the vehicle.

"Don't fucking say a word," he said pressing the barrel into the soft portion of her side. He slid in beside her and shut the door. It was smooth, done in one go and with little commotion. Her face was distraught. Shock. Horror. Surprise. It was all there. She knew this was coming. He reached into his pocket and pulled out zip ties that were already looped.

"Put them on."

"Aaron, please."

"Fucking put them on." He pressed the barrel hard into her side. Scared, she complied, and he pulled the end tight so her wrists were bound. He took the other and pulled off her flip-flops and looped it over her feet. A quick tug and it cut into her skin. She let out a cry, and he smiled. That was nothing to what was coming.

"Give me the keys."

"But — "

"The keys!"

She motioned to her pocket, and he dug around for them, then squeezed from the back to the front of the vehicle and turned over the engine. He kept one hand on her head, keeping her down. Slowly he reversed out and pulled up beside his truck. Billy was at the rear waiting for him. He gave Billy a nod, and he hopped in the back to keep her from freaking out.

That's when the pleading began.

It was a pitiful attempt at trying to appeal to his good nature. But it wouldn't work as he didn't have one. Not for her. Not for anyone in this Godforsaken town.

"Aaron, please, I have a daughter now. I'm sorry about what happened."

"Sorry?" He kept a firm grip on the steering wheel as they pulled out and headed towards the highway. "Sorry doesn't get me back the time I did inside. Sorry doesn't do shit for me."

"Look, you want me back. I'm back."

He laughed and eyed Billy in the rear. "You hear that, Billy. She's back. That's it. All is good. She's ready to spread her legs again and pucker up those lips. Just like that."

Billy chuckled a little but looked nervous. He wasn't used to dealing with backstabbing whores. But Aaron was. He'd had plenty of experience with the little games they liked to play. They would say anything to get out of a beating. The times he would make them give him head before beating them black and blue was too numerous to count.

"Well I'm afraid, sweet Bonnie, it doesn't work that way. You see, there are rules. You break those rules, there are consequences. Just like I had to do time because you opened your fucking mouth."

"I didn't say anything."

"No? Then how did Larson know it was me? You must think I'm stupid. Well, now you're going to learn."

"Aaron. I'll do whatever you want. You want me to turn tricks, it's done. You want me to quit my job at the bar, it's done."

"Oh it's done all right," he said heading south on Highway 219 for Watogo State Park. He knew the area well. He and Merle had spent many a night camping out underneath the stars when they were kids. Back then life wasn't as complicated. He smashed the wheel with his fists several times at the thought of his brother in custody. His eyes flitted to the mirror to remind himself of the one responsible.

It didn't take long to reach the narrow trail that

weaved its way into the heart of the 10,000-acre forest. It was the largest one in West Virginia, a sprawling woodland that was frequented by campers, hikers, and youngsters looking to get their kicks. Oh, he was going to get his kicks today. The car soared over bumps, and through thick brush that hadn't been touched. No one knew about this entrance, or where it led. People got lost out there all the time. He pressed the accelerator hard and gave it some gas so they could reach the destination faster. His heartbeat was pulsating harder from all the excitement.

As he burst out of the dense path, they arrived at the spot that had once been their camping retreat. A place they caught rabbits, cooked them over a fire and mulled over their dreams of the future. Most of those dreams dissolved because life had got in the way, the police had got in the way, and whores like Bonnie. Well, now he was going to make it difficult for her.

He brought the car to a grinding halt and turned around.

"Time for some fun."

He let out a laugh and pushed his way out of the vehicle. Moving around to the back, he opened the door, grabbed her by the ankles and dragged her out. Her head hit the hard soil and she let out a groan. He pressed his foot on her back to hold her in place until Dale arrived. The truck emerged and fumes poured out the back. As soon as Dale was out, he went around to where Bonnie was and dragged her to her knees, pulled out his revolver and forced it into her mouth.

"Go on... suck it."

He cocked the gun and tears began to stream down her face as her head bobbed back and forth over the gunmetal. He grinned in delight seeing the fear in her eyes. She had her hands up pleading for him to not pull the trigger. It came out as a garbled noise. Snot and tears mixed together and dripped off her face. He withdrew the revolver and tapped it on the side of her face.

"Don't worry, I'm not going to kill you — yet."

"I have a daughter. Please, Aaron, I beg of you."

"That's it, beg. Come on, beg for your life."

She dropped down and rubbed her hands over his boots, getting her face close to them. He looked at the other two who were watching, their expressions full of bewilderment, excitement, perhaps concern? It was hard to tell. But he loved it. In town, he was just a face, a nobody, but here in this forest, he was God.

He kicked her face away from him. "You're pathetic. Killing you would be doing your kid a favor. Who wants to grow up knowing their mother was a whore?"

She pleaded but her cries fell on deaf ears.

"What should I do with you?"

She crawled over, a task that wasn't easy as her wrists and ankles were still bound. She raked at his jeans, pulling herself up onto her knees and trying to undo his zipper.

"Oh really. You think that's going to make it all better, do you?"

He shoved her face away. "I wouldn't touch you if you were the last gash on the planet but the boys would, wouldn't you?"

He eyed them and motioned towards her. Billy swallowed hard and Dale shook his head.

"Go on. Do it. She wants it."

Her cries grew louder as they pounced on her like wolves on a sheep. A flock of birds broke from the trees and Aaron walked away, pulling out his cigarettes.

Chapter 20

After visiting Karl Fraser, Jack headed towards New Hope Church. He recalled hearing the name Tim Mathers several times as he pored through Jenna's files, and the church's number was listed in her phone contacts. She'd made multiple calls in the days leading up to her disappearance. Now the calls could have been to her brother but from what he was able to glean from the snippets of information about Tim and his connection to the Green Bank Five, he figured there was more to it.

The church wasn't far from Karl's home. The journey had been filled with silent tension. Meghan was still fuming. As they approached, Jack could see the outline of the white spire against the forest. Other than that, the church was enveloped by its surroundings, mainly because it was small. Unlike some of the behemoth-sized churches in New York, this had none of the expensive details. The walls were made from clapboard siding, and though it appeared as if it had received a fresh lick of paint, the building still looked weathered. To the right of it, was another building, larger and longer, though equally in need of restoration.

Gravel crunched beneath the tires as Jack eased off the gas and parked out front.

"You should probably wait here," Jack said hopping out.

The last thing he wanted was to agitate her any further. If any place was going to make her feel worthless, it would be the church. Of course, not all churches were like that, but small towns usually had narrow-minded attitudes. As much as they preached acceptance and love, sin was sin in their mind and some religious folks could tend to engage their mouths before they switched on their brains. Meghan had already filled him in on the way some electro-sensitive folks who had moved to Green Bank had been treated by the church.

"Sure," she said pulling out a pack of cigarettes. Jack walked towards the entrance. He pulled the heavy door and stepped inside. Glancing around, he could see the place was being renovated. Scaffolding was erected at the far end near a stained-glass window. The floor had unfinished concrete, a few sections of drywall had been taken down, and the rest of the room was filled with pews. Besides the light filtering in through the stained-glass window, it was rather dark and dingy-looking — certainly not a place that he'd want to spend much time in. Off to the right was an upright piano, and ahead a pulpit.

His entrance didn't go unnoticed. A tall man appeared off to the right from a room that looked to be the rectory or office area. It certainly didn't look like the small size of the church had affected his pocket book. He wore a tailored black suit, crisp white shirt, and red tie. He had a chiseled jaw and a pleasant smile that would have disarmed even the most cautious. What remained of his hair was trimmed short at the sides, and he was holding a book in his hand when he stepped out of the shadows.

"Can I help you?" he asked.

The moment Jack saw him he remembered his face from the photos. Jenna had taken some of him with several women, and had snapped them leaving what looked to be a trailer, as well as a motel room.

"Pastor Tim Mathers?"

"Yes, that's me."

"Jack Winchester. I'm a friend of Jenna Whitmore."

His mouth parted into a wide smile. "Oh, Jenna. Corey's sister." He shifted from his position and crossed the room to meet Jack. "How is she?"

"Corey hasn't told you?"

He frowned. "I haven't seen Corey in a day or two because he generally only comes in on weekends, and Tuesday evenings when we hold a Bible study."

"She's missing."

His eyebrows arched and his jaw dropped. "That's awful. I gather the police are looking into it?"

"They're aware. Not sure if anything is being done."

He took a few steps back trying to compose himself. "And you say, you're a friend?"

"That's right. I was hoping to have a few moments of your time. That is if you're not busy." He cast a gaze around the room.

"Renovations. A necessary evil," he said with a half smile. "Costs a fortune but we have put it off far too long." He paused for a second to take in the sight of his chapel. "Look, come on back. I'll put some coffee on. You drink coffee?"

Jack gave a nod. He noticed the title of the book in his hands. It was related to medicine. Tim led him back into a cramped office. There was enough room for a table, two chairs and a bookshelf that was packed with religious books, and ones on counseling, drug addiction, and missions. He motioned to a comfy chair and Jack took a seat. Tim went over to a coffee maker and added water, and a filter before tipping a few tablespoons of coffee granules into it. On the desk in front of him was a framed portrait of his wife and three kids. She was seated, and they were surrounding her. Tim must have noticed what Jack was looking at, as he made a comment. "That's my family. You married, Mr. Winchester?"

"No."

"You have a lady in your life?"

"Not currently."

His eyes scanned the room wondering why Jenna had an interest in this man. If Karl was right, and he was meeting prostitutes for sex, he wasn't exactly a smart man. Most pastors were known in their community and with a population of only 143, surely he must have figured someone would eventually see him nipping into a local motel.

"So no children?"

"One but she lives with her mother."

"I see," he said nodding before taking a deep breath. "Divorce happens all the time. It's too bad. It really messes up kids. They are always the ones that suffer the most."

"We weren't married."

"Oh, I see." He turned his attention back to the coffee maker.

"You have a good relationship with your wife, do you, Tim?"

He cast a glance over his shoulder. "I do. Been married twenty-four years this October."

"They say the secret to a good marriage is a healthy sex life. Would you agree?" Jack asked without even breaking a smile. He stifled a chuckle wondering how he would take the question. Would it put him on edge? Cause him to blush?

Tim replied without missing a beat. "Oh, there's more to it than that. I mean, what happens when that's gone?"

"Who knows? I'm sure people find an outlet."

Tim stared at him as if trying to decode what he was saying before breaking his gaze and pouring out two cups. He brought over some milk and sugar and placed it before him. He cleared his throat. "Do you live in Marlinton, Jack? I haven't seen you around these parts."

"No. Just here for a visit."

He walked back to his desk and took a seat.

"And you say Jenna is missing?"

"That's right. Did you know she was investigating the murders of the Green Bank Five?"

"Um. I think Corey mentioned it. Jenna doesn't attend church as much as she used to."

"You think something might have put a bad taste in her mouth?" Jack asked, prodding him in the hopes of making him feel uncomfortable. He was curious to see how he would react, and how he handled himself before strangers. Tim sipped at his drink before putting it down.

"She didn't see eye to eye with the work we are doing here."

Jack frowned. "With troubled women?"

He'd spotted a three-fold pamphlet advertising counseling on the counter. It had been cheaply made.

"That's right. We have a building across the way that we use to house those who are looking to get their lives back on track but are having some difficulty."

Jack gazed down at his coffee. "That's odd. By all accounts, I got the impression that she was very concerned for the welfare of such women."

Tim quickly shifted the topic back to him.

"Do you work in the media, Mr. Winchester?"

"No, but I do assist in getting to the truth if that's what you're alluding to?"

He cleared his throat again. It almost sounded as if he had something stuck in it.

"The truth of?"

Jack leaned forward and placed his cup on the table before him. As much as he didn't want to take an approach that would cause whoever was responsible to bolt, he knew he was pressed for time. With the trouble he'd had at the bar, and the officer looking for him, he didn't think it would be long before he would be dragged in. Besides, if someone had taken Jenna, who knew if she was still alive or not. He stood up and walked over to a window and gazed out. He was about to drop the ball on him when he noticed out the back, nestled into the forest, was the same silver trailer with a gold band around it.

"What's that out there?"

"What?"

"The trailer."

"Oh, it's used for counseling sessions."

"I would imagine you would do those in here or the building across the way."

"No. Like I said, the building is used for housing and we tend to get a number of visitors dropping in here throughout the day. The trailer provides privacy. A safe place where they can open up."

Open up. I bet they do, he thought.

He turned and sucked in air between his teeth. "Let's cut the crap, Tim. You and I both know that Jenna thought you had something to do with the disappearance and murders of the Green Bank Five."

"What?"

"That trailer out there. She has photos of you going in and out with several women, some of whom ended up dead."

He chuckled a little. "I think you have misunderstood what I do."

"I know what you do, or should I say, what you have

done." Jack leaned against the table placing both hands on it. Tim moved back in his seat. "What did you tell Jenna? There were numerous phone calls to this place on the days leading up to her disappearance. So what did you say?"

"I didn't say anything because I didn't answer her phone calls. After the first accusation that she made against me, I forgave her. But when she started pointing the finger at me for having some involvement in the disappearance of those women, that's where I drew the line."

"You forgave her?"

"That's right I did."

"Then how come your name came up as a person of interest in the case at the time of the disappearance? Was it anything to do with what Karl Fraser had to say? You know, the part about you getting serviced by multiple women at the Lodge on the Edge of Green Bank?"

The color in his face vanished only to be replaced by red cheeks.

"I'm sure your wife would be really interested to know why you were seeing these women. Or was the lodge a 'safe place' for getting them to open up to you?"

He gritted his teeth.

"How dare you come in here and insinuate that I would be unfaithful to my wife. I've never been anywhere near that place."

"I'm not insinuating anything."

Jack pulled out his cell phone and powered it on. With a few flicks of the finger, he brought up one of the many photos that he'd transferred. He held it out in front of his face and swiped back and forth so he could get a good view of the shots.

"You want to explain? Did you kill the Green Bank Five because they rejected your advances? Or were they going to speak out against you? Is that why, Tim?"

Tim clenched his jaw then rose from his seat. "I think we are done here. Please leave."

"Oh, I'm not leaving until I get some answers. Take a seat."

Tim stared at him for a second then went for the landline phone. Jack reacted fast and slammed his hand down on top of his, preventing him from lifting the receiver.

"Tell me the truth."

A look of fear crossed his face. When he didn't answer, Jack reached around and pulled out his Glock, grabbed him by the throat and lunged, forcing him back against the far wall before placing the gun against the side of his temple. "I've had enough of people wasting my time. Now I'm gonna give you one more opportunity to tell me the truth or I'll—"

"Alright. Alright! I had sex with a few escorts but I don' t know anything about the Green Bank Five or the disappearance of Jenna. I swear. I mean I knew a few of the women and I had several people point fingers at me. Yeah, sure. But that comes with the territory when you are trying to minister. It doesn't matter if they are escorts or housewives. My job puts me in a precarious position where anyone is capable of saying that I did something or said something. You ask any pastor in this country, and they'll say the same."

"And yet you're married."

"My... my wife is... disabled."

"Huh! I've heard a lot of excuses in my time but that one is fresh."

"I'm serious. She was in a car accident six years ago, she's paralyzed from the waist down." He reached over to the shelf behind him for another photo frame that showed her in a wheelchair. "She can't..."

He was unable to finish.

"Oh well, that just makes it all better." He let out a chuckle. "So let me guess, the missus has given you her blessing to go and screw a few women behind her back. Is that how this works? Or did God give you the green light?"

He looked as if he was about to respond but then tears welled up in his eyes. He cast his gaze down. Jack studied his face. A look of shame, embarrassment, and guilt washed over it. Was this guy capable of killing women? It was possible. He'd seen all types over his years. The best were able to put up one hell of an act. Hide their transgressions from family, friends, and spouses. Either way, it was pathetic. Jack removed the gun from the side of his head and tucked it back into his waistband as Tim turned into a blubbering mess.

"Stop crying."

Jack reached over and grabbed up a few tissues and threw them at him. Tim wiped his face before all the excuses began to roll over his lips. "I know it was wrong. I tried to get help but what am I meant to do? This is my whole life. I would have been ruined if this got out. You know I tried to stop but I…"

"You just couldn't do it. And let me guess, none of your church members know either, so you just continue ministering to those wayward women hoping that one day you'll be able to forgive yourself as much as God forgives you."

"He does."

"You sure about that, pastor?"

He looked down at the ground and shook his head. It seemed as if it was a little too overwhelming.

"I care. I really do."

Jack walked back to the desk. "Oh, I bet you do. Then why didn't you respond to her phone messages?"

"Because she threatened to tell my wife, and the rest of the church if I didn't resign. I can't have that. I just can't."

"And then she goes missing. How convenient."

Jack tapped the desk a few times with his hand, picked up the framed photo of his family and slung it down in front of him before getting up. "Nice family. They deserve better. Now how about you show me what's inside that silver trailer out back."

Chapter 21

Later that afternoon, Merle woke from his drunken slumber, completely unsure of where he was. He rolled to one side and took in his surroundings. It was clear he was behind bars and that only sent his mind into a rage. Slowly, bits and pieces of the morning came back to him. He recalled not opening the garage, Aaron getting a phone call, and hitting the bottle sometime around ten… after that, it was all a blur, nothing but fragments of arguing with cops, the smell of vomit in the back seat of a car and waking up.

He wasn't going back to jail again. Hell no. Not for his brother. Not for anyone.

The thought of being locked up, dealing with sudden fights in the pen and trying to survive around the clock sent a shiver through him. He'd rather die than endure that.

He rolled off the hard bed and worked out the tension

in his neck before staggering over to the steel bars that were painted in a thick cream paint. He was shaky on his feet. The number of times he'd ended up here while growing up were too many to count.

"Hello? Is anyone there?"

"Shut the hell up," a gruff voice answered from a cell just down from him.

He looked up at the camera just beyond the bars, and made a few gestures with his arms, hoping to get their attention. Getting no response he relieved himself at the tiny steel toilet. Now that all the liquid courage was out of his system, he was anxious, overwhelmed and unable to process it all.

Then a part of the puzzle came back to him.

Stupid. Stupid! Why did you go with him to the bar? You should have stayed back.

This was it. He knew how this worked. They were going to put him through the court system, drag up his history of violence, theft and drug use and make a case against him, just so they could get him out of their hair.

But it was just a bar fight. This wasn't drug dealing.

It didn't matter, his parole officer had been real clear. They had him under a microscope. Any violation could lead to re-incarceration. He could plead for mercy as much as he wanted but without something to use as leverage he didn't stand a chance in hell. They would toss him back in prison, and he'd have to wait it out. This wasn't going to be good for him. No, that couldn't happen.

He ran a hand around the back of his sweaty neck and paced up and down thinking of what he could do to turn this around. It needed to be significant. There was no way in hell he was going to give up his drug source or give out the names of those in the biker gang. They would have him killed immediately even if he got out. Those were dangerous individuals not to be screwed with. His mind clicked over, running through every scenario and illegal activity he'd been involved with. It had to be worth their while. They wouldn't be interested in a few low-end dope dealers. But murder. That was another thing entirely. The

Green Bank Five was what was getting all the attention nowadays. They had nothing on the killer. Nothing.

Desperation set in, he rushed to the door and began trying to shake the bars. "Let me out! Hey!"

Nothing. No answer. He was going to burn.

His only hope was to come clean on a series of murders.

* * *

Larson had been off shift for close to four hours when his phone rang. He was already out of uniform, showered and in a pair of shorts and T-shirt. He had plans for the day. The garage was a mess, there was all manner of crap inside that needed to be taken to the dump and Kerry had been on at him to repaint the porch. It was weathered, and the paint was starting to peel. He pawed at his eyes. Really, he just needed to get some more rest. After the morning he'd had, all he wanted to do was forget that he was a cop for a few hours.

But that phone call would put an end to that.

He took one last sip of his ice-cold tea before picking

it up. It was Sergeant Berringer. After some small talk he got down to the reason for his call.

"I need you to come in."

"Sarge, are you serious?"

"Look, Larson, I wouldn't ask if it wasn't important. Merle wants to speak to you. Only you. About the Green Bank Five."

He shook his head in disbelief. His interest might have been piqued had it been anyone else but Merle. But he knew he was just toying with them. He had a reputation for doing anything to upset the grand scheme of things down at the station.

"Can't someone else do it, Sarge? I've only been off a few hours and I have a lot to get done around the house. Besides, he's probably just blowing off steam. Now that he's sober, he's just pissed off at finding himself behind bars and looking for any reason to get out. Give him a few more hours, he'll calm down."

"Sorry, Larson. We have strict orders to follow up on any lead in the case and considering his reputation; we have to take this seriously. When can you get in?"

There was a pause as he stared into the garage. Kerry wasn't going to be pleased, not at all.

"Um. Give me ten minutes."

* * *

This was the last thing he wanted to be doing with his time. He figured he'd walk in and give him some half-baked story that would send him down a road that led to nowhere. It would be a waste of police resources, and most of all, a waste of his time. When he arrived at the department, Berringer pulled him into the office for what he thought was going to be a quick briefing.

"So what's the deal with you pulling your firearm?"

"What?"

"This morning when you brought in Merle."

"I thought I was coming down here to speak with Merle?"

"You are but Ethan said you got a little hot-headed this morning."

Damn you, Rigby! The guy was determined to throw

him under the bus. He was about to give him an excuse but he knew it wouldn't hold up. Berringer was a stickler for shutting down deputies. The only voice he liked hearing was his own. So he just told him the truth.

"Since putting Aaron away, there have been a number of attacks on my property, and an attempt on my wife's life. I know Merle or Aaron is behind it."

"You got evidence?"

"Nope."

Berringer exhaled and ran a hand over his chin.

"Look, you already have one mark against you, Larson, don't make the mistake of thinking we let this kind of behavior slide. Small town or not, that shit don't fly here. You're a good cop, don't screw up by letting your emotions get the better of you." He gave a nod with his head towards the door. "Go on, and update me on what he had to say."

* * *

Larson was even more pissed off than when he walked through the doors. Ever since he'd started in the department, he didn't feel he had the support of those around him. As for Ethan, he couldn't see what he had to gain by opening his big trap, other than to make himself look good.

"You wanted to speak to me?"

He stared at him through the bars. Merle was in a state. As he got closer, the aroma of stale vomit wafted in his direction. His T-shirt was stained, eyes sunken in, and his skin looked pasty and thin as though it was stretched tight over his bones. Alcoholics were all the same. They couldn't wait to get that next drink in them. He was pacing back and forth, agitated. It was to be expected. Merle turned and his face brightened. He crossed over to the bars and grasped them.

"Sam Larson, you and I need to talk."

"So talk."

Larson kept his distance. In the past, people they'd brought in would come up with some story that they were going to come clean only to spit in their face when they got close.

"What if I could give you the one responsible for the Green Bank Five? What would that be worth to you?"

Larson scoffed. "Please stop wasting our time," he said as he turned to walk away.

"I can lead you to some bodies."

As much as he wasn't buying it, he couldn't resist biting. Larson turned and walked back to him. "So tell me. What do you know?"

"No, I want it in writing that when I give you this, you are going to make sure that I'm released and all charges are dropped against me."

"You're full of it."

"Really? You want to take that chance, be my guest, but I figure someone like you. Someone who is new to the department and already has one harassment complaint against him isn't going to last around here with another one."

"If you think you are going to get me on pulling my firearm, you are sorely mistaken. They already know about it. You really think they are going to take your word over mine?"

"I don't need the cops to take my side. The media always wants a story. And there is nothing they like better than a public citizen who gets a beat-down by an angry cop."

"A beat-down?"

Merle's eyes bore into him as he gripped the bars and jerked his head back and drove it into the metal. Once. Twice. Three times until there was a trickle of blood pouring from his forehead.

In a slimy voice and with a grin on his face he said, "Oh, this cut? He lashed out at me. I tried to get him to stop but he wouldn't listen. Deputy Larson has always had it in for me and my brother." He started laughing. "You see. I just need to give them enough reason to doubt you."

Larson chewed over what he said before shaking his finger at him. "You are one screwed-up individual."

His eyes became wild and crazy. "So is that a yes? C'mon, deputy, you know this is a win-win situation for you. I lead you to a few bodies, you get me out of your hair and you get to act like the big hero. Who knows, maybe you'll close the Green Bank case and they'll wipe that complaint from your record."

"Or I can just walk away." Larson pointed to the camera. "You must be a real kind of stupid to think that we haven't dealt with lunatics like yourself before. That's why we installed them. That ensures there is a record of what happened in here. I never entered. Idiot!"

A look of panic spread across Merle's face.

"You're on your own."

Larson was about to walk away when he yelled, "Deputy. These are dead women that were escorts. Look, I admit. We don't like each other, there's no denying that. But I have done my time for my crimes. Whether you believe me or not, my past is that... the past. The other night things got out of hand. But you know as well as I do that no judge is going to take a bar fight seriously. What I'm offering you here is gold."

"And let me guess, you have nothing to do with these

dead women?"

"I don't."

"Who does?"

He rolled his bottom lip in. "I can't tell you."

"Then I guess we are done."

"They will kill me if I do."

"And those inside will kill you if you don't. So how about you stop playing games and tell me? Because think about it, Merle. You lead me to some dead bodies but don't give up how they ended up there, what do you think the court is going to say? Who do you think they are going to pin it on?"

He took a few steps back and tossed his hands up. "I didn't do it. I swear on my mother's life."

"Then give me a name."

Merle was squirming, rubbing his hands and clenching his jaw.

Larson shrugged. "Fair enough. You don't want to talk."

"Will you do up the paperwork? I want it in writing,

all official and shit. I get out of here today and all charges are dropped."

"If you give me a name."

"No, I'll take you to the bodies but that's it."

"No can do."

"Don't do this, man. I have valuable information. This could be what breaks this case wide open. All I'm asking for is a little give and take."

"And all I'm asking for is a name."

He was visibly shaking; sweat was trickling down the side of his temple. He began scratching his arms. They were covered in red track marks.

He's wasting your time, Larson thought as he turned away. He'd made it a few steps when the sound of his voice stopped him in his tracks. "Aaron. My brother."

Chapter 22

The search of the silver trailer along with the rest of New Hope property yielded nothing. Before leaving, Jack made it clear that if Tim went to the police, the photos of him would find their way into the hands of his wife and the World Wide Web. By the way he was shaking when they pulled away, he was certain that wouldn't be necessary. Was he capable of killing five women? It wasn't entirely out of the question. Killers were masters at leading double lives.

Outside the heavens had opened up. It was steady but not hard, a warm summer rain that made it feel even more humid.

"You hungry?" Jack asked.

She nodded without even looking at him. Jack took the Shelby down the twisted drive onto the highway again. Even though they could have returned to Marlinton, they drove instead to Henry's Quick Stop on

Green Hill Road. Though it was used more as a convenience store, they still had a small diner-style restaurant inside where they sold hamburgers, salads, hot dogs and pizza, along with coffee. When they arrived it was nearly empty, just one middle-aged lady manning the register, and a young girl going from table to table.

Meghan ordered a burger and fries, Jack went for pizza and they both had coffee.

When the waitress returned, Jack asked if Green Bank only had the one pay phone. She nodded and her eyebrow rose. Admittedly it was a strange question to ask but if the area drew in tourists, it must have been common. Outside there was a short break in the rain, and they could see others who'd been waiting at the door of the diner to get back to their vehicles, make a dash for it.

As Meghan ate, she stared at him.

"What?" he asked. "Do I have ketchup on my face?"

She smiled. "No." She swallowed and took a sip of her drink. "So what's the deal with you?"

"What do you mean?"

"Well, I've told you about myself. How do you know Jenna?"

"She hired me to assist her."

"Before she went missing?"

He nodded.

"Are you an investigator?"

"Not exactly."

She nodded slowly, gazing out the window at a couple who were arguing over something.

"What about friends and family?"

"They're out there but I haven't really spent a great deal of time with them. My work keeps me on the road."

She sniffed hard and wiped her lips with a napkin. "You really think he's behind it?"

"What do you think?"

"If anyone is capable, it's Karl Fraser. The guy gives me the creeps."

"What do you know about Peter Dixon?" he asked.

"Not much. I knew his wife, Rachel. She worked for a while at Ali's Bar. We used to go out for drinks together.

This was before she got involved in being an escort. The few times I met Peter, he seemed like a nice enough guy. She met him through being an escort."

"He was a john?"

She nodded, taking another bite of her burger. "Yeah, it's rare that it happens as most of the women don't mix their personal lives with business but they hit it off."

"So it was no surprise to you when you heard his name mentioned as one of the men frequenting the Lodge at the Edge of Green Bank?"

She shook her head. "That place was used for years as a central spot for women to conduct business. Before it got a reputation and the new owner tried to get the women kicked out."

Jack stirred his coffee. "What about the other four? You knew them?"

"No, just Rachel and Paula. The thing is, Jack, in this business there is a high turnover of women. Some get into it just to earn enough to get by, others are doing it to pay their way through college and some are talked into it by a friend or a pimp. Rachel had tried to walk away from it a few times but it just kept pulling her back. It's tough when you have an addiction. A bar job just doesn't pay the bills."

He nodded and then cast a gaze around the diner.

"So you know where Rachel and Peter lived?"

She gulped and reached across for a napkin then pulled out a pen and scribbled the address and slid it across to him. It was a location in Marlinton.

"You might not have much luck with him. After her death, the local media were hounding him. He struck one of the photographers and ended up in court over it. Charges were dropped, and he was released but he hasn't been the same since. He used to frequent Ali's Bar most nights but not anymore. Some say he's become a bit of a recluse, others say he knows more than he's telling. You got to remember, Rachel was the first one. I mean, the first one that was discovered. There's no telling how many others were killed. It's not like anyone is keeping tabs on us."

Jack downed the remainder of his coffee. It felt good to get a kick from the caffeine. He leaned back and got comfy in his seat.

"You mentioned Jenna went with you to a client on the night she went missing, and that she was acting a little odd."

She picked up a fry and bit the end off in a seductive way. "That's right."

"You mind showing me where the house is."

"Sure. I need to make a quick phone call. I'm meant to be doing the afternoon shift at the bar today." She rolled her eyes. "The boss has been on our case about the fight the other night. Which reminds me, did the cops show up?"

"That they did," Jack replied.

"And?"

"I didn't stick around to find out."

She laughed and tossed her napkin down. "I'll be right back."

She wandered off down a corridor and disappeared out

of sight. Jack sat there thinking about how they were being selected. Was it just random? Had he met with them before? From the photos he saw of the Green Bank Five, they each looked different, so it wasn't like he was focusing on a specific type of woman like some serial killers did. The fact that there was no mention of them having been raped indicated that the murders were not sexually motivated. That was the part that struck him as strange. These were women in the sex industry. Did he have a bad taste in his mouth towards women in general or only those considered women of the night?

Jack glanced off to his right and noticed that Meghan hadn't returned. The waitress came over with the bill and he paid, tossing down a few extra bucks as a tip. He waited another five minutes before getting up to see where she had gone. He followed the short corridor around a corner and noticed that the back exit door was propped open.

"Meghan?" He called out to her but there was no response. A guy brushed past him and apologized. Jack eyed him as he headed out the back. Jack followed the corridor around until he saw the cook through an open section of the wall.

"You wouldn't have a seen a small, dark-haired woman, blue eyes, would you?"

"Yeah, she asked to use our landline, around the corner." He motioned further down.

"Thanks."

He followed it around. As the phone came into view, he noticed the receiver was hanging by the wall. His eyes swept back and forth. Panic started to climb in his chest.

"Meghan. Meghan!" he shouted louder and rushed towards the exit, bursting out the back. Bright rays of light momentarily blinded him. He raised a forearm. The noise of trucks assaulted his ears. His eyes darted from one vehicle to the next. "Meghan!"

"Jack."

Jack turned at the sound of her voice. She was still inside the diner. *Thank God.* She immediately recognized his expression of concern.

He trudged back. "I saw the phone receiver hanging and thought…"

"I was using the washroom."

He exhaled a sigh of relief. For a second there he thought she'd been scooped out from underneath his nose. They went back inside to collect her belongings before heading out.

"Jack, sorry but unfortunately I won't be able to take you to see that client's cabin because they need me in early. Seems Bonnie didn't show up for work this morning. She probably got held up with her kid. Anyway… I'll draw you a map." She leaned over the table and scribbled out a rough map on a napkin, jotting down the address and marking the location of the cabin before handing it over.

"I'll give you a lift back in. I have to drop by Peter Dixon's house."

They ventured out unaware that someone was watching nearby.

* * *

Back on the highway, the rain started again. A light mist grew thick the closer they got to Marlinton, stretching across like a ghostly apparition. He kept his distance staying one vehicle behind them at all times. His headlights did very little to illuminate the road before him. The dark, heavy clouds squeezed out what blue remained. He'd come so close to them, sitting in his vehicle outside, watching them through the window. How could he associate with that whore? Did they honestly think they could ensnare him? He hadn't made it this far without learning how to deflect attention away from himself.

No one was going to stop him from continuing his work. It was a calling, of that he was certain. Still, he didn't like that they were getting close, snooping around and asking questions.

He gripped the wheel tightly and glanced down at his passenger side seat. Organized in a small pile were a pair of leather gloves, a taser and some drug paraphernalia. He'd passed by her, smelled her hair and wondered what it would be like to take one in the daylight. He'd always been so particular about how he conducted business. Nothing could be left to chance. There could be no witnesses. No one saw him. No one heard him. He operated under the cover of darkness and had perfected the art, like with that bitch Brenda Norris.

Oh, she was a sweet one.

The first that had given him a real challenge. She wasn't stupid like the others, but she sure as hell couldn't outsmart him.

As he followed the Shelby, excitement rose again. It would soon be nightfall. By now she would have got the message. He always offered more money than the rest of the johns. They usually nickel and dimed them. Not him. He hung money out like a carrot on the end of the stick. Two hundred was nothing. Four would entice them but he went far beyond that and offered them twelve hundred. None of them so far could resist it. One client. One night.

The door would close behind them. They would slip

into something comfortable.

He would lay them back on the bed, hold their hands over their heads as if he was about to kiss their neck, and then they would feel the click of metal as cuffs locked around their wrists. Some of them kicked and screamed, those he subdued quickly. The others thought it was part of the game, part of the fantasy he had. And it was. Except they didn't realize it ended in their death. Then, with them fully under his control and unable to escape, he would savor the final chapter of their life.

Rain battered against the windshield, the wipers flipped back and forth, like his mind between the present and the past. His hands grew sweaty from reliving it. It didn't take long to be back in the room, standing at their side with a needle in hand. He wasn't sure what he relished more, the thought of their demise, or the anticipation of taking another. Slowly but surely he watched the eyes in their head roll back as they succumbed to the cocktail of drugs, then he would lean in and watch, listening intently for that last breath.

It was always clean. No DNA could be left behind. He'd studied and learned how to avoid detection. It was a matter of attention to detail. Sometimes hours after the trash had been left beside the river, he would retrace his steps to ensure that nothing had been dropped, that nothing could lead back to him.

The rainfall was steady on the top of his truck. He watched them veer off into Marlinton and he continued to keep his distance. It would soon be evening and once again he would get to pluck one of them out, cleansing the streets of the filth. Like a garbage man collecting black bags off the side of the road, it was his duty. They might not understand it now but one day they would.

He couldn't pinpoint the moment he crossed the line between the thought of killing and the actual act, only that it crept over him like a warm blanket, slowly enveloping him and reassuring him that it was the right thing to do — for society, for them and for him.

Gravel crunched beneath the tires as he pulled off to the hard shoulder and watched her jump out. They exchanged a few words before she placed a handbag over her head and made a rush for the bar. He clenched his jaw and bunched a fist. Winchester lingered there a little longer. *What are you doing? Can you see me?* He thought to himself. The cold rain that pounded the ground like a distant train fogged his window up. Though it was still early in the day, the darkness of the storm was building in intensity and making it feel like night. A light came on inside the Shelby and he could see the silhouette of his figure reaching across to the glove compartment. This man was a problem and one that he would deal with once he had decided how. Minutes passed before Winchester drove away. He would have followed him again, but he had better things to do with his time. All he needed now was working inside. His eyes diverted back to the bar, the place that had become his home away from home. In the darkened corners he would sit with a drink, observing them from afar, watching how they interacted. Again he would do the same though this time he wouldn't let her walk away.

She was his. They all were, they just didn't know it yet.

Before getting out of the truck, he reached into the side compartment and pulled out a few personal items belonging to Brenda Norris. An earring, a bracelet, just small mementos from the collection of items he took from each of them — just a way to relive, and fuel his uncontrollable desire to follow through and give them what they so much longed for — peace.

Chapter 23

Larson slowed the car in the wet, murky darkness of Watoga State Park. Following close behind were two cruisers, one with a K-9 deputy. While Sergeant Berringer had given the go-ahead, he'd made it clear that while they'd drop the charges for the bar brawl, they wouldn't guarantee that Merle wouldn't do time for having known about the dead women. Forensics would have to rule out his direct involvement before any attorney could try to arrange a deal to ensure a lesser sentence. It didn't matter to Larson, the way he saw it Merle and Aaron were going away for a long time.

He still couldn't believe that in an attempt to avoid jail time, he had unwittingly thrown his own brother under a bus, and screwed himself in the process. Of course, Larson wasn't going to tell him that. He wanted him to believe he was going to get away without being punished, and in some ways he was, but not from this charge. A charge that he didn't even know was coming. *What a dumbass.* Merle thought he was going to walk after he'd shown them where these bodies were. He knew the guy was stupid, but that was just mind-boggling.

Had he been smart, he would have kept his mouth shut. Chances were the charges for what happened down at Ali's Bar would have been dropped. Now he was giving Larson exactly what he wanted and more — evidence to be used against Aaron, and a reason to put both of them behind bars.

"So you want to tell me how you came to know about these? I can't imagine Aaron telling you. Why this place?" Larson asked as they got closer to the location.

Convinced that Larson had agreed to his demands, Merle kept talking. Larson couldn't have gotten him to shut up even if he had wanted him to. His hands were locked behind him and he was leaning forward, resting his forehead against the plastic divider.

"We used to come up here when we were kids. You know — camp out overnight — drink a few brewskies, have some fun with the ladies and whatnot."

Larson eyed him in his rearview mirror and nodded.

"Anyway a couple of years ago, we were out here together, just him and me. He was acting all agitated, fidgeting and unable to settle. I thought he was taking some of the drugs he was selling but it wasn't that. He tells me that things got out of hand with this one girl that he was pimping out. Her name was Kayla. Anyway, he knocked her around a little too hard and she didn't wake up. So he brought her out here and buried her." Just as he said that he motioned with his head. "Just keep going a few more minutes and this trail will come out into a clearing."

He nodded.

"How many are there?"

"With Kayla, four more from what I recall."

"So you were involved?"

"Me? No. I didn't do shit to those women."

"But you helped bury them?"

"I just told you. I wasn't involved. I learned about this

recently from him."

"And yet you kept this from us."

"He's my brother, deputy, what do you expect me to do?"

"Still, you didn't say a word."

There was silence for a minute or two, just the sound of the tires sloshing in puddles and mud spitting up against the vehicle. Larson knew the cogs in his tiny brain were clicking over. Slowly but surely it finally dawned on him what he had just done by admitting to where the bodies were.

"They can't hold that against me, can they?"

Larson eyed him in the mirror without responding.

"Larson."

"It's not for me to decide."

"But you said I was going to get off."

"And you are. But this is an entirely different case."

"No. No! You can't go changing the deal now. Deputy, you get back to your sergeant and tell him that we agreed to…"

"Getting the brawl charges dropped. And we've done that."

"This is not what we agreed to."

"Of course it is."

His face contorted in anger. "You... You have twisted this. Used it for—"

"I've done nothing except let you talk your way into a deeper hole."

"Then I'm done. I'm not telling you where the bodies are."

Larson chuckled. "You idiot, you already have."

And that's why the dog came along. It was trained in finding human remains and had been used in previous situations where the information they'd been given was incomplete.

He bounced in his seat a little as they arrived at the end of the trail which opened up into a clearing. Nearby was a fire pit, several logs on the floor and... a burnt-out husk of a vehicle. He parked and pushed out of his cruiser. The smell of smoldering plastic still lingered in the air. He ducked his head back into the cruiser and stared at Merle.

"Well, looks like this place has had company. Now I wonder who that was?"

He slammed the door closed, sealing in the noise of Merle's protests and obscenities. Larson went around to the back of his trunk and pulled out a rain jacket. The rain was beginning to fall hard and turn the ground into mush. The other officers exited an SUV and a cruiser. The dog hopped out and began sniffing the ground. He covered himself up and pulled out some shovels. It was going to be dirty work, but he was confident that by the time they left that forest they would have enough to put away the Gance brothers for life.

* * *

Peter Dixon's home was located at the end of a quiet road, east of Seneca Drive. It butted up against the Greenbrier River. The property was part of a larger farm. A dilapidated red barn stood off to one side on the verge of collapse. When Jack pushed his way out of the car, he looked around but couldn't see anyone. He approached the door of the home and gave it a knock. There was no answer. Jack peered in through the dust-covered window and stood there for a few minutes taking cover from the downpour that was churning over the gutters. He noticed near the small barn a white F-150 truck. Figuring he was going to have to return later, Jack stepped down off the porch and hurried back to his vehicle. That's when he heard a door open behind him. Jack cast a glance over his shoulder and saw a young man no older than thirty holding back a storm door.

"You need something?" he hollered.

Jack returned, and the man stepped out closing the door behind him. He was dressed in a thin muscle shirt and a pair of cut-off shorts. His hair was tied back tightly in a man bun, and his jaw sported a goatee.

"I'm here to speak to you about your wife, Rachel."

"Look, get the fuck off my property. I told the media to stop coming here."

He turned to go back inside and had his hand on the

door handle when Jack continued. "I'm not from the media but I might have information that will help you find out what happened to your wife."

He paused and answered without even looking at Jack. "I already know."

"I mean who did it."

Jack figured that if he wasn't guilty, and he cared anything for her, he'd want to know. And if he was involved in the disappearance of Rachel and the rest of the women, he'd be curious. Peter looked around for a second, pushed the door open and motioned for him to enter.

"Come inside."

Jack stepped in and wiped his feet on the mat. From the second he entered he could tell the place was strange. There were clocks everywhere; small, large, modern, vintage and even a few grandfather clocks. All of them were ticking in unison. If that wasn't peculiar enough the hall and living room had mounds of newspapers, some of them dating back to the 1950s. It was as if the owner had collected every daily paper since the beginning of time.

"I'm sorry for being rude but I've had a lot of journalists from the local paper here since Rachel went missing, then even more after she was found dead."

He led the way down a narrow hallway. It was dingy and smelled musty like it hadn't been cleaned in years. The walls were covered in a patterned wallpaper from the '80s and dotted around in different spots were framed photos of family, and one of Peter and Rachel in better times. Jack paused and gazed at it.

"That was taken a year after I met her. She was stunning, absolutely beautiful. Hard to believe that's she gone."

He pressed on and they entered a kitchen. The sink was piled up with dirty dishes, the table covered in newspaper. Heaps of clothes that had been taken out of a hamper were strewn over the floor. He started scooping them up. A look of embarrassment crossed his face. A gray and white cat slinked inside and purred, sliding up against Jack's calf.

"Please excuse the mess. It's my grandmother's house. She tends to hoard things and since Rachel's gone I haven't been able to bring myself to do much of anything."

He cleared off a chair that was stacked with books and shoe polish and then offered him a drink. Jack declined, and he took a seat across from him.

"What can you tell me about your relationship with Rachel?"

He frowned, confused. "I thought you had information about her?"

"I do. I'm curious. You met her through backpage, is that right?"

"Not exactly. It was through a friend."

"Another escort?"

He nodded.

"Do you still use the escort service?"

He cleared his throat. "From time to time. There's no law against that."

"Well, that's debatable. I think you'll find it is illegal."

He snorted. "Whatever, man." He got up from his chair, went over to the fridge, pulled out a can of beer and cracked it open. It hissed, and he chugged it back. "Look, I met Rachel, we seemed to connect and she moved in with me. I wanted her to get out of the escort business. It's not a life for anyone but she had a lot of drugs and money problems. Both of her kids are with a foster mother so she was struggling. I told her I could help. You know, slowly get her back on her feet and whatnot."

"And?"

"I managed to get her off drugs, and she even got a job working at a local convenience store for about eight months but... uh... well, she started to think that perhaps she could get her kids back. You know, be a mother again and so forth."

"And what did you think?"

"I thought she could do it. Man, look, there are a lot of people that wrote her off because of what she did for a living but she was a good person. She just happened to fall in with the wrong crowd. She hated prostituting herself, but she continued so she could pay for her drug addiction. It didn't help that Aaron Gance kept showing up and sticking that shit under her nose any chance he got."

"Aaron Gance. I've heard the name."

"Trust me, you don't want to know him. He's bad news around here. Him and his brother. Word has it they were involved in the disappearance of several escorts. At least that's what Rachel said. She was going to turn him in," he said nodding. "Yeah, until she went missing. Anyway, that's who I think did it but getting anyone to believe me is just pointless." He sighed and took another swig.

"People think you did it, don't they?"

He scoffed. "Hell, people have said a lot of folks in this town did it, all except the police. They are still treating it like a drug deal gone wrong, or an overdose. But I know the truth. Yeah…" He walked over to the sink, set his beer down, gripped the counter tightly and gazed out the window. Water streaked down the pane of glass like wriggling worms.

"I loved Rachel."

"What can you tell me about those last days?"

"After eight months of regular work, she got back in contact with the foster parent. Just said she wanted to speak with her kids. They wouldn't let her. They told her that the kids didn't want to speak to her." He turned around and faced Jack. "That killed her. She took that personally. I tried to tell her that it was probably the foster parents and not the kids. It didn't matter. It sent her back over the edge. The next time I saw her she had a needle in her arm. Two days later she was back turning tricks. Aaron Gance was back in the picture and within a week she went missing."

He exhaled hard and shook his head before finishing off what remained in the can and crumpling it and placing it beside a stack of about twenty.

"Anyway. What can you tell me?"

"A journalist by the name of Jenna Whitmore. You know her?"

He smirked then pursed his lips and nodded. "Jenna was one of the good ones. You know, the only one that actually seemed to give a damn about what happened to Rachel. The rest of them were like ravenous wolves. All they wanted was a headline or a sound bite for the TV, nothing more. But her—"

Jack cut him off. "You said 'was'?"

"Yeah, she was one of the good ones." He paused. "Is there a problem?"

"Jenna is missing."

His eyes widened. "I..." He glanced down before shaking his head. "I... didn't know that. I just meant that back when they were coming around, she was one of the few that took the time to listen instead of film me."

Jack blew out his cheeks. He was feeling on edge. Unsure of who might have been responsible and ready to jump on anyone who gave even the slightest inkling that they knew more than they were letting on. That's when he was reminded of what Meghan had said.

"Why do people think it was you?"

"What do you think? She was the first one to go missing and show up dead. Everyone immediately thinks the husband is guilty. I mean, don't get me wrong, we had our arguments, but it was never about us, it was over drug use, trying to get her to stay away from Aaron Gance. I would be surprised if it wasn't him who started the rumors."

"That's it?"

He hesitated before he spoke again. "I failed a polygraph three times. And before you say anything, those things aren't accurate. The cops said I had my dates and times mixed up. But they don't take into account the stress I was under at the time. There is no way I would have hurt Rachel. I cared for her."

"What do you do for a living?"

"A plumber. Not that I've managed to get much work as of late. Her death has created upheaval in my life that I can't seem to get out from underneath."

A voice called out his name. It sounded elderly.

"I'll be right there," he responded before he turned

back to Jack. "Look, I have to get going. You said there was some information you could tell me about who might be responsible."

"Yeah. I'm still working on that," he said rising from his seat and walking towards the exit. "Jenna was close to finding out. If I have any news, you'll be one of the first to know."

He shook his head in disbelief, a look of anger flashed across his face.

"Get out! Get out now!"

He pushed the storm door open and Jack stepped out into the humid rain.

Chapter 24

It was an absolute mess. Larson's lower legs and arms were covered in thick wet mud. The storm began to force waves of rain against the deputy's jackets like handfuls of tossed pebbles. Larson jabbed the shovel into the earth and scooped up another heavy layer. They'd already found the remains of Bonnie Ratlin. She was laying face down, naked in a shallow grave. She'd been stabbed multiple times. The method of death was astonishingly brutal. There had to have been more than twenty wounds to the chest and neck. Whoever stabbed her, showed no mercy. It was savage. Every now and again Larson would look over to the back of the cruiser, wondering what role Merle had played in the murder. He acted as if his hands were clean but that was bullshit. There was no way in hell Aaron had done this all by himself. Someone had helped him. It was possible that Billy and Dale had chipped in. They were as crooked as the other two. Both had done time for petty theft, fighting and possession of narcotics. One had been accused of rape but the charges were dropped before the case reached the court. No, all Merle cared about was avoiding prison, even if it meant passing the blame to his younger brother. At thirty-six years of age, Merle looked like a rat. Not only did his forehead slope backwards, and his chin jut out, but he had barely any hair left and what remained was slicked back into a small ponytail. It was embarrassing.

"Sam, over here! Looks like we've got another one," Deputy Wallace said. Larson crawled out of the small pit he was creating, eyeing Merle with disdain. His boots made a slurping noise as he trudged through mounds of waterlogged earth. Wallace was about twenty feet away. As soon as he arrived, he looked down at the partially uncovered female. Her body was in a much worse state of decay.

"Same MO," Wallace said.

Behind him he could hear the K-9 deputy, Mansfield, giving instructions to his dog. So far that dog had been spot on. Now they had two bodies on their hands. Exhausted, cold from the weather and with rain pouring off the brim of his cap, he shouted over.

"Anything?"

"Not so far. Though by the looks of it, this whole place could be a graveyard."

Larson started giving Wallace a hand to uncover the woman's frail body. She had a tattoo on the back of her neck, and a small locket around her neck. Wallace crouched down and wiped it off, shone his flashlight on it. "Well, I'll be."

"What is it?"

"You remember that nineteen-year-old that went missing two weeks ago. Laurie Jones?"

"That her?"

"Yep. Poor girl. No one deserves to die like this. These bastards are animals. I hope they give them the electric chair for this."

They continued unearthing her. They would have to leave the bodies where they were for the time being until

JON MILLS

the forensic team came in, took photos and did their preliminary work. The radio on Larson's shoulder crackled, static came through the speakers before he heard Ethan's voice.

"Larson, you there?"

He straightened up and wiped off his hands before leaning back against the mud wall. "Go ahead."

"Still no sign of Bonnie."

"Don't worry. We found her. Dead."

"Shit." There was a long pause. "It gets worse. I swung by Ali's Bar and spoke to the owner. You are never going to believe this." He paused as if trying to give some dramatic effect.

"What?"

"Meghan Palmer has now vanished."

His eyes widened. "Are you kidding me?"

"The owner said he called her into work early because of Bonnie. She was serving customers for a while, and then the last time he saw her was when she stepped out back for a smoke break. She never returned. I've checked her apartment. No answer. Phone messages aren't getting through."

"Doesn't she have a kid?"

"He's with a babysitter."

Larson wiped his soaking wet hand across his tired face, smearing mud over his forehead and then sighed heavily. He looked around at the dug holes and Mansfield still searching. They'd already been out there several hours. Who knew how many bodies were buried. Up until now the disappearance of the women from Marlinton hadn't garnered much attention beyond local news but this find was liable to go national.

"Listen, I need you to contact State Police," he said looking around him. "This is bigger than we anticipated. And who knows, maybe Meghan is among these shallow graves."

"I hope not."

"Contact State Police, put out an APB on Aaron Gance and set up a few roadblocks on Highways 219 and 39. We need to find that asshole before he kills again."

"Will do."

Larson removed his hand from the radio and looked off towards the cruiser. He scrambled out of the grave and headed towards Merle. He wanted answers, and he was going to give them. Larson opened the rear door and yanked him out.

"What the hell?"

"How many bodies are out here?"

"I told you, four that's it. At least that's what Aaron said. There could be more for all I know."

"For all you know?"

Larson hauled him up and slammed him against the cruiser.

"Get off, man."

Larson leaned in close to his ear. "I swear you are going down for this, and your brother. This time you aren't getting out."

"We made a deal."

"Screw your deal."

"This is police brutality."

"Brutality?" Larson clenched his jaw and gritted his teeth. "I'll show you brutality."

With that said he dragged him towards the grave where Bonnie lay. Still in handcuffs, he stumbled and fell to the ground. Larson didn't bother to help him up. He hauled him like a huge sack of potatoes across the ground, creating deep lines in the earth. The other deputies looked over and Wallace called out but Larson ignored it. He forced Merle onto the ground and pressed down on the back of his neck, pushing him towards her lifeless frame.

"That's brutality. You get off on that?"

"Please. I didn't do it."

"Sick sonofabitch."

Wallace came rushing over and placed a hand on Larson's jacket sleeve. "Sam. Let him go."

Larson stared at him intently before releasing his grip. Merle coughed and spluttered and put on one hell of a show. That's how he'd managed to get the judge to be lenient with him last time, but not this time. This time he was going to make damn sure he received the stiffest penalty possible.

* * *

After returning to the inn to collect Jenna's hard drive, Jack ended up at Dories Lounge at half past five and had been sitting there for close to three hours. He'd had dinner, dessert, and several cups of coffee and was now drinking a glass of beer — anything to keep the owner off his back. She'd approached several times asking if he wanted the check but he didn't want to head back to the inn yet. He was still poring over the information that Jenna had left on her voice recorder, though now he had a pair of headphones on and was leaning back in a booth near the window. Most of the other tables were already occupied.

"Look, I'm just going to leave the bill here," the waitress said.

"I'm not done yet. I'll take another beer." He slid out from his seat. "I'll be right back."

She looked concerned when he headed out and dashed across the street to the parking lot to retrieve his small laptop from the car. He wanted to hook up the external hard drive and see what else she had dug up prior to going missing. Outside, the rain came down in sheets. When he returned to his table, he plugged in the unit and powered everything up.

Karl Fraser had mentioned Officer Rigby, however, there was no mention of him in the hours of statements, interviews, and videos she'd taken. She hadn't even snapped one photo of him. Had Karl just been lying, and pointing the finger, hoping to distract him from the one who was really responsible?

He hit play and leaned back closing his eyes. Jenna had this soft voice that could almost lull a person into a trance. He knew he was missing some vital information and that eventually, he'd stumble over it.

"I'm sure now that Aaron Gance is behind the recent string of phone calls. Though, Pastor Tim Mathers isn't without fault. The sighting of him entering the Lodge on the Edge of Green Bank with Dixie Stokes last week leads me to believe that he knows more than he's telling. He's refused to

take my phone messages and has somehow convinced Corey that I'm deluded. Still, regardless of the setbacks, I have been able to establish a timeline. In every instance that a woman was taken, they were found within a two-week window, however, after chatting to Doug Whethers from the coroner's office, it appears they were able to establish that the bodies were only in the water for eleven days, which means you aren't killing them for three days. So where are you keeping them in that time? Why do you keep them alive for three days? Why is it always three days? Is it related to your work? Note to self, I must cross-check the dates they went missing. Was it a weekend? Maybe that's it. You are doing this on the weekends. You are holding down some job in the week that prevents you from taking women. You are keeping them over the weekend to have your fun with them and then dumping them. But... you're not touching them sexually. Why? Are you impotent?" Jenna chuckled a little. *"I bet that's it. Isn't it? You can't get it up so you lash out at them."*

Jack forwarded the recording, hit play and then did it again a few more times until he found another spot that interested him. *"Tuesday the 31st of May. I'm convinced that Karl Fraser is behind the murders of the women. Actually, let me rephrase that. I'm concentrating my efforts on observing him both day and night as his nine-month sentence coincided with the timeline of the murders. No disappearances occurred in that time. Within a week of his being out, Dixie Stokes went missing. Did you take her? I bet you were eager to get your hands on another the second you got out."*

Jack hit stop and chugged back on his drink before turning his attention to the folders on the hard drive. He clicked through two folders full of audio snippets, most of which were comments made by women who knew the Green Bank Five. Jenna had been trying to obtain as much information as she could from them on johns they had been with over the past year. She seemed convinced that the key to figuring out who was behind it, was in the statements made by escorts. Those who might have come across the Green Bank killer and lived to tell the tale without even knowing they were in his presence. He pressed the button again, glancing around the restaurant. Several locals scrutinized him, and he wondered if the killer was close? Was he watching him? Did he know that he had Jenna's files? Jenna's voice brought him back to attention. *"If it is you... When did you start? If it was you, Karl, you let Bailey get away. That was sloppy. How many others did you take before you decided to kill? What shifted? How did you graduate from letting some go to killing others? Had you been thinking about it while locked away in that jail cell? And why the water?"*

Jack stopped for a second, distracted by some of the photos on the hard drive. These weren't people she was investigating — it was photos of her family — Jenna, Corey, her mother and father on vacation. Some were of locations in Colorado, others from local spots. They were skiing, boating, and fishing. There were hundreds of images. Among the many, he came across a letter addressed to her mother. It was an apology. In the top left-hand corner was her mother's address in Durbin. He read some of it but felt like he was intruding. It was private. Not related to the murders but to her father's passing. It was an apology that she wasn't able to make the funeral because she was away in New York at college and hadn't got the message, been too busy and… Jack stopped reading. He felt his chest become heavy at the thought of what she must have been going through. Had she printed it and sent it to her mother?

Jack transferred a number of the photos and the letter onto a small flash drive he owned and placed it in his duffel bag among the rest of his belongings. After he breathed in deeply and glanced out the window, he saw a brown sedan pull up beside his vehicle. It was too dark to see the occupants' faces. It was a couple from what he could tell. It wasn't anything out of the ordinary so he returned to listening to the recording.

A few minutes had passed when he was suddenly startled by a knock at the window. Jack jerked his head to see someone wearing a dark hoodie and a white mask. He could make out their eyes but that was it. Slowly, under the glow of the light outside, they lifted an arm to window level to reveal a baseball bat, and then slapped it a few times in the opposite hand in a menacing gesture before dashing off into the darkness. He looked across to the parking lot but the brown sedan was gone. His eyes swept from side to side, then he noticed it farther down, slightly angled and facing the restaurant. Wipers sloshed water back and forth as rain drops glittered in the reflection of the headlights.

Jack collected his belongings. He tossed some cash on the table to pay the bill and then headed towards the door. Through the blurry, rain-covered window he could see the sedan. The engine roared a few times just as he stepped out the front door. He was so focused on the car that he didn't see what happened next. Instead, he heard it. A crash, the smash of glass, then again, followed by the sound of crunching metal.

Jack jerked his head to see the bat-wielding lunatic smashing the shit out of his Shelby.

"Hey!" he yelled. They looked up and made a break for it just as Jack dashed across the road narrowly avoiding getting blindsided by a truck. Brakes screeched, and tires squealed as the truck swerved to miss him. That split second delay was all they needed. The masked stranger hopped into the back of the sedan and it revved its engine a few more times, almost taunting him. He reached around for his Glock but it wasn't there. Shit, he'd left it in the car. The last thing he wanted was to get raked over the coals again by the police for carrying one, so he'd tucked it in the glove compartment.

The brown sedan jerked forward a few times like an angry bull getting ready to charge.

Now he could see the other occupants. They were masked like the one in the back, and there were three of them. Jack made a mad dash for his vehicle but had to dive for cover as shots rang out. A window had dropped in the back, a handgun was sticking out and several rounds were fired in his direction, tearing up the gravel nearby.

"Motherf—"

Not wasting any time, he scrambled to his feet and

bolted out from behind one car to the next, steadily making his way towards his vehicle that had the windshield busted in. Bastards. It was a mess. Several more shots were fired, and then he heard tires squeal.

"Oh, hell no!"

He hurried over to his vehicle, hit unlock on the key fob and dived inside. Through the passenger window, he could see the red taillights of the vehicle as they tried to escape. He turned over the ignition, and the engine roared to life. Rearing back his legs he pushed out the windshield that was barely hanging on by a fragment of glass around the edge.

Then, he smashed his foot against the accelerator and tore out of the lot.

Chapter 25

Aaron Gance couldn't stop himself from laughing. The brown sedan blasted out of the lot with the Shelby behind them, closing in fast. It soared over a rise in the road hitting ninety miles an hour. Billy rammed the stick shift into gear, threw the wheel and they swerved down 5th Avenue.

"Oh, you should have seen his face. It was priceless."

Dale's face lit up. "The way he hit the ground. I thought he was a goner."

Aaron frowned as he looked out the back window at the headlights cutting through the night. "Pick it up, he's gaining on us."

"I'm going as fast as I can," Billy yelled.

He tapped the back of his seat. "Well, go faster."

"I'm telling you, Aaron, that was a dumb move. We already have enough to deal with and now you want to rile this stranger up."

"Screw him, he fucked with the wrong guy."

Aaron brought the window down and leaned out. "Keep it steady," he shouted as they swerved a little before he took aim with the revolver and unloaded two rounds in rapid succession at the car behind before slipping back inside. "Can you believe this guy? Who in their right mind chases after someone shoots at them?"

"I told you, man."

"Ah shut up," Aaron growled.

As they burst out onto Highway 39, Billy hung a right swerving into oncoming traffic. A large truck with monster wheels was heading in their direction. Dale yelled, "Watch out. Shit!"

Billy veered to the right, and the truck tried to avoid hitting them. While they narrowly escaped being squashed beneath its monster wheels, a parked Mini wasn't as fortunate. The truck soared over the back of it, squashing it like an ant. The truck roared on to its final destination — a phone line.

Meanwhile, in the back, Aaron was loving every

second. He fished into his pocket, pulled out a small baggie of coke, took a pinch and snorted it up his right nostril, then the left. Just a quick pick-me-up before he looked back at the devastation the truck had caused. It had taken down the phone line. Sparks were flying, and the occupants were hurrying away from what was likely to be one hell of an explosion.

"Fuck. He's still coming!" he yelled noticing the Shelby. "Veer on to 8th Street, head down 8th Avenue and back onto 9th." Billy didn't question it. He plowed his foot into the accelerator and roared past multiple parked cars, slamming the shifter into the next gear. Aaron returned to laughing. It was partly because he hadn't had this much fun in ages, but it also was a nervous habit. There was a motorbike up ahead, and a compact car. With parked cars on either side, there was no way they were going to be able to get through so Billy eased off the gas.

Aaron leaned forward gripping his seat.

"What the hell are you doing?"

"What do you expect me to do?"

"Go through them."

"But…"

"You heard me."

Billy knew not to argue, he plowed into the back of the bike sending the rider soaring through the air and landing on the hood of a parked car. The bike was destroyed. In the process, Billy lost control of the vehicle and it hit the left and right bumpers of the parked cars in front of it, knocking them forward. It took everything he had not to cause that vehicle to spin. Aaron jerked back in his seat feeling every knock. Metal crunched and sparks flew as the sedan blew through two more cars like bowling pins.

Somehow he managed to keep it going.

Aaron twisted in his seat expecting to see the pursuing vehicle stopped, but it wasn't. He just kept coming. The Shelby slalomed through the wake of dented cars and accelerated after them.

As they burst out onto 9th Street, they flew past a

parked cruiser. The deputy was outside his vehicle speaking to someone when the sedan took off his wing mirror. He scrambled into his cruiser, hit the siren and lit up the night with his cherry top lights.

Like a kid viewing a theater screen, Aaron gazed out the back window and watched as the cruiser went to veer out only to be sideswiped into a spin by the Shelby. "Holy shit! Now we're talking." He roared with laughter. "Hell, yeah!"

The cruiser didn't take long to correct itself before charging after the Shelby and sedan.

Fifty yards farther down the street, Aaron noticed traffic blocking up the road on 10th Street.

"Is there a fair in town or something? What the hell?"

It was very rare to see the roads clogged up at any time of the year except Christmas but this was after nine o'clock at night. Most of the streets should have been deserted barring a few vehicles.

"Go up onto the sidewalk."

"What?"

"That's the only way we are getting out of this."

He kept turning his head back and forth. No sooner had he said that to Billy than all of them jerked forward. "Asshole!"

Twisting he saw the Shelby had rammed into the back of the sedan. This time Aaron aimed the revolver at the back window and fired several times causing it to shatter. Then the gun clicked. He fished into his pocket for more ammo and was about to reload it when they were struck again, this time it nearly caused Billy to lose control.

"Get on the sidewalk," he yelled again. The sedan shot over the edge and screeched back and forth between the walls of buildings and parked vehicles until he eased off the gas to take the corner.

"Don't ease..."

Before he could say it the Shelby smashed into the back as they tried to take the corner, knocking the sedan into a spin. The vehicle slammed into traffic. Glass exploded, metal crunched and sparks ignited like sparklers.

* * *

Everything happened in a split second. A truck hit the front end of Jack's vehicle after he plowed into the sedan and he found himself knocked sideways across the street, colliding with a wall. A horn could be heard blaring away as the world came back into view. He wasn't sure how long he'd been out — minutes, seconds? But he was aware of warm blood trickling down the side of his face. He reached over and pushed out of the vehicle, the door groaned, bent and twisted by the impact. There was a ringing in his ears that he couldn't seem to shake. On his hands and knees, he could hear people yelling. The first thing he remembered was the brown sedan. As he rose to his feet, his eyes scanned the chaotic scene. Vehicles were lined up, farther up the road were red and blue lights flashing. A roadblock?

He winced and reached up to touch his forehead. Right then, he saw the sedan as it started pulling out from the aftermath of wrecked cars. He blinked hard, willing his mind to snap into focus. Turning, he staggered back to his vehicle, reached inside and over to the glove compartment. It was already open; his Glock was on the floor. He scooped it up and hurried out of the car, heading for the brown vehicle when....

"Police! Drop the gun and get on the ground now."

Off to his left two officers came into view, both had handguns trained on him.

"I said now!"

Jack froze, he knew that common sense had to prevail in that moment, though everything in him wanted to turn and shoot. Slowly but surely he lowered to the ground and before he knew it they were on top of him, digging their knees into his back and pummeling his legs into position. With his head turned sideways all he could do was lay there watching as the brown sedan peeled away.

* * *

The drive to the station was short as it was located on 10th Avenue not far from where the collision had occurred. Along the way, Jack saw multiple police cars, many of which were State Police. There had to have been six, maybe eight cruisers blocking the road and officers were stopping vehicles and shining their flashlights inside.

Something big was going on.

The cruiser parked out front. A few lights shone down providing light to the smooth, wet tarmac and sidewalk. Even at night, the building looked ugly. Brown brick, dismal and uninviting, just the way they liked it. Nothing about it was new or tidy except for the surrounding landscape. Under the light of the moon, everything looked refreshed by the downpour.

The one deputy got out and headed in while the other remained in the front seat. A minute or two later, two more officers appeared, though these were State Police, dressed in green. One of them opened the rear door.

"Time to go," he said leaning in and helping him out.

The other officers were scanning the area as if expecting trouble.

"Look, you've got the wrong guy, my vehicle was vandalized by three men in a brown sedan. That's the only reason I was after them. The officer on scene will be able to tell you that."

They ignored him and pushed him forward. The handcuffs were tight. The evening was humid. Ahead were five steps that led up to two double doors. Above it engraved in concrete were the words: Pocahontas County Sheriff Department. The deputy pulled a door open. It hissed a little. The state cop pushed Jack in and the door closed.

Inside, the air conditioning provided much-needed relief from the humid air. The floors, walls, and ceilings were white with wood moldings. It reminded Jack of an old schoolhouse. Fluorescent lights lit up the place, with one of them flicking on and off. One of the officers spoke to another behind glass, and he buzzed them in.

Shoved forward, Jack was led to a desk while one of the deputies left him with two female state troopers. The department was buzzing with activity. Phones were ringing off the hook while the front desk clerk punched keys at his computer.

"Wait here."

Jack was forced into a seat. He shivered a little. Though it was warm outside, he was drenched to the bone from the rain, and the air conditioning wasn't helping. When the officer returned he had him stand against a wall while he was patted down and the contents of his pockets were removed. There wasn't much on him. His cell phone, a few receipts, the napkin Meghan had given him and some loose change. The rest was in the car. He was told to remove his shoes, chains, watch and anything else that was loose. It was procedure, they didn't want him trying to hang or choke himself. All his personal belongings were put into a plastic bag and placed inside a large brown envelope. The deputy scribbled on it and handed it off to a woman dressed in office clothes.

"Take a seat."

Besides one officer, sitting off to the side, no one else kept an eye on him. It wasn't like he could escape. The office was crawling with cops. He saw a few suits. Someone mentioned FBI. Five more minutes passed before two deputies were discussing whether his prints were in the system.

"Let me save you some work. They are."

"Figured as much."

Right then the buzzer on the door went off and none other than Deputy Larson walked in.

He shook his head and crossed the room after speaking to an officer who pointed towards Jack. "Why am I not surprised to see you again? You know you're a hard man to track down." He pulled up a rolling chair and sat down in front of him. "Breaking and entering into a home, a brawl in a bar and now a high-speed chase through my town? Not to mention open carry of a handgun."

"What can I say? I'm innocent."

"Everyone is. You are in a whole heap of trouble, Mr. Winchester."

Jack leaned forward. "Like I told the other officers. You have the wrong guy. My vehicle was vandalized, and the assailant took off in a brown sedan with two other men. I gave chase but—"

"You get a look at these men?"

He frowned. "No. It was dark, and they were wearing masks."

Larson tapped his fingers against the desk and squinted.

"If you don't believe me, speak with the officer who attempted to give chase when his side mirror was taken off by the sedan. Hell, there is probably still some brown paint residue left behind."

"Which officer?"

"How the hell should I know? I was on my face before I could get a word in edgeways."

"And the men in the sedan?"

"They drove away. Great police work, deputy. First class!" Jack leaned back in his seat and sighed.

Larson gave him a blank stare before telling one of the other officers to process him. He rose from his seat.

"That's it? You're throwing me in a cell?"

"We are holding you while we complete this investigation."

Jack scoffed. "Tell me, deputy. All those State Police out there aren't here for the hell of it. You've found something, haven't you? Who is it? Is it Jenna?"

He looked as if he was going to speak. His lips parted and then closed again, before nodding to the officer who hauled Jack up and began strong-arming him away. He remained fixed on Larson.

"Who is it, Larson?" he bellowed.

Larson waved him off. "I'll be back to speak with you later."

"I need to speak to you now."

"Later."

Shoved through a door and led down a series of steps, Jack was fuming. Everything about the situation was spiraling out of control. There was no chance in hell they were going to let him walk now, not after this. On the way down to a holding cell, Jack didn't bother protesting. His words would have only fallen on deaf ears. Cops were used to it. Fighting back, whether that was in word or action, would have been a dumb move. As far as he saw it, it was a situation that could be resolved with a little bit of time. Problem was, time wasn't on his side. If the abducted women had lived for three days before their bodies were placed into the rivers, that meant Jenna's time had nearly run out. She'd gone missing the night he'd arrived, and he'd already been in Marlinton two days.

As he was led on, a door opened up to the right and in walked Deputy Rigby. He passed by casting Jack a serious look.

"Ethan, Larson wants to speak to you," said the deputy that had a firm grip on Winchester.

"He's back?"

"Yeah."

Rigby gave a nod and went to turn when Jack spoke. "Officer Ethan Rigby?"

"Yes?"

Jack shook his head and cast his eyes at the floor. He recalled the name mentioned by Karl Fraser. Rigby walked over to him, his eyes narrowing the closer he got.

He wagged his finger in front of his face. "I remember you. You were brought in only a day ago — the guy who broke into the apartment. That's right." He scoffed. "Back here again. They never learn," he said to the other deputy before walking away.

He was tossed into a cell and the heavy steel door clanged behind him before a key was turned. The cell wasn't much to look at, just a run-of-the-mill holding cell; a chrome toilet, sink and a hard bed. They didn't want him getting too comfortable. Jack exhaled and slumped down on the bed. Who knew how long he would be in there before a lawyer showed up, if they even bothered to call one. Outside the door, he could hear phones ringing, keyboard keys being tapped and the swell of conversation. Now and then, he'd hear another man in a cell farther down slam fists against the door and demand to be let out.

He lay back and put his hands behind his head. It didn't matter how many times he saw the inside of a cell, he never got used to it. It was empty, cramped and capable of breaking down the hardest of men.

He sighed.

This was going to be a long night.

Chapter 26

It was his description of the vehicle that piqued his attention. Billy Irving drove a brown sedan. Larson had stopped him on numerous occasions for speeding around town. He had the thing pimped out with an LED under-glow light, and his entire trunk was full of speakers that let out a heavy bass beat. When he was cruising the neighborhood, he could be heard long before anyone laid eyes on that sorry excuse for a human being.

He ran his hand over the busted-up cruiser that belonged to Deputy Hodgkins. It was just about to be towed away. Someone was going to have to pay the thousands of dollars in damage. The department's budget was already tight, and they'd had one other cruiser that got banged up a few months back when Wallace lost control of it on the way to an incident. The boys were still ribbing him over that. Larson felt sorry for Hodgkins as he was the one that was liable to get pulled into the office on this. He'd joined the department a few months after Larson did and was still in his first year of probation.

Hodgkins made his way over to him after being checked out by a medic.

"How are you feeling?"

He ran a hand around the back of his neck. "I've got a bit of whiplash but beyond that, I'm good."

"So you want to tell me how the brown sedan managed to get away?"

Hodgkins let out a heavy sigh. "Aargh, it was chaotic, Sam. Both vehicles crashed ahead of me into multiple vehicles, by the time I hopped out the one guy had a firearm in his hand. My main concern was for the safety of civilians. When I looked over to the sedan, the occupants didn't look like they were going anywhere. I figured we'd cuff Winchester and then the backup would haul them out of the vehicle, but when I looked back, they were gone. Sorry, man."

"It's not me you have to answer to, it's the chief."

He tossed his arms up. "What was I supposed to do

with all our guys helping State Police at the checkpoints? They came out of nowhere, sideswiped the cruiser and took off at a high rate of speed. I did the best I could under the circumstances."

Larson rested a hand on his shoulder. "I know." He looked over to where Winchester's Shelby was. "Was he pursuing the brown sedan?"

"Yeah, I caught sight of him just before he busted into me."

"The damage to his windshield. Was that there before or after he collided with the truck?"

"Before."

So he was telling the truth. Larson wandered over to where a State Police officer was gathering together Jacks belongings from the vehicle.

"You mind if I take a look at that?"

"Knock yourself out. In fact, you can take it."

He handed him a duffel bag and Larson carried it back to his cruiser. With gloves on, he fished through it and pulled out a cellphone then powered it on. At first, he thought it was Winchester's, but upon closer inspection, he was able to determine it was hers. An image of Jenna Whitmore and her family came up on the screen. *What are you doing with her phone?* He pulled out the external hard drive, hooked it up to the laptop in his cruiser and accessed it. His eyebrows arched as he browsed through folder after folder of images, videos, and audio. These were folks he'd seen around town, some that held prominent positions in the community. He shook his head. He knew the situation with escorts was bad but he had no idea the kind of people that were using their services. It was another world, a dark underbelly full of lost individuals. He knew that much of it was fueled by drug use and that the flow of drugs into the town was coming from the Gance brothers, but he had yet to prove that. With Merle in custody and Aaron soon to be locked up, perhaps it wouldn't matter. With them off the streets, their source would have to seek out a new dealer. He clicked through on a few more photos before unplugging. Right now he needed to speak with Winchester.

* * *

The clang of the door startled him, forcing him out of a light sleep. Larson walked inside and closed the door behind him.

"What are you doing with Jenna's cell phone?"

"And hello to you, deputy."

"Cut the bullshit. Did you steal it from her apartment?"

Jack swung his legs off the bed and leaned forward. "No, I found it hidden inside the toilet tank."

"But this wasn't on you when we brought you in."

Jack chewed on the side of his lip and didn't reply. His lack of response was the answer.

Larson snorted. "Of course, you went back there."

"I had to. Deputy, she's a journalist who is obsessed with the Green Bank Five case. I was convinced she would have kept some record of her work, and I was right. Now if you go through that, you'll find some interesting information that perhaps your guys have overlooked."

"I already have."

"Then you know that time is against us right now. All those women who were taken were kept alive for a period of three days before their bodies were placed in the water. Jenna has been gone for almost three nights. If we don't find her tonight, chances are she's dead."

Larson leaned back against the wall. Jack could see he was chewing it over.

"Look, that call I got the night before I showed up here, came from a pay phone in Green Bank. There is only one pay phone, which means she managed to escape."

"You still think she's been taken?"

"Positive. The phone calls in the night, the warning letter and then her last comment to me about how close she was. I don't think she was just getting close, she knew who it was. Now the last person to see her alive was Meghan Palmer. She went with her to a client's home in Green Bank. Now if you go through my possessions, you'll find a scrap of paper with an address. It's a cabin on the east side near Hamilton Hollow and the North Fork River. I was about to go there but, well… Speak to Meghan, she'll confirm this."

He breathed in deeply. "I would but Meghan has vanished."

Jack's brow furrowed. "What? I dropped her off at work."

"I know that's where she went missing."

"But…"

The cogs in his mind turned over, faster and faster.

"Did you know Bonnie Ratlin was gone?" Larson asked.

"Meghan mentioned she hadn't turned up for work."

"She's dead. Found her body along with several others out in Watoga State Park. All of them were buried in shallow graves."

Jack ran a hand over his head unable to process the bombshell he'd just dropped on him.

"It's Aaron Gance, Jack. We've been on to him for a while but haven't had proof. I finally managed to get a confession out of his brother Merle. The dead women out in Watoga are escorts as well. Chances are he is responsible for the Green Bank Five." He paused. "That's why the State Police are involved right now. They've set up roadblocks. If that was him in the brown sedan, we'll get him. As soon as we find him, he'll be charged with the murders of the Green Bank Five."

It was coming at him way too fast. First Jenna, now Meghan.

"How long ago was she taken?" Jack asked.

"Five hours, maybe six."

"Listen, deputy, Meghan said Jenna was acting strange the night she went to see a client out in Green Bank. The client never came to the door. The appointment was canceled. Once she dropped her off, she headed back in that direction." He let his words hang in the air. "We need to get to that cabin. I'm gonna go out on a limb here and say that there is a strong possibility that Meghan is there, and maybe, just maybe Jenna."

Larson stared back at him before heading over to the

door.

"So you'll be dropping the charges now that you have proof?"

"Just hang tight here. I'm going to find that scrap of paper with the address and run a check on it."

"Larson."

"Jack, just wait."

He was flustered. Overwhelmed much like Jack. They were closing in but dealing with fragments of information. The door slammed behind him and Jack headed over and called out to him through the bars. Larson didn't respond, he took off up a flight of stairs and disappeared out of view.

* * *

Larson immediately got on the radio to find out if the State Police had spotted the brown sedan. The response was negative. He figured they dumped the vehicle, took off on foot and headed back to the garage where they would have been able to change into a different vehicle.

"Send a few of your men over to Gance Garage,

Hodgkins will give you the address."

As soon as he got off the radio, he headed into a small room that was used for keeping evidence. It was organized by day. He wandered up the aisle until he found a box containing files with belongings. He retrieved Jack's and emptied out the contents onto a countertop. There he spotted a scrap of paper.

"Summers. Are you there?" He shouted over his shoulder as he went through what Jack had on him at the time.

"What do you need?"

"Is Merle Gance still here or has he been taken by State Police?"

"No, he's still down in the holding cell," a gruff voice replied.

It was a gut instinct; call it a hunch but one that he wanted to follow up on before going through the process of bringing up the details on the owner of the address. If the location had been used as the killing room for the Green Bank Five, chances were if they did own the cabin, it might have been registered in someone else's name. The Gance brothers were shady in their business dealings; he didn't expect anything less now. He figured the quickest way to find out was to head down and speak with Merle.

He jogged out of the room and was on his way down when Wallace got on the radio. "State Police are now at the dig site. We're heading back."

"No. Stay where you are. They have things covered here. Besides, they probably could use the help and we don't want State fucking this up. Anyway, any more bodies found?"

"Another four."

"Any we know?"

"None that we or anyone could recognize. It's a mess. Pretty much all bones."

"Shit."

He continued on towards the cellblock housing Merle.

Chapter 27

From the moment he arrived at the cell, Merle was belligerent. He rolled off his bed and sauntered over to the bars.

"Finally! You assholes gonna let me out of here or what?"

He shook the bars expecting Larson to let him out. Of course, he refused to answer the question, it would only lead to him making things difficult and right now he needed answers. He raised the scrap of paper up in front of the bars.

"You want to tell me who owns this?"

Merle squinted and leaned forward slightly. He smirked. "Not without my glasses."

"Don't fuck with me, Merle." He knew he didn't wear any.

"Who cares? I want out of here. I fulfilled my end of the deal. Now unless you guys want a civil lawsuit, I suggest you release me."

"Not gonna happen."

"Then you can go fuck yourself and your address."

He turned and ambled back to the corner of the room. Sniffing as he went.

"I know what both of you have been doing. You, Aaron, probably Billy and Dale. Now tell me. Did you take them up to the cabin for a little bit of fun, huh? Did they not want to put out so you killed them?"

"I don't have a clue what you're on about but you really should seek mental help."

"Is that where Meghan is? Is it?"

"Again. Don't know. Don't care. Now unless you're going to let me out, we're done talking."

He leaned back on his bed and crossed his feet.

"Whose address is this, Merle?"

"Not listening," he said in the most obnoxious tone.

"You better hope she's alive," Larson added before turning to walk away.

"She might be, but your wife won't."

"What did you say?" Larson screwed up his face and charged at the cell. He unlocked the door and lunged at Merle. Before he could say another word, Larson lashed out at him and struck him twice in the face with a right hook. "Motherf—"

"Larson."

Behind him, he heard the sound of heavy soles against the floor. He'd completely ignored the camera angled down at the cell. He'd also lost touch of how long he'd been laying into him. Seconds, maybe minutes? Nothing but rage fueled him, blocking out what common sense should have told him. Ethan burst into the cell along with another officer and hauled him back. Merle's face was bruised and cut up, he spat blood onto the ground and tried to say something but it just came out as a garbled mess of snot, blood, and spit. Ethan slammed the cell door and locked it.

"What did I tell you?" Ethan bellowed. "You want to lose your badge?"

Larson shrugged them off. He looked off to his right

and saw Winchester looking at him.

Ethan followed his gaze. "Look, I just got word the brown sedan has been found burnt out on the north side of town. K9 is trying to track those guys down but a few leads have come in from witnesses in the area saying they bolted on foot across Old McGee's Car Lot, heading north." He pointed towards the exit. "Get out there and help track them down. In the meantime, I'll handle this and deal with the footage. But you owe me."

"That's it, I knew you cops were crooked. Going to wipe the video, are you? Oh, you are all going down for this."

"Shut up, Merle," Ethan replied.

Larson scowled at him. All he wanted to do was go back in and finish what he'd started. As he turned away, he wiped his mouth, shot a glance back at Jack and shook the scrap of paper in his hand.

* * *

Jack had to admit, he was impressed. Larson was full of spit and vinegar. The kind of man that was liable to do the department a world of good. They needed someone who wasn't going to take shit. Police work had become nothing but a political game. Avoiding civil lawsuits and bad press. It had made them weak. Perhaps that's why he got on well with his late friend, New York Police Detective Frank Banfield. Ethan Rigby, on the other hand, was something else. Wiping a recording, seeing escorts, probably some of the same women he'd busted in the past for soliciting. He shook his head.

"Hey, Larson. You said you were going…"

Larson disappeared before he heard him.

Ethan came strolling over. "Keep it down."

"But…"

"I said…" He bellowed at Jack, pulled his baton out and slapped it along the bars. "Shut the hell up before I come in there."

"Is he coming back? That's all I want to know."

"Not tonight, so get comfy. You'll get your turn to go before a judge tomorrow."

Shit, Jack thought as he returned to his seat. This was

not how he intended it to play out. If those three guys were somehow connected to the disappearance of both Jenna and Meghan, who knew if they were heading back to the cabin. He needed to get out and fast. Jack began pacing in his cell looking at the clock outside and listening to the sound of Merle's rant.

"I'm going to sue every last one of you. You better have good lawyers," Merle yelled before breaking into a string of curse words. There was no shutting him up. Other prisoners yelled and banged on bars to get him to be quiet but he wouldn't listen. It didn't take long for Ethan to return, this time he began cracking the metal baton across the bars.

"Enough!"

Merle, however, wouldn't settle easy. In fact, he only became even more belligerent. Ethan took out his keys and unlocked the cell and rushed in. It was out of view so all Jack could hear was the noise of his beating before Ethan came out, wiping the blood off the baton with a small cloth. That's when Jack had an idea.

"I bet you like it rough, don't you?" Jack muttered gripping the bars.

"What did you say?" Ethan eyed him with a look of disgust.

"You know, the women you see. The escorts. Do you beat on them too?"

He stared back at Jack. An expression of shock? It was hard to tell but he had his attention.

He pointed the baton at him with an outstretched arm. "You better watch your mouth."

"Is that what you told them?

Ethan approached his cell and smacked the baton against the bars. "Don't make me come in there."

"I get it now." Jack nodded. "Yeah, you get off on it. That's why you go see them. Your girlfriend probably doesn't let you do the things you want to do, am I right?"

"I warned you."

He took out the keys and unlocked the door. Jack took a few steps back, readying himself. He was just putting away the keys when Jack spoke.

"Oh, I think you forgot something, officer." He pointed to the camera.

Ethan snorted. "Don't worry about that."

Jack didn't give a shit about the camera. Whether it saw what he did or not, it didn't matter. Though he had a feeling that whatever it captured would mysteriously disappear once it was over. Ethan clenched his jaw and came in swinging. As his arm came around with the baton, Jack lunged at him closing the distance. He grabbed his weapon arm and forced it upwards. Ethan let out a high-pitched yell before Jack slammed the side of his hand twice into his throat. On the third time, he grabbed him behind the neck and head butted him as hard as he could. His nose exploded and he dropped to the ground. Jack moved fast, grabbing him by the back of the collar and dragging him out of the cell and out of view of the camera. There was a fifty-fifty chance someone had been watching but with all their resources funneled into the roadblocks and hunt for the three men, he figured he stood a chance. Still, he wasn't going to take the risk, while Ethan was groaning and writhing around on the floor gripping his nose, he removed his baton and double-timed it over to the stairs, waiting for the next influx of cops. All the while the other prisoners yelled.

"Yeah! Fuck him up! Dirty pig!"

Jack stood off to one side waiting. Sure enough, he heard the sound of boots pounding the steps. "Ethan," a voice cried out. Before he had a second to respond, Jack was on him. A few sharp blows across the head and the young officer was out cold.

"Let us out," said a burly man who was dressed in nothing but white pants. Who knew where the hell his shirt was. His gut hung over his dark leather belt like a balloon full of water on the verge of bursting.

"No time."

"Hey. Hey!"

Jack didn't waste another second, he unclothed the officer and changed out of his attire and quickly slipped into his uniform. It wasn't an exact fit but the guy was close to his size, though slightly on the larger end. He tore off the name tag, pulled the police cap down to cover his face as much as possible before heading up the stairs. He hadn't made it a few steps before he heard Ethan mutter something. Jack turned and noticed he was still conscious. He hurried back.

"Sorry, got to go."

A few hard kicks to the jaw and it was lights out.

* * *

When Meghan came to, her throat was dry and she had the taste of bile in her mouth. Light stabbed her eyes, as her eyelids fluttered. What was in her mouth? Some thick material cut into the sides of her gums. Her wrists hurt, really bad. She tugged a few times and then realized they were bound with cuffs and secured to a metal post. She tried again, another attempt to free herself but it was pointless. *Where am I?* She'd been in and out of consciousness since… she couldn't remember. She gazed around at her surroundings. It was some unfinished basement; concrete floors, rough-hewn walls, and a blacked-out window. Someone had painted over it with dark paint, or was it material? She couldn't tell. She shook her head trying to get her mind to focus. Slowly, her memories came back like a flood. She remembered being dropped off at work by Jack, serving customers for an hour or so, and then having a smoke before... pain, severe pain. That was followed by her muscles twitching uncontrollably, and then hitting the ground.

The basement didn't have any furniture, except for a workbench that had some tools on the side, along with cans of paint. It smelled musty. There were no voices, no sound except — water. She could hear a river or stream. She felt her stomach churn within. Fear gripped her as she came to the realization that she was going to die. This was it. Just like the others.

The only light in the room came from a few small candles. The dim flicker of flames created shadows on the walls making it seem even eerier than it was.

How long had she been here?

It didn't matter. All that mattered was escaping. Meghan tugged hard on the cuffs that were wrapped around the steel foundation pole. She leaned forward and used her lips and tongue to try and push the gag out of her mouth but it was impossible. It was too tight. She let out a muffled scream. Frustration, anger, fear; all of it rolling into one.

Her head dropped and she closed her eyes, exhaustion overwhelming her. What drug had she been given? She could barely keep her eyes open.

Right then she heard the sound of tires on gravel. A few doors slammed and she heard voices. Male. One, maybe two? It was hard to tell. Was it a neighbor? Help? Or... her captor? She would have screamed a few times to get their attention but the gag in her mouth kept her silent.

Their boots pounded against wooden planks, then a door opened above. In between the cracks of the floor above her, dust fell.

"We need to stay off the grid for a while. Keep our heads down. No one is going to come up here."

"What about Merle?"

"He's on his own."

Meghan could hear them walking back and forth. She managed to determine there were three of them. Had they brought her there? What were they going to do to her? She tried to recall the news articles that she'd seen about the Green Bank Five. Had they raped them? How did they die? She could barely breathe. Panic rose in her chest. All she could think about was staying alive, getting back to her kid. That was all that mattered now.

They were loud. One of them started laughing. "Oh God, that cop's face. I'm surprised he didn't come after us."

"And that guy. Fucking guy."

"Well, we don't have to think about him now."

"This weekend, Billy, you'll head into Green Bank and pick up some food. I'm sure there is enough here for a few days but it's not going to last. Chances are the streets are going to be crawling with State Police."

"Why do I have to risk it?"

"Because they are probably looking for me. No one

knows you."

"Of course they do."

"Just do as I fucking say."

"Don't I always?"

A bucket was kicked across the floor.

"Hey! Don't give me any attitude. Go down and bring some beers up."

Meghan looked across the room and saw a large fridge in the corner. The door opened at the top of the stairs and light flooded in. The guy was bitching and complaining as he stomped his way down.

"I don't want to go back to prison, Aaron."

"That's not going to happen."

She watched as his legs came into view, then when the rest of him emerged, he got this wild look in his eyes. "Holy cow! Aaron. Hey, Aaron, you are going to want to see this."

"What the hell are you on about?"

His boots stopped at the top of the stairs.

"Down here now."

Protesting all the way, he trudged down. "This better be good."

As he came into view, he sighed. "Oh, you have got to be kidding me. I told him — not here. That damn fool never listens."

"Well at least we can have some fun," Billy said hopping down off the last step.

Chapter 28

Larson drove on autopilot, fully aware that he'd stepped over a line. Ethan might have been able to cover up the incident in the cell but he wouldn't be able to keep Merle's gums from flapping. Still, Ethan was right, he couldn't afford to have more harassment complaints on his file, not at this stage in his career. Heading north on Highway 28, he grumbled to himself. It should have only taken forty minutes to reach Green Bank but the road was clogged up. A little after ten at night, and it should have been clear sailing but there were still tourists packed into SUVs and minivans towing boats. His cruiser crawled behind traffic that was being forced to take a different route due to the multiple blockades that had been set up by State Police.

As he drove, he thought about Jack Winchester. Why would a man risk so much for someone he didn't know? It didn't make any sense. Even if Jenna was paying him, no amount of money could be worth placing himself in the line of fire. Aaron Gance wasn't a man to back down. Merle's words haunted Larson. *She might be, but your wife won't.* He couldn't take that threat lightly. Not after all that had happened. The thought of finding his wife buried in a shallow grave because he didn't put the Gance brothers away ate away at him. That's why he was on his way to Green Bank. He should have remained with the State Police, helped them stop vehicles but something told him that Aaron would be avoiding the main arteries. Though he'd made foolish decisions in the past, he wasn't an idiot.

Larson cast a glance at the scrap of paper. Ten more minutes and he would be there. *Let's hope your hunch is correct, Winchester.*

* * *

Aaron sat in a chair sipping on a beer, wondering how he was going to strike back at Larson. They initially had plans to visit his wife at her home. That's what the masks were for. They would scare the shit out of her, drag her out and bury her in Watogo with the other women. That was until they saw the Shelby. It was a lot of fun but it had seriously thrown a wrench in the works. Now the county was crawling with cops. Any chance of being able to get close to Larson's wife was all but gone.

He took a hard pull on his cigarette and watched as Billy taunted Meghan. He had to admit she was pretty hot, stripped down to her underwear and cuffed. Dale sat off to one side, tossing pieces of scrunched-up paper at her face.

"C'mon, Aaron, I don't see why we can't have a little fun with her. It's not like anyone's going to miss another whore."

"I told you assholes that no one is doing anything until I've spoken with him."

"Just a taste then," Billy said, smirking before running his tongue up the side of her face. Meghan reacted by jerking her head in a whiplash fashion and driving it into his nose. Billy's nose burst and blood began streaming out.

He cupped his hands over his nose. "What the fuck?"

Dale and Aaron started laughing. "Oh God that was good. She is a feisty one."

"Bitch."

Billy grabbed her by the hair and jerked her head back.

"Let her go," Aaron said. Billy shot him a dirty look.

"Oh, I see how it is." He scoffed before releasing his grip. "You just want her all to yourself."

"Shut up."

"No," he crossed the room and snatched up some tissues off the counter to block the scarlet flow. "You've had a thing for her ever since she turned down your offer to be her pimp."

"You don't know what you're on about."

"Isn't that right, Dale?" he said seeking additional support from him. Dale shrugged. He wasn't getting involved.

"Just go and get the rest of our stuff in from the vehicle. And Dale, start a fire, it's getting cold in here."

"No, Dale, don't. Let him do it."

Aaron's eyebrow shot up. "You calling the shots now, Billy?"

He patted the sides of his nose while keeping an eye on Aaron. "No, I'm just tired of taking them."

Aaron looked over to Meghan who was watching intently. She was wearing nothing but a black bra and panties. Her dark hair hung past her shoulders. Billy was right. He did like her but he wasn't going to tell them that. He knew why she turned him down. She was smart, unlike the others. Pimping out women had changed. It was harder to convince girls to go with him now that they had the Internet. They could post an ad in minutes and have four or five calls within the hour. Without a pimp, one hundred percent of the money from clients went to them. They were in control. They were their own boss. Whereas if they worked for him, he took all the money and made sure they had a place to stay, food to eat and protection from abusive clients.

Meghan's dark eyes darted back and forth between them. She looked like a scared mouse.

Aaron rose to his feet but before he could bitch slap him, Billy withdrew his handgun and aimed at him. "Don't do it."

Aaron laughed and tapped his own chest. "You gonna shoot me, Billy?"

Dale tried to intervene but Billy was beyond the point of listening.

"Billy."

"No, fuck it. We are in this mess because of him, because of his brother. I said we should have split a few months back but oh no, you wanted to stay."

"You wanted to split?" Aaron asked.

"You're a fucking idiot and so is Merle. Like did you really think that the cops wouldn't figure it out in the end? All these women showing up dead. Are you that egotistical?"

Aaron was enjoying this. This was a different side to Billy. He'd always been so compliant; definitely not a guy to square off to Merle or him.

"I'm not going to jail for you, Aaron."

"A little late for that now. Your DNA is all over those women."

Billy pointed the gun at an angle like he was some kind of gangster.

"Billy," Dale interjected. "Put the gun down."

"You want to wake up in a cell again, Dale?"

Billy didn't threaten Aaron. He knew he wouldn't pull the trigger; he didn't have the balls to do it. Initially, he stood a few feet away but slowly he inched his way forward.

"Get back, Aaron."

He smiled. "You're not going to shoot."

Billy spoke through gritted teeth while shaking the gun in front of him. "Don't tell me what I will or will not do. I'm tired of listening to you."

"I know you won't because you're a pussy. You always have been."

"Fuck you."

Aaron kept moving forward and Billy took a few steps back. Slowly but surely, Aaron crossed the room until the barrel of the gun was pressed against his chest. He reached up and adjusted the angle so it was against his forehead.

"Go on. Shoot."

"Don't push me."

"Shoot. You're a big man now. Squeeze the trigger!"

He pressed hard against the gun, clutching it and feeling the cold steel embed into his skin.

"DO IT!"

Billy's hand was shaking, Dale looked on nervously.

Seconds passed before Aaron slapped it out of his hand, grabbed Billy by the throat and lunged forward, pinning him against the wall. Billy released his grip on the gun and it clattered on the hardwood floor. Aaron stared into his eyes, teeth gritted. With his other hand free, he reached around to the small of his back and yanked his own revolver out.

"Aaron," Dale immediately tried to get between them but Aaron pointed the gun at him.

"You want it?"

Dale threw his hands up and took a step back. Aaron

turned his attention back to Billy; he placed the barrel against his chest, right over the center of his heart.

"Feel that?"

Tears began to well up in Billy's eyes as Aaron cocked the gun.

He was about to pull the trigger when the sound of tires breaking through gravel caught his attention. Dale hurried over to a window and pushed back the drape a little.

"Fucking cops."

Aaron released his grip on Billy and he let out a relieved breath.

"Shut off that light, and get her downstairs. How many, Dale?"

He snorted. "One. It's Larson."

Chapter 29

Jack burst through the exit door of the sheriff department, staring wildly at the vehicles in the back lot. After knocking Rigby out, he rooted through his pockets for his keys. He pressed the button on the key fob and lights blinked to life. There were two cruisers. One was State Police; the other belonged to Ethan Rigby.

He didn't bother to drive slowly through town; he'd heard sirens long before he turned his on. He sped up through the uneven streets, veering towards the east side of town. He figured he would run into a blockade but being as he was wearing a uniform and driving the cruiser they would let him through without even stopping.

However, that didn't stop his pulse from racing as he drew close to four State Police cruisers. Jack kept his head low and the lights flashing as the cruiser crawled up to the one guy who shone his light inside then waved him on without stopping him. Jack's eyes swept side to side as he waited for them to pull back their cruisers. His heart slammed in his chest thinking that any minute they would get a call from the department telling them to look out for a stolen cruiser. He slapped away the paranoia from his mind and eased his way past them and on to Highway 28, leaving the lights of the town behind in his rearview mirror.

* * *

The place was located at the end of a sparsely inhabited street. Nestled in the surrounding forest, the old place was a ramshackle cabin, fronted with a porch and dirty white siding. Whoever owned the place hadn't taken the time to do any yard work. Overgrown bushes and wildflowers hemmed it in. A rusted-out mailbox at the end of the driveway had no name on it, just the number 669, except the nine had dropped and turned a little making it look like another six.

As Larson made his way into the drive, he saw a black Ford truck parked off to one side. His eyes flitted to the windows but there were no lights on. Was there anyone home? He brought the cruiser to a crawl and sat there for a moment; the engine idling. He stared at the windows that had shabby-looking drapes. He stepped out of the car with his gun drawn and moved around the truck, stopping only to place his hand on the hood. It was still warm. Someone was home. He backed up a little and radioed through to get them to run the plates. He pulled out his flashlight and positioned it across his other hand holding the Glock. Static came from the radio as he waited for them to get back to him.

A minute or two and they came back with some name he didn't recognize. There was no report of it having been stolen and yet it didn't match the address.

"Copy that."

He pressed on towards the cabin pushing past the overgrown bushes and climbed the steps onto the porch. He listened intently for any movement inside. His nerves were on edge. His hands were clammy and though he knew he should call for backup, he didn't because the chief would want to know why he had left his post without permission. There was no denying it. He was treading in hot water and this was liable to cost him his badge but something about Winchester's run-in with the Gance brothers, along with what he'd unearthed told him that this wasn't his first rodeo. He knew a thing or two about tracking people.

Larson peered in through the front window, he saw the silhouette of a few pieces of furniture; a table, four chairs, and a sofa. By any measure, the place looked peaceful like any ordinary cottage in the country. A nearby river could be heard rushing in the background. After trying the front door, he gave it a knock and stepped off the porch with his gun at the ready. Seconds, then minutes passed without any answer. He worked his way around the back, peering into different windows through thin, dirty drapes that blocked out most of the view. It was hard to see anything at night.

He returned to the truck and peered in through the window. There was a packet of smokes on the dashboard but beyond that nothing to indicate who might own it.

He cast a glance around before heading back towards the cabin.

Finally, he made it to the back door and gave it a twist. It was locked.

He shone his light down and saw four cigarette butts on the ground. Larson crouched and picked them up. One of them had recently been put out. He wasn't feeling good about this. Again for a few seconds, he contemplated calling in backup.

Everything inside him told him this was not a good move but the way he saw it, if the owner was asleep, he could just make up some bullshit about having received a noise complaint and that someone had been spotted lurking around their property. It was a page right out of Ethan's handbook but it worked. He'd seen him do it. That was the thing about the public, most didn't really know what the police could or couldn't do. If they did, they would realize their hands were tied more than they knew.

He looked again through the window, this time

cupping his hand over the pane of glass and waiting a few more seconds, just in case the owner had heard his first knock and was taking their time to crawl out of bed.

It was dark inside. No movement. Only a faint glimmer of light from a crescent moon illuminated a few spots in the cabin. He shone his light at the door. He could hear his wife's voice reminding him that he had a daughter.

He ground his teeth together. *This is your job, do your job!*

Screw it! He thought, before kicking in the back door. Wood splintered and scattered all over the floor. "County Sheriff Department."

There was no answer, so he stepped inside, hoping that Winchester was right about this.

Chapter 30

The cabin was darker than any residence he'd been inside. Larson's flashlight started to flicker, so he tapped it a few times against his leg. *Not now. Don't die on me now.* The farther he ventured inside, the less of the moon filtered through the drapes. Nothing but endless black was before him. Every step he took made a floorboard creak. Every so often he thought he saw a shadow move until he swept his light over it. As he swung around into the living area, he raked his gun back and forth, his heart pounding in his chest. Most of the furniture was covered in white sheets except for the four chairs. There was an ashtray on the ground; an open bottle of beer and what looked like loose binds around one of the chairs. He stepped forward and bent down to touch the bottle. It was ice-cold. Someone was here, of that he was sure.

There was a sound, barely noticeable. *What is that?*

Was his mind playing tricks on him? Remaining where

he was, he crouched, brought his ear to the floor and listened intently. It sounded like muffled cries. Slowly he walked towards a doorway that led back into the corridor on the far side of the room. As he came out, he hugged the wall with his back while holding his Glock out in front of him.

No. Again his flashlight started flickering, and this time it went out.

Enveloped by darkness he waited a few seconds for his eyes to adjust before giving the flashlight another hard smack. It didn't turn back on. *Shit!*

Up ahead he noticed the faint glimmer of light below a doorway.

His pulse sped up as he got closer. He placed a hand on the knob and gave it a twist. It opened. He couldn't escape the feeling that he was somehow making a mistake by entering alone, whoever was in here could be waiting for him.

If he wanted to back out, he needed to do it now.

Pushing his fears aside, he opened the door and gazed

down the steps that led into the basement. For a brief second, he cast a glance over his shoulder and it was then as he stepped inside that Larson felt as if he was being watched.

* * *

Jack brought the car to a crawl as the cruiser and truck ahead of him came into sight. He switched off his lights while the car idled. It was probably Larson but it could be anyone. He might have sent a different officer to check the cabin out. He contemplated backing up and putting the vehicle out of sight. He gripped the wheel tight as his eyes took in his surroundings. Every nerve ending was on high alert. Ahead he could just make out a faint glow coming from a window at the foundation of the cabin.

To be on the safe side, he shifted the gear stick into reverse and slowly eased out of the driveway before parking just a few yards away from the mouth of another road.

Cracking the door, he pushed out and pulled the Glock from its holster, and proceeded to head back to the cabin. There was no telling what trouble he was about to encounter.

* * *

At the bottom of the staircase, the woman came into view. It was Meghan Palmer. Her wrists were tied with rope to a steel pole in the center of the room. Surrounding her were four small candles. Each flame flickered, providing a small amount of light, enough to see her but keeping the rest of the room shrouded in darkness. He swept the corners with his gun for a second, one last check before moving towards her.

With every step, her eyes grew wider and her cries louder. She was trying to communicate but with her mouth gagged it was impossible for him to make out what she was saying. Instinctively Larson holstered his weapon and crossed the room, crouched down and began untying her binds.

"It's okay, you're safe now."

She was yelling even louder now.

"Don't move. I'll get you out."

She wriggled hard and her eyes kept flaring. Larson's brow furrowed as he realized she was trying to motion with her head towards the corner of the room. He reached up for her gag so he could make sense but it was too late.

It happened so fast Larson couldn't even comprehend it.

One second he was untying Meghan — or trying to free her, when all of a sudden he felt a dull smack to the back of his head. He was struck with so much force it knocked him to the floor.

Before he had time to react, he could see Meghan reacting. Fear flashed across her face. As he tried to go for his Glock, he was struck again, this time even harder causing his ear to bleed. His head throbbed and he could taste blood in his mouth.

Behind him, a voice echoed off the walls.

"Oh, I've waited a long time for this."

As Larson tried to get up, he felt a boot force him down. Coming into view from two of the darkened corners were Billy and Dale. He didn't even need to turn his head to know who was behind him. He recognized the asshole's voice long before his face loomed over.

"I'll take that," Aaron said reaching down and removing his firearm. He then grabbed the handcuffs from his pouch on the side of his duty belt and used them to cuff him. He kicked Larson in the back, pushing him towards the steel pole. "Move it, asshole!"

With her hands released, and all the focus shifted to Larson, Meghan had untied her ankles. In a sudden burst of energy, Meghan shot to her feet and raced towards the staircase. Wincing in pain, Larson watched as Billy rushed towards Meghan and grabbed her by the back of the hair as she tried to escape.

"Where the hell do you think you're going, bitch?"

Billy lashed out with a hook but she ducked and drove her shoulder into his stomach like an NFL player, driving him to the floor. Vaulting over, she catapulted herself to the staircase and began clambering up, raking each step with her fingers. She managed to make it three steps before Dale grabbed her leg and brought her crashing to the bottom.

"Come here, you whore."

Even as she hit the floor, she didn't give up. She didn't care about the weapon in either of their hands. Survival mode had kicked in and she was going to do everything she could to escape, even if it meant dying in the process.

"For fuck's sake, grab her!" Aaron said while keeping his revolver against the side of Larson's temple. All Larson could do was watch and hope.

Dale drove a fist into her gut and she cried out before raking his face with her hands. The punch barely slowed her down. In a flash she was up again crawling on her hands and knees up the stairs, tears falling from her face. Larson took it all in, every second of the violent attack on her. By now Billy was up and cursing and gripping his stomach. As Dale grabbed the back of Meghan, she lashed out with a donkey kick and struck him in the nuts so hard that he doubled over. Billy hurried over and scaled up the stairs as she disappeared out of sight.

The next thing he heard was Meghan screaming hysterically.

"Come here, bitch," Billy yelled. There was a loud thud, then another and then silence.

A few seconds passed and Billy came back into view, dragging her down the stairs by one leg. Her body bounced off each step. Meghan let out a faint groan, tears dripping from her face.

"Get up," Aaron said.

He staggered on his knees and fell forward close to Meghan.

"Others are coming," Larson muttered, hoping to buy himself some time and put a little fear into the three of them.

"Yeah?" Aaron said leaning over him. "Billy, go check outside."

He hurried away, his boots pounding against the staircase as he went up.

"You dumbasses must be the biggest idiots in West Virginia. The county is crawling with State Police. It's only a matter of time and you're going to be locked up with your brother. No getting out this time, asshole."

Aaron clubbed him across the back of the head with the butt of his gun. "Shut the hell up."

It didn't take long for Billy to return.

"Nothing, Aaron. Just his cruiser."

Aaron let out a chuckle and circled around both of them jabbing the air with his revolver. "I've got to say this is sweet. I was going to take your wife but now I have you, it doesn't really matter, now does it?"

"I can't wait to see your face when they toss you inside and throw away the key."

He stopped for a second and crouched down beside Larson. "Well, that's not going to happen. As you don't have shit on me."

"No? Your brother told us everything. Everything," he spat back.

Aaron spoke through gritted teeth. "You're lying."

"Am I?" He smiled. "Then why are officers digging up bodies of women you have killed and buried in Watogo

State Park?" He let out a laugh. "You are fucked!"

Rage filled Aaron's face; his breathing became faster before he looked at Meghan.

"Billy, get her out of here. Take her to the river, kill her."

"How?"

"I don't care. Just do it."

Meghan let out a whimper. "No. No. NO!"

Billy got this big grin on his face as he stepped in and untied her. She screamed and tried to fight back but was soon quieted by three sharp jabs to the side of her head with the butt of his gun. He hauled her up and slung her over his shoulder and trudged off up the stairs.

"Listen up, Aaron. You don't have to do this. She's done nothing. It's over."

"Over?" he chuckled. "It's not over. It's just begun."

With that said, he bounced Larson's head off the metal pole.

* * *

Jack stood in the shadows, his lips forming a tight line

as he took it all in. The stranger was lugging her over his shoulder. Gripping her with one arm and holding a handgun in the other. Jack nearly walked right into his line of sight as he came up to the mouth of the driveway. He half expected the guy to see him as he dumped the girl into the back of the truck's cab, but he didn't look down the driveway.

The surrounding darkness was punctuated by the faint flicker of stars providing just enough light to make out who he was carrying. It was Meghan.

If that was her, where was the officer? Or had they simply stolen a cruiser? Perhaps Larson hadn't even made it here. The truck's engine roared to life, the red taillights glowed like eyes in the night as it began backing up. *Where are you taking her?* She had no one. No one who could help her. His eyes darted over to the house. What if she was dead? He had to know.

Rounding the thick bush, Jack hurried back to the cruiser, knowing he had to follow, if only to punish whoever had taken her.

* * *

Larson felt his ears being crushed from both sides as Aaron's boot pressed down on the side of his face. The sole cut into his cheek and he was sure that his teeth would break at any second. Aaron kept tapping the barrel of the gun against his temple.

"Now, what to do with you?"

Larson fell back on his training. Communication was key in extreme situations. Hundreds of people had been talked down from a ledge, coerced into dropping a weapon and giving up through negotiation. But Aaron wasn't one to negotiate.

His radio crackled, and Aaron tore it off and had Dale stamp on it.

"You won't be needing that."

"Aaron, don't make this any worse than it already is. If you want freedom, go now, but if you kill me you are going to end up in the chair for sure."

"Stop with that negotiating shit. That won't work. I don't care."

Larson swallowed hard, it tasted like he had vomit in his mouth. Aaron leaned his weight onto the leg that was over Larson. The pain was getting worse and Larson tried to shift but he was pinned so tight, it was impossible. He wasn't going to plead for his life. Not in front of this guy. He squinted as he looked up at Aaron, trying to get him to listen to reason.

"We are beyond that. You and I know that."

"So why did you kill them?"

"Because they were whores."

"That's it?"

"Do I need a better reason?"

Slowly he released the pressure from his boot and stepped back. "Dale, get him up. Let's take him upstairs." Larson struggled as Dale hauled him up and Aaron kept his gun on him. He could have fought back but it wouldn't have helped. If they were willing to kill women and dump their bodies, they wouldn't think twice about putting a bullet in him. All he could think about was Kerry and his daughter. He had to stay alive for them.

That alone prevented him from taking a risk. Instead, he inwardly berated himself for stepping foot in the cabin in the first place. His need for retribution outweighed common sense.

He was forced into a chair. Dale tied his legs and made sure his hands were locked firmly behind his back before he stepped out of the way and Aaron got close.

Aaron placed his gun down and began rolling up his sleeves.

"I'm going to enjoy this."

He fired off two gut punches, and a hook to his face causing the whole chair to topple over.

"Get him up," he commanded Dale as he took a few steps back. Larson coughed hard. Pain coursed through his body as Aaron grabbed him by the throat and unloaded one jab after the next into his face until he had broken his nose. Warm blood coursed down his face.

"What a mess," Aaron continued speaking. "If you had just minded your own business, this could have been avoided. But oh no, you had to go sticking your nose in where it wasn't wanted. And just look at what's happened. Bonnie is dead. So you didn't save her. And soon you'll join her."

He reared back his fist again but this time Larson muttered something as blood dribbled down from his lips.

"What's that?" Aaron asked, leaning forward. Larson lifted his head flashing him a bloody grin.

"I said… Is that all you've got? Pussy!"

Aaron's eyes went wild with fury before unleashing the next vicious beating. He knew death was coming but he wasn't going to give that asshole the satisfaction he wanted. Not before, not now, not ever.

Chapter 31

Jack waited until the truck passed by the alcove of trees where he'd parked the cruiser before he stabbed the gas and rolled out behind the truck. He flipped on the flashing blue light. There was no point attempting to follow from a distance as there was no traffic to hide behind on the narrow dirt road that led down to a rushing river. He figured the simple approach would work best — it didn't. Jack saw the driver of the truck cast a glance over his shoulder. Instead of pulling over to one side, he floored the gas and took off at a high rate of speed.

Did he honestly think he could outrun a police cruiser? These things were custom-built for speed. Jack ground his foot against the accelerator and sank back into the seat as it exploded forward. Quickly, he caught up with the truck and tried to go around him but the truck began swerving erratically.

As the truck tore up the road ahead of him, Jack tried to make a pit maneuver. Cops were notorious for doing it in high-speed chases. It required getting up alongside until the front wheels were in alignment with the rear tires, and then with a sharp jerk of the steering wheel, it would send a vehicle into a spin.

He was fully aware that Meghan was inside and there was a chance it would flip but if he didn't take drastic action, he might cross onto the surrounding fields and lose him, and cross-country was one thing cruisers weren't built for. The truck rumbled like a jackhammer, moving side to side to prevent him from pulling up.

A cigarette butt was flicked from the driver's side out the open window. It hit the road, ashes sparked before the cruiser streaked over it. Again he tried to come up alongside him. Tires screeched, and the cruiser nearly left the road at one point. On either side was nothing but forest, dense, dark and all consuming. The truck was eating up the dirt as Jack roared after him. He slapped the gears into action, maneuvered tightly around turns before feigning to go left. *Yes!* The cruiser squeezed in scraping the backside of the truck.

As they burst out into a clearing that was heading for a bridge that went over the North Fork River, Jack knew it was now or never. There was no way both of them were going to cross over the bridge side by side. He accelerated hard, and then slammed the brake to adjust to the rear tires before jerking hard to the right, then left. The cruiser crashed into the rear tires, sending the truck spinning like a corkscrew. The driver must have attempted to stop because smoke was coming off the tires. All he could do was watch as it struck the corner of the bridge and flipped over the edge, down the embankment, and into the river.

Jack hit the gas and launched forward like a missile, turning sharply before the bridge and hopping out. He hurried over to the edge and spotted it. It was upside down and taking in water. The guy had managed to get out and was splashing around. His head was barely above the water that was frothing and slapping up against him as he clung to the sinking truck.

"Help! I can't swim."

Jack didn't give a shit about him but Meghan... he vaulted over the small bridge down twenty feet into the frigid waters. He gasped as the cold took his breath. The current was strong, dragging at his legs. He swam over to the truck and dived beneath the surface. Below it was even darker than it appeared from above. It didn't help that it was disorienting. That's when he spotted her. She was up against the window banging on it. He tried to point to the other side that was open but she was in a state of panic. He came up for air, and swam around to the other side. He was just about to dive when that asshole latched on to him.

"Help me please."

He was struggling and making it even harder for Jack to move.

"Get the fuck off!" Jack cracked him on the side of the face with a hook but he didn't let go. Jack grabbed him by the neck, placed another hand on his head and shoved him under. The man desperately raked at Jack's skin, his jagged nails cutting in and tearing his shirt. All the while the truck was slowly sinking. He knew if he didn't act fast, she was going to drown if she hadn't already.

There was no time to keep him under, he released his grip and pushed away, taking one big deep breath before diving. Jack kicked his legs and swam against the current until he came up alongside the open driver's side window. He pulled himself inside only to find Meghan no longer struggling. He grabbed a hold of her, yanked her towards him and slipped back out the window while tugging hard. It took every ounce of strength to keep him from being torn away and carried off by the river.

As they breached the surface, he let out a gasp and swallowed more water.

Jack gagged at the taste.

There was no time to drag Meghan back to the embankment. While trying to keep her head above the water he began breathing into her mouth. *C'mon, c'mon!* All the while he could hear the man yelling nearby. That fucker was still not dead. He ignored his cries for help and kept breathing in. He needed to pump her chest.

He was about to drag her back when she let out a splutter. Water spewed from her mouth, and her eyes went wide.

"You scared the shit out of me. I thought you were gone."

"Jack?" she asked as she started to come to grips with where she was.

He grinned. "Let's get you to the edge."

Jack guided her and had taken just a few arm lengths when he felt a hand grab his back. It happened fast. Meghan let out a scream before his ears were filled with water. One second he was on the surface, the next dragged under. He spun around to find the man trying to clamber on top of his back. Fighting underwater wasn't easy. It was even harder when dealing with a guy desperate to survive. It also didn't help that his clothes and the ten-pound police officer's duty belt were weighing him down. Circling around and around, he tried to pry the man's herculean grip away. A sudden whoosh of the undercurrent and both of them were swept away towards the truck that was now fully engulfed in water. The current smashed them into the side of the steel as if they were nothing more than loose leaves.

In that moment the man released his grip and Jack watched as the current sucked him away. He'd never forget his eyes — wild, swollen and full of fear.

Jack, however, was pinned against the vehicle, above, he could see the shimmering reflection of the moon on the surface getting farther away. He turned and noticed that his ripped shirt was caught in the twisted metal. It was pulling him under, down into the deep, down into a watery grave.

He tugged at the shirt a few times, but it was no use. It was lodged in tight, caught up and tangled around the metal. It also didn't help that he'd used most of his strength just trying to fight off the man beneath the water.

His chest started heaving for air.

Desperation was setting in.

His eyes went wide.

Instead of fighting it, Jack tore at the front of his shirt until the buttons snapped and he was able to slip out from the shirt. Like a snake shedding its skin, Jack slipped away from the tangled clothing and headed for the surface.

Gasping for air, he inhaled deeply; feeling the surge of oxygen hit his lungs.

"Jack!" Meghan yelled swimming over to him. He grabbed a hold of her and slowly but surely both of them swam back to the edge. When they made it to the muddy embankment, both raked at the earth pulling themselves out of the water until they collapsed from exhaustion.

Chapter 32

"They have him," Meghan blurted out.

Five minutes later, speeding around turns along the long stretch of dirt road that snaked its way through the forest and thick brush, they were now getting closer to the cabin. Out of breath, chilled to the bone and furious, Jack could still see the cruiser as he eased off the gas and hopped out. Before heading in, he leaned back inside.

"Get on the radio, call for backup. If I don't come out, you get the hell out of here, okay?"

"Jack."

"Just do it," he said. Removing the shotgun from the center of the police cruiser, he checked that it was loaded before jogging towards the cabin at a hunch. Lights were now on inside. Through the thin drapes that shielded the windows, the silhouette of a stranger glided back and forth ahead of him. Jack felt a nagging sense of recognition. The way his shoulder bounced a little, the

jabbing of the hand in the air and the way he moved...
Jack had seen that before. Aaron Gance. He would have
thought he'd learned his lesson the first time he whipped
his ass but some men didn't learn. In the shadows of the
night, he watched trying to decide the best course of
action. There was no easy way to do it but an officer's life
hung in the balance.

That's when a second man came to the window and
peered out. Jack shifted back behind a tree trunk and
waited until he moved away. Slipping out he faced
forward again and ran up, now parallel to the front
entrance of the building. He drew near focusing on the
window that gave him a clear shot of those inside. He
took in the scene. Chairs toppled on their sides, the
muffled noise of a man groaning while someone laughed.
He could now see Larson slumped forward in his chair
while the other two were chugging back on beer. They
placed the bottles down and Aaron took another swing,
knocking him to the ground.

As he watched and crept forward, his boot touched

one of the steps on the porch and it let out a creak. Aaron and Dale froze.

"Billy?"

That's right, you're expecting him back, he thought.

"Get your ass in here and stop messing around," Aaron's voice came in a rasp as he stared at the window. Could he see Jack? No, it was too dark outside.

When there was no response, a different expression crossed Aaron's face, one of comprehension. He pulled out a revolver from the small of his back and nodded to Dale. Dale strode over to the window and peered out. Jack pulled back into the shadows expecting them to come out. He raised the shotgun anticipating the door to swing open. It didn't.

What he heard next was movement off to his right. It was quick but not quick enough that he couldn't move. By the time the trigger was pulled, Jack had already dived out of the way, taking cover in a thicket of trees. He glanced back over his shoulder towards the cruiser — Meghan was still in there, the dome light inside illuminating her. *No.* He waved trying to get her attention but she was on the radio, completely distracted.

* * *

Coughing and spluttering, another wave of pain coursed through his body.

Larson was unable to move, tied to the chair, but from what he could hear and see through blurred vision he was able to make out what was happening.

Was it backup? Ethan?

Someone was causing enough trouble that they had left the room. All that mattered was Aaron's beating had stopped and they were gone. Larson tried to slip his hands through the cuffs but they were too tight. He wasn't getting out of here. And whoever had shown up had just bought themselves a one-way ticket to the grave.

From his scrunched-up position on the floor, he could hear gunshots outside and Aaron yelling to Dale. The silhouette of a figure dashed past the window. The flash of a gun muzzle and a cry as someone hit the ground in agony.

All the while he tried to at least free his legs. They were held in place by nothing more than rope. Now that he was on the floor, tilted on his side, he shifted his legs down towards the ends and forced the loops off the chair legs. A split second of relief was followed by panic as more gunshots ricocheted, then he heard Dale cry out and start cursing.

He heard Aaron's voice nearby as if he had stepped back into the cabin for a brief second before firing his gun wildly and racing out into the night.

What followed was an explosion as glass shattered on one of the windows. Fragments sailed across the floor stopping near his face. Some of the slivers of glass rained down on him, nicking his skin. Whoever was out there, they were giving those two assholes heck. Rocking back and forth, Larson tried to get onto his knees so he could get up. The awkward position he was in made it almost impossible. He shifted his feet across the hardwood floor moving a few inches at a time towards the wall. If he could get close to that, he could push up against it and stand.

He winced in pain as he tried to move. His teeth were broken, and his mouth was filled with blood. He was pretty sure that he had several broken ribs and something had ruptured inside, as every movement was extreme agony.

Outside he could hear the banging of someone against the side of the cabin as if embroiled in a brawl. Something hard connecting with a wooden beam was followed by the faint sound of Dale groaning.

Aaron appeared in the doorway, staggering a little and reaching for his arm that was bleeding. "Motherfucker!"

He was paying no attention to Larson; his entire focus had shifted to the attackers. He assumed it was more than one person attacking otherwise they wouldn't have stood a chance against these two. They were known for playing dirty and wouldn't have batted an eye in killing someone in cold blood. Aaron raised his gun around the wall and fired a few times before bolting out again. The sound of his boots pounding the wood ended as he exited the cabin.

More shouting, scuffling and the sound of a body being slammed up against the side of the cabin with such force that it caused the floor to vibrate.

Dale let out a high-pitched cry before he came soaring through one of the windows. The glass erupted in an explosion. He landed in a heap a few feet away from Larson, letting out a faint gasp before going limp. His skin had been slashed to pieces. He would have cracked a smile if his face didn't hurt so damn much.

More yelling ensued, this time coming from Aaron.

"Come on, you sonofabitch. Where are you?"

More running. From where he was he could see the rear exit. Aaron stumbled backward and fired off a few more rounds. He shouted again and staggered in, now holding his leg. When he came into view, he could see that he'd been shot. His eyes darted over to Dale.

"Dale, get up."

But Dale wasn't going anywhere. If he wasn't dead already, he probably would be soon. He'd received several shots to the stomach and was bleeding out. Aaron dragged his leg, keeping an eye on the doorway while he crossed the room to Dale to check on him.

Larson squinted, his eye sockets were swollen and he was barely able to make out what was going on around him. That's when the sound of boots on the roof could be heard. Running back and forth. *What the hell?*

Aaron was in full panic mode. His eyes flitted back and forth before he fired a few rounds upward. "You want some of this? Come on then!"

He unleashed everything he had left in that revolver before loading it again. All the while he was muttering to himself. It was the incoherent babbling of a man that knew he was about to die.

Aaron fired another wild shot at the ceiling, and then there was silence.

"Who the fuck is this guy?" Aaron asked Larson as if he would know.

Guy?

Right then a figure dashed past the window and

opened fire on Aaron. A round caught him in the shoulder and spun him like a spinning top. Desperation kicked in and he fired again, unloading another six rounds at the wall, peppering it.

That's when he heard the stranger enter the rear door.

Aaron reached into his pockets to load his gun again but he was all out of ammo.

"Shit. Shit," he said over and over again as the sound of boots got closer. Larson was in so much pain, and barely able to see, but he watched through slit eyelids as Aaron tried searching Dale for a weapon. Then he saw Aaron backing up, his hand lifting.

"Look, man, we can talk about this."

Larson tried to shift around to see who it was but it wasn't easy. That's when he saw a mass of darkness race forward, bull-charging Aaron and knocking him out of the shattered window onto the porch outside. He was sure he recognized it as a police uniform. *Ethan?* Though he couldn't see what going on, he could hear Aaron pleading for mercy. The sound of bone colliding with bone seemed louder in the silence of the forest. It continued for a few minutes. A hard pounding as if a fist connected with a jaw over and over again.

What followed was a single gunshot.

Then, it was silent, nothing but heavy breathing. In the distance, the faint sound of sirens echoed. A minute or two passed and he heard the stranger enter the rear of the cabin and make his way into the room. When he crouched in front of him, Larson couldn't believe his eyes.

"You?"

"Let's get you out of here. Where's the key?"

"Uh… Over there."

Jack crossed the room and picked up a handcuff key on the table.

Questions swirled in Larson's mind as he went about freeing him.

"Meghan?"

"She's safe," Jack answered.

"But how…?"

"No time for questions."

He helped Larson up and carried him outside before laying him on the porch, not far from the dead body of Aaron Gance.

"The flash drive, where is it?" Jack asked.

Larson winced in agony. "What?"

"The flash drive. It was in the duffel bag."

Larson gave a nod towards his cruiser. Jack hurried over and retrieved it from the back seat before returning. The sound of sirens were almost upon them. He crouched down and placed a hand on Larson's shoulder. "You good?" Jack asked.

He nodded gripping his ribs. The squeal of tires captured his attention. Blue lights flashing. Police. Medical. Ahead of him he could see Meghan step out of the vehicle. An array of headlights cut into the night. He turned back to say something to Jack, but he was gone.

Chapter 33

Three days later, Jack sat inside a black, rented 4 x 4 truck outside the home of Jenna Whitmore's family in Durbin. The small town was a blip on the map, having a population of only two hundred and ninety-three people. It was north of Green Bank. He looked down at the fresh copy of the *Pocahontas Times* in his lap and read the article:

SEVEN MORE BODIES FOUND IN WATOGA STATE PARK
Cops say locals murdered the Green Bank Five
Two suspects shot dead by police, one in custody
Missing journalist among 12 dead

The discovery of seven bodies three days ago in Watoga State Park brings an end to a killing spree and the total number of murder victims to 12 including journalist Jenna

Whitmore who was investigating the case.

Merle Gance, 34, a mechanic, reportedly told investigators he had nothing to do with the murders and that all responsibility fell on the shoulders of his younger brother, Aaron Gance, and friends Billy Irving and Dale Markoff, who were killed during the rescue of another intended victim.

However, investigators aren't convinced. Merle Gance denies any involvement with the Green Bank Five or Whitmore, and states that he only knows about the women found in Watoga State Park. He is being held without bond on accessory to murder charges and is scheduled to appear in court Wednesday.

Behind the mask of public service, there was evidence of something terribly wrong with the Gance brothers — all ignored until the skeletons were found in shallow graves. Pocahontas County authorities declined to comment until a thorough investigation is concluded.

Police said they would release more information as it becomes available.

Outside the sun was high in the sky. A few birds broke away from a cluster of trees. Jack breathed in deeply and shook his head. Though he had managed to save Meghan, it burned him to know that Jenna had died before he could reach her. He figured she was probably killed not long after the phone call, long before he arrived in Marlinton. He turned his head towards her mother's residence.

It wasn't going to be easy, but it was the least he could do.

Jack pushed out of the truck and crossed the quiet street.

Her mother lived in a single-wide trailer at the west end of town on the outskirts of Durbin. The place wasn't much to look at. The cream plastic siding was cracked and fading. The trailer itself was crouched on stacked cinder blocks with weeds and tall grass growing up beneath it. Though it was in a run-down neighborhood, she'd obviously taken the time to try to make the yard look inviting. A small patch of grass was cut short; a bed full of flowers brought some color to a low-income area. A small series of stones snaked up to the doorway. Outside a wind chime jangled in the breeze. He gazed around. It was quiet, and from the looks of her neighbors, it appeared to be part of a small retirement community. A few trailers down, an old man watered his flowers, minding his own business. An elderly lady rode past on a bike before stopping at a mailbox to collect mail.

Jack gave a short knock on the red door and stepped back.

He heard shuffling before it opened wide.

"Can I help you?"

The woman was frail. She wore a small flowery dress, the material practically hung off her shoulders without form. She had to have been in her mid-seventies but time had not been kind to her. There were dark circles and bags under her eyes, and she had some bruising on her lower leg as if she'd recently had a fall.

"I'm a friend of Jenna." He extended a hand. "Jack Winchester."

She shook it and he noticed how clammy and cold her hands were.

When she didn't invite him in, he reached into his pocket and pulled out the small flash drive. "I have something that I think your daughter would have wanted you to have. Do you mind if I come in?"

She looked nervous.

"I won't take up much of your time."

"How did you know her?"

"Through business."

"Oh, journalism. Okay, come on in," she said, turning and heading back inside.

Jack climbed the four metal steps up into the cramped living space. There wasn't much to it. The trailer stretched before him leading down to a single bedroom with a bathroom. The kitchen had barely enough room to turn around. While the floors were covered in a new carpet, it was unable to hide how warped it felt. Humidity, he assumed. Jack stepped inside and felt like he was walking on a slant. The vinyl flooring in the kitchen was faded, scuffed and turning up at the corners and the countertops were scratched.

It really didn't look like a home for anyone, let alone an aging woman.

Every single wall was covered in framed photos, some in color, others in black and white. She walked over to a small table and took a seat, picking up a lit cigarette that was perched in a dirty ashtray. Beside that was a copy of the newspaper he'd been reading earlier. There was an old Windows laptop nearby, and two coffee-stained cups that looked in desperate need of cleaning.

"Can I get you some coffee?"

"It's fine. This won't take long."

"Do you work for the *Times*?"

"No. I mainly do freelancing," he said, just giving her an answer off the top of his head. He could tell she was nervous or had some arthritis. Her hand twitched ever so slightly.

"Yeah, my Jenna did that for a while. She always had these aspirations to work for the *New York Times*. Big lofty goals, that was my Jenna. Never satisfied with the Status quo. Always after the truth."

"Do you mind?" Jack asked motioning towards a seat.

"Oh please. Where are my manners?" She got up and wiped off the seat and he sat down. Then she picked up a cup and went into the kitchen and began making coffee.

"So you live alone?" Jack asked.

"For the past six years. I used to live with a friend but she passed away from cancer. Before that I had my husband, Harold, but he died back when Jenna was in her early twenties."

"Did she get along with him?"

"She adored him. I think more than me." She went still, holding a spoon in her hand and looking out a window as if recalling the past. She sniffed and continued pouring hot water into the cup and giving it a stir. "We had our issues. Small things now that I think about it but both of us were as stubborn as one another."

She shuffled over and took a seat.

"Does your computer work?" he asked.

"Yeah, you need to use it?"

He held up a flash drive and tapped the air with it. "I want to show you something."

It took a minute or so to load up the computer into Windows and then he stuck the flash drive in the side and brought up a window full of folders and files. He clicked on the one that had the photos and letter, and then dragged it across to her laptop, and then he removed the flash drive. After he clicked on a few of the photos and they enlarged. Jack turned the computer.

Her eyes lit up, and a smile formed at the sides of her mouth, creating tiny creases. She tapped the keys a few times and rotated through the photos. "I never knew she kept these. They were from a long time ago. When things were good, less stressful. When..." she trailed off and glanced at him, and for a second looked as if she was going to say something but then returned to browsing through the photos. She laughed a couple of times and it brought a smile to Jack's face. He could see the strain of her daughter's death had taken its toll on her.

"Beautiful. Thank you."

"There's one last thing."

Jack turned the computer and brought up the letter, then handed the computer back.

He rose from his seat and started browsing the photos on the walls. Many were from when Jenna and Corey were much younger. He could hear her mother mumbling to herself as she read it. Once she was done, she closed the laptop and reached for a few tissues to wipe away the tears. Despite their disagreements, Jack didn't want to suggest that Jenna cared for her mother more than she knew. That wasn't for him to say. Instead, he hoped the letter she'd penned clarified, even if it was late.

"Did Corey always want to be a church leader?" Jack asked, seeing old pictures of him dressed in heavy metal clothing and smoking cigarettes. It was a stark contrast to the way he remembered him — clean-cut, shirt and tie, polished shoes.

She let out a snort. "My Corey? No, he was a handful when he was a youngster — a real troublemaker. Drugs mostly. My husband and I used to attend New Hope, so my kids grew up in that world. When they hit their teen years, they both rebelled. You know how kids are but the pastor, Tim Mathers, never gave up on either one of them." She sighed. "If it wasn't for him I don't know where Corey would be today. He had a tendency to run around with the wrong crowd."

Jack nodded and smiled as he saw a photo of Jenna holding Corey's head in a headlock. His eyes drifted from photo to photo and then, he narrowed his gaze towards a photo that looked familiar.

Jenna's mother must have noticed him staring as she spoke up. "That one was taken about eight years ago. It belonged to my father."

In the photo was a picture of Corey standing beside Jenna with his arm around her, and off to the right was Aaron Gance perched on the hood of a Mustang with a beer in hand. Behind them was the cabin. The same one he'd visited a few nights ago, the same one where Meghan and Larson were held.

"Those goofballs used to spend the summers up there. They absolutely loved it. When my father passed away, Corey took it upon himself to look after the place."

Jack nodded. "You get up there much?"

"No. I can't bring myself to go there. Not after losing him."

"Did Corey spend a lot of time with Aaron?"

"Oh yeah, back in the day they were best friends. I used to always tell him that Aaron was a bad influence on him but he would wave me off and say, 'Oh Mom, give it a rest.'" She took a sip of her coffee. "When Corey returned to being involved in the church, he tried to get Aaron to go along but he wouldn't have anything to do with it. Corey kind of took it hard but was determined to reach him. He never gave up on him. It's strange but even after all these years they still remained friends. At least that's what Corey says." She shook her head and gazed down at the newspaper. "That's why it's hard to believe Aaron did what the cops say he did."

Jack turned and nodded. "Yeah, it is."

"Corey will miss him."

"I bet he will. Where is he by the way?"

"Corey? Oh, he left for the cabin this morning, said he had to clean the place up."

Jack smiled briefly. "Do you think I could use your phone?"

Chapter 34

Corey Whitmore stood in the ramshackle cabin, his hands clasped around a broom as he swept up the shattered glass. He grimaced, thinking that it was going to cost a small fortune to fix the two large windows, siding that was peppered by gunshots, the busted-up back door, along with the porch rocker that had been obliterated.

Were the police going to foot the bill? Like hell they were. They didn't even have the decency to remove the yellow taping. A black bag off to his left was crammed full of the stuff. He'd considered putting a claim into the insurance company but that would have only caused a spike in payments, and he was already paying enough.

As for Aaron, Billy and Dale, well, they got what they deserved. *Idiots.*

He stared down at the pool of dried blood. There was no way he was going to be able to get that out of the wood. It would require replacing the flooring. He gritted his teeth, his mind churning over his disgust and hatred for the police. They'd been in touch with his mother a day after the incident and told them that Aaron had broken in but withheld the details of the damage, only saying it was probably best to contact their insurance company. *More idiots.*

Corey swept up the slivers of glass into the pan and disposed of it in a large cardboard box. He carefully picked it up and headed out the back. In the distance he could hear the babble of the river, he'd become attuned to its rhythm. With the box under one arm, he navigated around the tall pine and fir trees and made his way down to the water's edge. There, in the soft soil, he emptied the box of glass into a three-foot hole he'd dug earlier, then covered it in loose soil. He removed his flip-flops after and took a moment to let the cold water cover his feet. There was something refreshing and cleansing about water. Corey closed his eyes and thought about all the news swirling around. The capture of Merle and the death of Aaron and the others had become the talk of the town as well as across the country. National media had swarmed the quiet county over the past couple of days. Fortunately, details about the cabin where the men were shot had been left out for privacy reasons. He was pleased, as the last thing he needed was the place getting any more attention than it already had. Rumors, gossip and innuendos had begun swirling and as usual, people took it as the gospel truth. Him? He was just glad it was over.

He leaned his head from side to side to work out the tension in his neck before heading back. Turning away from the river, he scanned the forest; it was quiet, almost too quiet. Once the cabin was clean, he would step away from his ministry for a week or two. He needed time to reset. Think things through. He threaded his way back to the cabin with his mind deeply troubled. While events had unfolded the way he'd expected, it hadn't come without a price. One that he wished he could change. But he couldn't. What was done was done.

With his mind occupied as he entered the back door, he didn't notice the truck parked out front. Corey headed back into the living area and gazed down at the stain. Though certain it wouldn't come out, he would at least try to remove it. He ventured into the kitchen and dug out a large bucket from the cupboard to fill with hot water. Next, he rooted under the sink for some bleach and a bristle scrubber.

When he returned, he got on his hands and knees and started scrubbing. It didn't matter how much elbow grease he put into it, the darn thing wouldn't budge.

"Some stains are permanent."

A voice behind him startled him. Corey turned, feeling his heart pound. He broke into a smile when he saw him.

"Jack, holy cow, you ever think of knocking?"

"The door was open. You always leave it unlocked?"

He smiled but upon studying his expression he could tell Jack was asking a serious question.

"No, it's always locked."

"Funny," Jack said rising from a seat in the corner of the room. He was almost hidden by the shadows. "Officer Larson said the place was locked the night he showed up here. Meghan, now she can't recall much from the night she was taken, as her eyes were covered but she did have a faint memory of arriving here. She heard a door unlock when she was carried in, but she never heard it unlock when Aaron showed up. Which is strange since the police reported that he broke in."

Corey made a face and shrugged. "Not sure what you're getting at." He quickly changed the subject to try to break the tension. "Anyway, are you staying for the funeral?"

"Jenna?"

"That's right."

"No, unfortunately I have to leave today but I just had one more thing to do before I left."

He shrugged and a nervous smile danced on his lips. Before Jack said anything Corey pointed at the windows. "A lot of work to be done here. It's going to take a while to get this place back together," he muttered.

"I didn't know your grandfather owned this place."

"Yeah, it's been in the family for years."

He nodded slowly, his eyes never left him, making him feel even more nervous. Jack turned ever so slightly looking towards the windows. That's when Corey noticed the Glock sticking out of his waistband behind his back.

"Did you love your sister, Corey?" Jack asked without even looking at him.

Corey frowned. "Of course."

"Yeah, you look real torn up."

Corey clenched his jaw. "We each deal with grief in our own way."

Jack glanced over his shoulder and offered a smile. "That we do."

Corey tapped his fingers against his leg while Jack lit a cigarette.

"So… why are you here, Jack?"

"Came to see you. Your mother said you were here."

"Really? Well you can tell her that I'm fine. She worries too much."

"Yeah, she said you were a real troublemaker when you were younger." Jack walked around with no particular purpose, his eyes drifting around the room. "Said you used to hang out with Aaron."

Corey felt a lump in his throat. "Did she?"

"There was a photo on the wall of you and him." Jack turned as if waiting for him to acknowledge it.

"Oh, yeah, that. That was some time ago."

Jack reached around and pulled his handgun and placed it on the table. "Oh, that feels better." He put a hand on his lower back and stretched out. "Have you spoken to the police yet?" Jack asked

"Not yet," Corey replied.

"I bet you're glad they caught them, right?"

"Of course. Yeah, those bastards deserved what they got."

"You see there is one thing that's been niggling me about this case though. Two actually."

"Really?" Corey remained poised, his breathing speeding up ever so slightly.

"You see, I spoke with Officer Larson today and he told me that all the women that were found in Watoga

State Park were raped, stabbed and buried in shallow graves, barring one."

"Is that so?"

"Yeah, you see, this is what I don't get. The Green Bank Five weren't raped, nor were they stabbed. All of them were found with a large quantity of narcotics in their system, all of them were placed in water."

"And?"

"Jenna wasn't stabbed or raped and her body had a large quantity of narcotics in her system. Essentially, by all accounts, she died of an overdose... seemingly displaying all the outward indications that whoever killed the Green Bank Five, killed her... And yet she wasn't placed in water."

"She was buried."

Jack frowned. "How would you know that?"

Corey cleared his throat and shrugged. "It was in the paper."

"No, I read it today. There was no mention of it."

Corey chewed on the inside of his lip then tapped the

air with his finger. "Oh, that's right, I read it online. I think it was one of the media outlets from outside of town."

"Ah," Jack said, as a faint smile lit up his face. "Then there was one other thing that bothered me." Jack shifted his weight from one foot to the next and ran a hand over his stubbled jaw. "The night Jenna went missing, Meghan took her to meet a client, a client that cancelled at the last minute and a client who was located here. Yeah, Meghan said she was acting all strange after that. Jenna dropped her off in Marlinton and appeared to be heading back out of town, possibly towards here?"

Jack looked across to him. Corey's head shook ever so slightly. He could feel himself becoming overheated. "Look, I'd prefer not to speak about this. With my sister gone and all, it's very upsetting."

He cast his eyes down at the ground and rolled the scrubbing brush around in his hands.

"Sure. You got a drink, Corey?"

"What?"

"A drink. A beer? Water?"

Corey's eyes darted across to the gun on the table and then back to him. "Yeah." He jerked a thumb over his shoulder. "Give me a second, it's in the fridge."

Jack put up a hand, pursed his lips together. "Oh, don't worry, you've got your hands full there. I'll get it."

Corey leaned against the broom and smiled ever so slightly as Jack passed by him.

* * *

Jack wandered out of the room into the kitchen and retrieved a cold Budweiser from the mini-fridge. He took his time, cracked the top off using the counter and downed some before heading back towards the living area. As he rounded the corner, the first thing he noticed was the broom on the ground. To the right of that was Corey standing there holding Jack's gun with both hands. He was shaking ever so slightly.

"See, you just had to go stick your nose in, didn't you? Just like Jenna. Couldn't let up."

Jack took a swig of his drink. "She knew it was you,

didn't she, Corey? That night when she arrived here, she came back, didn't she?"

"I tried to tell her. But she wouldn't listen. She just wouldn't listen."

"That was you at the pay phone, wasn't it?"

"She was going to tell. I had to do something."

"Like you had to do something with the Green Bank Five?"

"That was different. Those... they were whores." He spat through gritted teeth.

"That's why you didn't rape them, isn't it?"

He was seething, changing in front of him. Like a caterpillar might break out of its cocoon, except what lay below the surface was something much more unpleasant.

"Rape? I freed those women. Gave them what they wanted. Freedom."

"Three days. The water. What was it, Corey, some kind of religious rebirth?"

He jabbed the gun while a smile broke on his face. "See. You understood it. The media. They didn't get it. I wanted them to, but they didn't get it."

"But Jenna did, didn't she? She was getting close, that's why you made the phone calls and sent the threatening letter to her."

His eyes went all over the place, a mixture of confusion, regret and utter dismay.

"I tried to warn her. I didn't want to hurt her."

"No, you didn't. That's why you injected her with narcotics and buried her out there in Watogo. You knew Larson was narrowing in on Aaron. It was only a matter of time until they unearthed those bodies that he was responsible for, and this way, he would get tied to Jenna's death and the other five, wouldn't he?"

Corey sneered, shooting him a look of disgust. "Get on the fucking ground. Now!"

Jack chugged down the remainder of his beer and dropped down to his knees; he set the bottle off to one side.

"If you had just left it alone, the killings would have stopped."

Jack scoffed. "Really? You were going to stop? Tell me, Corey, who pushed you over the edge? Was it because you knew your old friend Aaron was killing them? Did you do the same so you could show him that God accepted him, just as he accepted you? An attempt at reaching him? Was that it?"

"Shut up."

"Or was it Pastor Mathers? Did you see him cheating on his wife and assumed you could do the same? Except you couldn't do it, so you killed them instead?"

"Shut up," he said getting louder.

"Or let me guess... the devil made you do it!"

"I said... shut..." As he spat the words he lunged forward and squeezed the trigger. It clicked but nothing happened. He pressed it again, then again before staring at it. His eyes widened. In an instant, Jack grabbed the bottle of beer, smashed it against the side of the wall and lunged at him. Corey stumbled back and Jack fell on top of him pushing the shattered glass against the side of his throat.

"Do it. Do it!" Corey cried out.

Tears welled up in his eyes, streaking out and slipping down the side of his temples. Jack stared at him, contemplating ending his life. If he were dead, he wouldn't lose sleep over it. After all the misery he had caused others it seemed like a fitting way for him to die. But it would have been too easy.

"They weren't whores. They were sisters, wives, daughters, mothers and friends," Jack said. "You're a pathetic excuse for a man. I'm not going to kill you. No. Your mother has suffered enough, and you haven't suffered at all."

Jack tossed the bottle away, it rattled across the floor.

* * *

It had been less than twenty-four hours since Larson had been released from the hospital. He was now at home sipping on iced tea through a straw and watching a ballgame on TV while Kerry fed the baby across from him. His face looked like he'd been through five rounds with a professional cage fighter, even though the doctor said he was on the mend.

Since getting out he'd been put on a soft food diet because of his injuries. He'd suffered multiple lacerations to the face, a broken eye socket, broken nose and multiple broken teeth but had narrowly avoided a broken jaw. It was going to take some time to heal but with all the media attention the town was getting, he was happy to step out of the limelight for a while.

The phone rang, he groaned as he went to get up but Kerry told him to stay put. He didn't argue as he'd already received an earful from her after she saw him in the hospital. He fully expected her to say, *I told you so*, but she didn't. That wasn't her way. That's why he loved her. No matter what he went through she'd been there by his side, supporting him. Reality was she was just pleased that he was alive and finally taking some well-deserved time off.

She stepped back into the room holding the phone out for him.

"It's for you. It's Ethan."

He gave a nod, put his drink on the side table and took the phone out of her hand. He watched Kerry sit back down and dangle a toy in front of the baby. She cooed, and he smiled.

"Hey, you old dog, you sitting down?"

"Would I be doing anything else? She won't let me stand even if I wanted to." He smiled at Kerry and she screwed up her nose and wagged her finger. "I keep telling her it's not my legs that are damaged. Anyway, please tell me this isn't a call to cover a shift as I'm not coming in."

"No, I just thought you needed to hear this."

"What is it?"

"An hour ago, we received a phone call from an unidentified male. He insisted on speaking to you. Obviously staff told him you weren't on shift but they would take a message."

He heard Ethan clear his throat.

"And?"

"Okay, so he tells us that he has the man responsible for the murders of the Green Bank Five, and a confession to prove it. And get this... he said he was calling from that pay phone, you know the old rusted one in Green Bank... and..."

"Are you serious?"

"I know, right? Now had I taken the call I might have hung up and written it off as a prank but Shelly on the front desk called it in. We had an officer up that way so we had them swing by."

Larson swallowed hard. Up until that point they were treating the Green Bank Five as part of the same case with the Gance brothers, even though Merle kept denying any involvement in the deaths of the five women or Jenna Whitmore. No one believed him. He was notorious for telling lies.

"Anyway, the officer shows up and guess what he found."

Ethan paused for effect.

"Spit it out, Ethan," Larson said growing frustrated.

"Corey Whitmore hog-tied, and a voice recorder with him confessing to the murder of the five women and his sister. And here's the thing, Corey didn't even deny it. The guy was scared shitless. Pissed his pants and everything. He just wanted the officer to take him."

"You're kidding me?"

He tried to catch his breath as his pulse was beginning to race. Kerry looked over at him with a concerned expression and mouthed the words: *You okay?* He nodded and waved her off.

"But that's not the weird part. The voice recorder was taped to the inside of the pay phone. So they play it and get this... As well as Corey's confession, there is someone else's voice on that recording. You remember that guy we brought in, the one who broke into Jenna's place, the one who was involved in the bar brawl and..."

"The one who escaped your custody," Larson added, ribbing him over that.

"Okay, okay, that's not funny."

Larson cracked a smile. "I kind of thought it was."

"Yeah, yeah, anyway it was him, Sam. The same guy — Jack Winchester."

Larson let out a lungful of air and cracked a smile even though it pained him to do so. He nodded a few times, exchanged a few more words with Ethan before hanging up and then leaning back in his seat.

"Well I'll be damned."

THANKS FOR READING

Now read book #10: Trail of the Zodiac

Please take a second to leave a review, it's really appreciated. Thanks kindly, Jon.

NEWSLETTER

Thank you for buying Debt Collector 9: Her Last Breath

Building a relationship with readers is one of the best things about writing. I occasionally send out a newsletter with details on new releases and subscriber only special offers. For instance, with each new release of a book, you will be alerted to it at a subscriber only discounted rate.

Go here to receive special offers, bonus content, and news about Jon's new books, sign up for the newsletter. http://www.jonmills.com/

A PLEA...

If you enjoyed the book, I would really appreciate it if you would consider leaving a review. I can't stress how helpful this is in helping other readers decide if they should give it a shot. Reviews from readers like you are the best recommendation a book can have. Without reviews, an author's books are virtually invisible on the retail sites. It also lets me know what you liked. You can leave a review by visiting the book's page. I would greatly appreciate it. It only takes a couple of seconds.

Thank you — **Jon Mills**

JON MILLS

Jon Mills is originally from England. He currently lives in Ontario, Canada with his family. He is the author of The Debt Collector series, Lost Girls, I'm Still Here, The Promise, True Connection, and the Undisclosed Trilogy. He also writes under other pen names. To get more information about upcoming books or if you wish to get in touch with Jon, you can do so using the following contact information:

Twitter: Jon_Mills

Facebook: authorjonmills

Website: www.jonmills.com

Email: contact@jonmills.com

Made in the USA
San Bernardino, CA
17 August 2019